THROUGH THE ROCK

MAGGIE CLARK

GOLDPANNER BOOKS
DEVON
UK

First published in 2006
By Goldpanner Books

This book may be purchased on-line from www.goldpanner.org

A catalogue record for this title is available from the British Library

ISBN 0 9550461-2-2

Printed on recycled paper in Great Britain by Bookchase, London

Goldpanner Books is a division of Eco-nomic Ltd

Eco-nomic Ltd
Edgcumbe House
Bere Ferrers
Yelverton
Devon
PL20 7JL
United Kingdom

Maggie Clark lives on Dartmoor. She writes poetry, has won two short story prizes and co-written and produced a play 'Snaily', based on a Dartmoor legend, performed in Exeter's Phoenix Art Centre. She has recently written a second play with co-writer Nels Rodwell. Through the Rock is her first novel.

Acknowledgements

I would like to thank the following

Inspirational creative writing tutor Roselle Angwin, editors Julie-ann Rowell and Christina Bastumante, publisher Goldpanner Books, and all my family.

'One cannot shut one's eyes to things not seen with eyes'
The River Line, Charles Morgan (1894-1958)

CHAPTER 1

I saw the Rock for the first time in 1970, when I was seven years old. I had wanted to see it for as long as I could remember. Each time we visited Burrow, Great Uncle Ted's farm, I would hear the grown ups talk, listen to their murmurings which rolled around the kitchen while I played quietly in a corner, or under the table, straining to hear their words — evasive sounds — like dreams caught and let go of all at the same time. Yet the words came into me and I mulled them around and around in my head, knowing better than to ask directly about the Rock; knowing that Mother anyway would clam up at once if she thought I was interested. No, it was better to keep my secret and listen; make what I could of the whispers. I could guess, through the low tones of their voices, that the Rock held secrets too terrible to mention out loud.

I gathered that the Rock stood in the middle of the river Teign. The river born of two streams that rose far above the farm, on the high moor, and melded into one mighty stream, that gathered strength and speed as it fell into the valley, within sound, but not sight of Burrow. I realised as time went on that when the grown-ups' voices dropped during a conversation it was because the Rock had been mentioned, and they were talking about dark things — death and illness or bad luck.

Dad had sometimes made light of it to Peter and me, telling us that if you climbed through the hole in the Rock you would never get rheumatism. And, what's more, you'd see your true love in your dreams. Great Uncle Ted would chortle to himself when he heard Dad talking like that and shake his head, which made me feel that Great Uncle Ted knew a great deal more about it than Dad. Even to this day, when teacups clink in a quiet room, I am back at the farm with that sense of terror instilled in me by those whispers of Great Uncle Ted and his cronies and Mother pouring tea.

On the day when I finally set eyes on the Rock, soon after my seventh birthday, we were again on holiday at Burrow Farm, and I was glad to be there away from home, away from our life in London. Even so, despite the relief of being away from city streets, away from the nuns at the London convent school, I dreaded such days. The awful silent afternoons, like this one, which seemed endless and empty with Mother ill again and Peter floppy and sleepy, and the house groaning as though dreading the arrival of some unnamed thing. My child's mind knew it could be a monster of some sort or God Himself, who the nuns had taught me was to be feared. I knew also that somehow the Rock was connected to all those things.

I was too small to be out of doors, where I would have been happy on the hillside helping Dad and Uncle Ted. Why, even Uncle Ted's son Monty, Dad's cousin, who was a grown up but would play with me and Peter as though he was no older than us, whose head had been put on wrong (according to Dad) and limped, was able to do outside work and was now helping move sheep on the moor. Instead I was in my parent's bedroom. My brother had fallen asleep next to Mother on the oak bed, which dominated one end of the low-ceilinged room like a throne. At the foot of the bed was the dark chest from which Mother had pulled a blanket before she had settled down. I could still smell the camphor.

I was kneeling on the floor, my pencils, crayons and drawing paper scattered around me, in the shadow of a vast wardrobe. It leaned slightly into the room and away from the wavy white walls, obscuring much of the light that hung dense and damp outside the tiny window. As the afternoon dragged on I had gradually become conscious of a silence surrounding me — isolating me.

One of my pencils began to roll slowly away across the sloping boards, eerily interrupting the all-pervading silence. It reached a dip in the floor and came to a halt, just by the door leading to the landing, and my heart thumped loudly in my chest. I felt a sudden draught blow under the door and my drawing paper moved. Then it stopped. All was still.

Sometimes in moments of solitude and isolation, a feeling, a sensation, some unknown longing, would creep around me. I dreaded that feeling. It was as though some monster was prowling near me; waiting — waiting — to pounce on me — consume me. Once it started its prowling I could do nothing to stop it. I would stay still, trance-like, staring into the space around me, waiting for the horror of its attack. Then, unable to bear the suspense one more second, I would rush from the room terrified.

And the monster was here now in my parents' bedroom. It was going to consume one of us, maybe me. It would know who I was because I had written my name clearly in black crayon at the top of my drawing: 'Cleo Endaton.' My thick blonde plaits swung forward as I leaned over the paper to hide it. I knew seeing my name would give me away, give the 'thing' — this man-beast or whatever it was — power over me.

I thought I could hear something coming, looked up and stared towards the door hardly breathing. Mother groaned and I got to my feet and hurried to her bedside. I stretched my hand toward hers, tentatively, for some reason afraid to touch the pallid fingers that rested on the bedclothes. She went on sleeping. My brother's head close to hers made them twins, pale-faced, mousy-haired twins, with an ethereal quality about them that made me think of death. Perhaps it was Death here in the room. Had he come to get one of them?

Too terrified to warn them, I turned my face away, threw my pencil to the floor and fled from the room across the landing's creaky floorboards to the stairs, almost falling down them to the empty kitchen below, where the monster's breath still hovered in the silence. Then, rushing to the back door, standing on tiptoe, I unlatched it and ran outside, crossing the farmyard as fast as my legs could run, towards the moor. Out there, in the open landscape, I would be safe.

Once through the orchard and stumbling up the hillside towards the open moorland beyond, the air seemed friendly and I began slowing my pace, catching my breath as I struggled up the sheep track. Scrambling over the remnants of a granite wall I gasped as my knees, grazed, began to trickle blood. Still I would not allow this to stop me. I was determined to reach the top.

When I came to what I thought was the top of the hill, I was consumed with disappointment. There was another rise. Gripped by dismay I sank down on the ground, tears pricking my eyes. I had never ventured farther than the orchard before and wondered fearfully what I would find at the next summit.

My monster was far below in the farmhouse, probably breathing over my brother or mother, and my stomach turned at the thought of them being breathed on like that. Would Mother be taken away to the death place? I had heard of people 'being taken', having 'gone', and I often wondered where they went. "God has taken them," people said. God was likely I thought to take anyone at any time. I did not want to be taken and I did not want God to take Mother or Peter, though I despised the way they waited there for this monster god to come and get them. Why did they not run from its presence? I knew when it was around, why did they not know?

I sobbed at the thought of what I had escaped and was devastated that my mother and brother were too pathetically tired to run away like me. I rose from the ground and struggled on up and up, reaching the top breathless, the blood now dry on my wounded knees. I felt the tingling anticipation of being somewhere I had never been, somewhere my mother would never have allowed me to visit alone, and certainly a place she would never have taken me or Peter.

Slowly I turned around, peering into the misty landscape, following with my eyes wisps of grey, as though someone had taken Dad's biggest brushes to smear a smoke-like trail across the half-hidden land. For a moment I felt a swell of excitement, the same as when I saw one of Dad's landscapes of the moor for the first time. But now as I gazed enraptured, the surge of excitement was turning to a chilling fear.

I could see the brush strokes gathered into a swirling fog that was descending towards the river below. It was then, as I looked down the steep drop to the river, that I saw it — saw the Rock. Though I was above it, looking down on it, it was close enough for me to see the light and dark patches of its great granite body.

I held my breath at the sight, for it was unmistakably special, standing like a giant with a huge hole for an eye, staring up to the sky. I was drawn to its majestic beauty, yet frightened by it, knowing already, in my child's heart, that there was something vastly important, potentially threatening and secret about it, that its power would influence my life forever.

I was alone, vulnerable, knowing there was more to the Rock than Dad had told me. I was shaken, stunned by my close proximity to its great presence.

The advancing mist became a shape that hung over the eye of the rock, a wide-open eye now, like a hungry mouth. Unnerved, mesmerised by the sight, I forced myself to turn away, to run for home. For now I realised that this enormous Rock that stood amid the rushing waters, dominant above the minion rocks fawning at its feet, was the home of that fearsome thing that threatened and dogged my life. It was the home of Death itself. I could see its dense spirit, like a tornado, twisting as it disappeared into the huge mouth-eye. And the Rock became the monster once this evil spirit had gone into it.

I ran blindly back towards the farm, my heart pumping, and as I ran I saw striding down the hill in front of me two big figures and a third one limping beside them. It was Uncle Ted and Dad with Monty. Trotting fast behind them came a boy on a white pony. They must have heard my running footsteps, or maybe I cried out, for they all stopped and turned; I sensed Dad's surprise seeing me there on that hillside, out of hearing from my mother. The boy on the pony said something to Uncle Ted, and then rode away. My father picked me up as I ran into his outstretched arms. He stroked my head and I buried my face into his neck, stifling my sobs. Over Dad's shoulder I could see the white pony galloping away. Mud flew from the hooves.

"Showing off," Dad said.

"Yeah," Uncle Ted agreed. "'Tis the time for it." He chuckled. "The boy is young; 'tis the time for showing off."

I buried my head deeper into Dad's shoulder, crying soundlessly. We went back to the farm in silence. Mother was sitting in the kitchen with Peter, looking anxious. He was crying too and I felt my father's anger and heard Mother's grief at her inability to look after me even for an afternoon.

Later Dad laughed when I told him that a monster lived in the Rock.

"Nonsense," he said. "Who told you that? Uncle Ted, I suppose."

"No, it wasn't Uncle Ted. I saw it. I saw its spirit going into the hole at the top."

"Don't make things up, Cleo," Mother said severely. "You mustn't tell such stories; you'll frighten your brother. You mustn't go as far away as theRock on your own, it's dangerous. Promise me you won't go there, Cleo."

I nodded my head obediently, for the very image of the Rock was now frighteningly huge to me. Of course I wouldn't go there again, for the monster lived there. Mother must have known too or she wouldn't have warned me in that frightening tone. I wished she would be more honest, explain things to me. Uncle Ted was honest.

"Everyone hereabouts goes through the Rock at some time in their life," he told me later. "You have to really, if you want to be lucky."

"Mother says it's dangerous," I told him.

"It is," he said. "People have fallen, banged their heads and drowned. You see, maid, climbing through that great hole is only the beginning; then you've got to get through the slit in the far side of the Rock before steppin' out into the river. Tidn't somethin' to be taken light, little maid, 'specially in winter, when the river's 'igh." Uncle's expression was serious and he had stopped what he was doing while he spoke. "Don't go there on your own, maid," he warned, "not to climb through, that is."

I felt myself shiver at the very thought, but listened intently as Great Uncle Ted continued. "When I was just a little tacker, one woman went there alone." Great Uncle's voice sounded shaky. I could tell by the way he was looking at me and lowering his tone that he was uncertain if he should be telling me this. Instinctively I knew that in Mother's eyes it would be wrong – yet I longed for the story to be told.

"What happened, Uncle? Tell me what happened to the woman you remember who went there all alone?"

For a moment he hesitated. We were in the cowhouse. Uncle Ted had been milking the red-brown Devon cows. I watched as his big hands went back to squeezing the huge pale teats and milk streamed out. I loved to see the creamy white liquid frothing into the bucket. When the cow moved a leg, Uncle hissed soothingly. I waited happily enough, for I loved the sound of his hissing and the milk swishing against the galvanised bucket's side. I half closed my eyes, inhaling the sour sweet cud cow-breath that hung in the low granite milking shed. When he had poured the last full pail into the churn by the doorway, he gestured for me to come outside. We sat together on the bench, our backs against the cowhouse wall; we could see across the yard out to the moorland valley where stood my monster's home — the Rock.

Waiting for Uncle Ted's story to unfold, I could hear the lap lapping of the farm cats as they drank cow-warm milk from a saucer at Uncle's feet. At last he began.

"Her name was Betty. Betty Barton. She was married ten years or more and wanted to have a baby." Uncle had taken out his pipe and was sucking on it. He had not filled it.

"She thought if she climbed through the Rock her luck would change and her wish to have a child would come true. So maid," he continued, "one evenin' at dimpsey time, when her husband was down to the pub drinkin' cider — he had a terrible temper on him when he'd had cider mind — she went to the Rock, secretly. He didn't believe, you see maid, and would have stopped her."

"What happened?" I asked in a whisper, almost knowing, certainly dreading his answer. He had filled his pipe now and held a match to it. I was afraid that at any moment my mother would look out of the farmhouse kitchen door and call us to come indoors. She would be angry and would know somehow that Great Uncle had filled my head with what she knew were 'silly' stories, 'lies at that'. But we were undisturbed and Uncle cleared his throat before continuing the story in his slow and deliberate way, sucking on the pipe between words.

"She went and slid over the edge," he said. "Must have hit her 'ead as she fell and drowned in the deep water below." Uncle Ted stopped talking, the only sound now the suck, suck on his pipe. Its sweet smell was one I had already added to the long list of stored memories of Uncle, the moor and the farm, which I was to feel comforted by long after I had grown up.

Now he was speaking in a voice that sounded unfamiliar to me because it was both shaky and grave. He told me that Betty Barton had been 'swep' away in the fast waters. Away from the Rock, down the river, down, down for a long way. They had searched in vain all night. A terrible wind got up and rain had lashed down on the rescuers and poor old Barton.

"After that night he never touched a drop of cider. They found her next day, Cleo. Yes, they found her next day." Great Uncle Ted took his big red hanky from his jacket pocket and blew his nose before carrying on with the story of Betty Barton's fateful attempt to climb theRock.

"All torn to shreds she was and nearly gone as far as the bridge down to Crediford."

I leaned against Uncle, felt the rough tweed of his coat against my face, breathed the rich gorse and heather smell of it. We sat silently for a while listening to the evening sound of the river in the valley as it raced down to Crediford.

"Did Aunty Gwen climb through it?" I asked, for I knew that Monty had been born soon after Uncle had returned from fighting in the Second World War. Uncle Ted looked sad.

"Maybe she did, maybe she didn't. I wasn't here to know, chile'. She was fair unlucky come the finish though." Uncle dropped his head and looked down at his boots and I put my hand in his, for I could feel his sorrow. He squeezed it and said, "You'm a queen, that's what you are, a queen."

We walked together towards the house, me feeling quiet and thinking I did not feel much like a queen. Our Queen was grown up and married to a Prince. She was rich and happy. But then, perhaps this bit of me is like the Queen, I thought. This bit, for with my hand in Uncle's I felt safe again, almost happy.

I saw the boy again, in the distance, on his fast white pony when Peter and I were playing on the wall between the moor and the orchard. We watched him as he galloped along the hillside on the other side of the river. I felt envy. Oh, to be free like that and sit on a pony and fly across the land without fear. The boy, who was hardly older than I, seemed adult in the way he chose where he would go. He stopped the pony, turned it round, charged up the hill and vanished. Peter and I stood still, staring after them. Then he returned, at a slower pace, behind a flock of sheep, a sheepdog trotting behind them, nipping this way, that way.

The boy wheeling his pony around would not have seen us, he was far too busy working, driving the sheep down the valley on the far side of the river. Peter and I watched until he was gone. The sight of moving sheep, dog, pony and boy all gone.

Peter wanted to go on playing but I couldn't. I was too drawn to that life, that wonderful life the boy on the white pony had. I felt angry. It wasn't fair. Here was I, having to go back to London, go to school, sit on buses and do my homework, when what I really needed to do was be like that boy, the one Uncle Ted said had been showing off that day I'd seen the Rock. He wasn't showing off now, he was working alone on the moor with a dog and a pony to help him. I was more than envious, I was jealous. Games with Peter lost their attraction completely.

I asked my parents about learning to ride, about having a pony. Uncle Ted said nothing. Dad said it was no good because we had to be in London for school.

"Why don't we just live here?" I'd asked.

Uncle Ted agreed it would be nice for him and young Monty if we left London and moved to Burrow Farm. But Dad said it was too far for his work and anyway Mother would hate it. It was bad enough spending holidays here. She needed to be near her doctor's, too.

I felt helpless but knew my father was right. There was nothing I could do to change things, so I kept quiet and calm behind the mask I had become adept at wearing at such moments. The mask was something I had learned to wear early in life.

Once my father had answered my ever-constant questions about living at Burrow with Uncle Ted with the reassuring words, "We'll live here one day, poppet," I was relieved and glad, but wished my mother would not wear that tight expression.

"Over my dead body," she had said sharply, and there had been a dark silence that seemed like a bolt of electricity travelling across to where I stood. It entered my being under my feet, moved up through my legs, up my spine, tingling my stomach, my chest, my heartbeats, through into my throat which tensed, almost closed, made me gasp as it shot up through my face and head and out to the ceiling.

The light went out.

"Another bloody bulb gone," my father had said as he scraped back his chair and reached for a candle and matches from the sideboard. It wasn't completely dark yet, but the candle threw a long, welcoming light around the room. The spell was broken. The house had come to life, and I left the room, my mask firmly in place.

***

I had worn the mask the day my brother and I painted the mural in the hall at Burrow when we were still quite small. Dad had been digging Uncle Ted's vegetable patch and we were helping. It was comfortable with Dad, just plodding about doing things.

"There's our head gardener," Dad would say, as a fat wiggly worm was brought to the surface on his spade. We would rescue the worms and put them where they would be safe and could burrow down into the ground again.

"Ugh," Peter said. He wandered away and Dad said: "You'd better go and find him, make sure he's not up to any mischief."

I knew he wouldn't be. Peter wouldn't do anything to upset Mother. He was playing with his toys in the front hall. I said, "Let's paint a big picture on the wall, Peter."

"Mum wouldn't like it if we drew on the wall."

"We won't draw on the wall," I assured him. "We are going to make a mural. She and Dad will love it. There is such a big space and Uncle Ted said he'd like a nice picture there. If we make one, it will mean Dad doesn't have to do one for him. Uncle Ted likes real pictures of things, and Dad hates doing those sorts of pictures. He only likes doing his flashy things. Uncle Ted would love our picture and Dad and Mother will love it too."

Peter caught my enthusiasm and we raided the dairy studio. Dad was never cross when I used his paint, so we took lots of colours and plenty of big brushes and some smaller ones, "for the details," I told Peter.

"What are details?" he asked.

"Small things, of course," I answered.

We squeezed the paints out of the tubes and stared at the huge blank wall, which continued along the hall and stretched up the stairs. We made a blue sky with little hills of green dotted with brown trees, a beach and a vast sea, which rolled along the stairwell to a bay.

"It's called Stairs Bay and it's a surprise for you," we chimed, sensing our mother's dismay when she appeared at the top of the stairs. She didn't scream at us but shrieked at our father, who stood with earth on his boots and a lopsided grin on his big face, staring at the wall. Uncle Ted stood beside him, two big men grinning.

My brother shrank against the stairs, not sitting on them but seeming to be held up by them. He was white-faced. I ran to my father, put my hand in his big muddy one and said in a small voice: "It was a surprise for you."

"It most certainly is, my darling." He threw back his great fair head and roared with laughter. My mother's anger wiped the smile from his face.

"You should have kept an eye on them," she accused. I was indignant, for I felt I could keep an eye on myself. Though frightened by her tone of voice I put my mask on.

Uncle Ted walked away, shaking his head. "Young varmints," he said, but he was laughing. In fact he laughed off and on for several days every time he thought of what we'd done.

"Them young varmints, I'm blessed if they bain't be artists like their dad," he wheezed to himself.

***

In those days, when I was small, I found my father as easy to get on with as Uncle Ted, though he was often in his studio, preoccupied with his painting. He let me be with him there, giving me paper and paint, which I daubed all over the pages. He was never cross or critical.

"The child knows what she wants," he told my mother once. She was dressing me for church. I hated going and would glumly refuse to put on my best clothes.

Mass was held in the village hall, which smelled of stale tobacco and people's feet from the whist drives and dances held there on a Saturday night. Dad would drive us and wait outside for the service to finish. On one cold January Sunday we were driving slowly along our bumpy lane, when we reached the spot where, the day before, Dad and I had seen a fox. It had appeared suddenly over a low bank. In its wake came a swarm of hounds 'speaking' in the unforgettable way of hounds 'giving tongue' when hard on the scent of their prey. The fox had landed almost at our feet, had stared straight into my eyes, then turned and raced away. I clutched Dad's hand, terrified as the hounds surrounded us, giving chase. I began shrieking out loud: "Stop them Dad, I don't want them to kill my fox." For in that moment of eye contact I believed that the fox had become part of me.

Dad, disconcerted, had briefly comforted me. "Don't take it to heart Cleo. He's a strong fox — got more brains than the hounds too — he'll likely live to run another day." Unconvinced, but sensing Dad's disquiet, I stemmed my screams and, ashamed of my outcry, put on my mask — stored the memory — the day spoiled.

Father Smith, a dour Hebridean, preached damnation. I was frightened of his 'woe betide' words, even though most were meaningless to me. That January Holy Family Feast Day he had reached his zenith of hatred for sin, and warned the congregation that family life was in grave danger of becoming extinct.

"Unless you turn to the example of the Holy Family and do as they did, living simple holy lives, you will be damned." He began to talk about pop stars and the evil of their ways. "The Rolling Stones," he told us, "are evil." I sat up at his words and really listened, for I knew Dad liked the Rolling Stones and played their music in his studio when he was painting, and I knew it off by heart, for sometimes I used to make Dad laugh when I waggled my bottom and danced around the studio to the sound of the Stones' music.

"Mick Jagger is a bad example to the youth of today," Father Smith ranted. He was white with red patches on his cheeks, as he denounced my heroes, Dad's music – my music. He spoke in a hoarse stage whisper and I, despite the chill of the stark January hall and the sensation of cold in my bones causing my teeth to chatter, felt the back of my legs on the uncomfortable chair hot and damp and I knew I had wet myself.

Later, we were having Sunday dinner: Uncle Ted, Monty, Dad, Peter, Mother and me. My legs felt sore at the back.

"Come on, Cleo," Mother said, looking at my plate.

"Maybe not hungry today?" Dad asked with a smile. I didn't smile back.

"Father Smith says that your music is bad, and that Mick Jagger is evil," I announced. Uncle Ted looked up.

"Don't know about evil. Mazed though, very likely," he said.

My father said: "You can't believe a word that bloody priest tells you."

I was shocked at his anger, put on my mask and struggled with my food.

CHAPTER 2

I was nearly ten when Uncle Ted bought me the pony. We had already spent most of August at Burrow and to my utter delight were to stay even longer, 'well into October' Dad had said. 'With so much work there's no choice but to stay.'

I had woken early to watch the ancient transport lorry being loaded in the yard. Uncle Ted was going to market with some bullocks and it was hardly light when Bert, the driver, jumped down from his seat. He wore a flat cap like Uncle Ted.

"Right then?" he asked.

"Right then," Uncle Ted answered.

Dad, Mother and Peter were still asleep. My feet were cold, stockingless in my wellies. I pulled my jacket around me and followed behind the two men, then climbed the gate to watch as they opened up the inner yard gate to let the cattle out. Six brown bullocks to go, Uncle Ted had told me. The bullocks ran out and turned towards where I was sitting on the gate. Fear gripped me, for they had their heads down — were snorting as they trampled the ground towards me.

Uncle Ted growled loudly and Jumble the sheep dog flew past to head them back. I imitated Uncle, saying "ged on" like he did, waved my arms, growled like a farmer. Jumble bit at their heels and the bullocks were soon back on track and out in the pound, where they had no choice but to clamber up the ramp into the cattle truck.

Uncle Ted was lifting the back doors of the lorry. There was that boy again, the dark haired one I'd seen on a white pony. I hadn't noticed him earlier. He helped Uncle Ted slam the back doors, deftly dropping the latches before lifting his flat cap back off his head and pulling it down again like I often saw the grown-up men do. Then he was out of sight up in the cab, silent, quick. The driver nodded towards me.

"Got some extra help then, Ted?"

"Yep," said Uncle Ted. "She's my helper."

I felt proud. The men were glad I'd been on the gate waving my arms at the bullocks.

Uncle Ted put his hand under my chin. "I'll bring you back a pony, maid, you mark my words. I'll find one for my little helper."

I was speechless. I wanted to say, "Oh yes, please," or "Oh, please can I come too," but my lips would not move. A pony from Tavistock market!

I watched the lorry ambling down our track, envying the boy in his privileged place between Ted and Bert. But I stopped myself feeling miserable with the thought of the pony.

Later that day, Mother told me she had agreed that if Ted bought a mare to breed from, I could learn to ride on her if she was nice and quiet.

"Oh, thank you, Mother," I said, breathless with disbelief. I ran to her side, wanted to put my arms around her, but she had already turned away from me, bending to reach something from a cupboard. Kneeling on her haunches she had looked flustered and sounded severe again as she said, "She won't be your own horse, Cleo. You are not in any position to own a horse. It is purely part of Uncle Ted's farming enterprise." I did not feel dismayed: Uncle Ted had said he'd bring me back a pony, and I believed him. I knew he meant the pony to be mine — my very own.

The day dragged on and on, I must have run down the track a dozen times thinking I could hear the sound of the lorry back from Tavistock, its wheels trundling over the rough farm lane. My heart sank when it turned out to be my imagination or a delivery of cow cake from Crediford or the afternoon postman in his red van.

Then at last, as evening drew near so did the sound of the cattle lorry. We were having tea and I spilled my cup as I leapt to my feet when I heard the sound of the horn beep beep beep warning us, telling me that Uncle Ted and the lorry were here at last. I ran outside, down the garden path, through the little green wrought-iron gate and out into the yard just as the lorry came into view. Bert beeped the horn again and my heart thumped with anticipation and doubt. Would it be really true? Had Uncle found me a pony? Suppose he hadn't? How would I bear the disappointment? I hardly dared look at Uncle as he descended from the cab. He was grinning at me.

"Come on, maid, come an' see what I got for you."

He took my hand in his. Bert had backed the lorry into the middle of the yard and switched off the engine. Breathless with excitement, I ran behind the lorry. There was a cacophony of sound coming from inside, sheep baaing and thudding about, causing the lorry to shake. Uncle told me to stand aside while they let down the ramp. I strained my neck to see if I could see the pony, but through the open hurdles that had kept the animals securely bunched together for the journey, sheep started pouring out, eyes peering wildly from black faces.

"Scotties," Uncle announced proudly. "Pure-bred Scots blackface ewes, six of 'em an' a fine ram."

They leaped and bucked down the ramp, the ewes following their magnificent curly horned husband. These were closely followed by a gaggle of squawking geese, a breeding pair of white parents with their four well-grown goslings. Everything seemed to clatter and screech at the same time. I barely believed there could be anything left in the back of Bert's lorry. But when the sheep and geese had taken themselves hurriedly across the yard to a safe corner, I dared to peep inside again and there I saw her. My very own beautiful Dartmoor mare. Tied by a rope halter, she surveyed me with an expression that spoke to me of the wild nature of the Dartmoor pony, dignified and free-spirited.

Stunned with excitement I could hardly speak as Bert and Uncle, one on either side, began leading her. I wanted to run up, throw my arms around her; but it was impossible. Suddenly the animal plunged down the ramp, tossing her head as she leapt from the lorry.

Rooted to the ground, I watched her antics. Her sturdy body rose high above me as she reared and plunged. Her mane, long thick and wavy, dark as peat, swung wildly. Her eyes, almost covered by a thick dark fringe, flashed white through the movement of the forelock. She threw her head from side to side, resisting the ropes that tugged tight around her neck.

Suddenly Mother was there beside me, hurting my arm as she pulled me away, back towards the safety of the garden gate. But I could still see the men holding on to the rope while my pony thrust herself up and down, thrashing her legs, bucking, pawing and snorting.

Then all at once she stopped, put her head down to the ground, breathing heavily, blowing and sniffing the earth and mud. Uncle Ted was blowing too; whistling with each breath through his teeth like he did with the cows, but the noise of hooves and snorting had stopped.

Dad was watching from his makeshift studio in the old dairy. I was aware that Peter was peering from around the half-open back door. His view would be long, all the way down the garden path to where we stood; Mother, one hand on me and one on the garden gate was shaking her head slowly.

"Not a very suitable mount for you, Cleo," she warned. But I scarcely heard her critical tone. Pulling away I ran quickly across the yard down to where Uncle Ted and Bert were standing next to the pony, whose body gleamed with sweat.

"Here you are, maid, the mare's giv'd in now." Uncle Ted grinned. "Take your pony, take the rope, chile, and come down to the orchard."

I held the rope with a sense of ownership and love. It was love at first sight. Even as she had plunged and dived to escape I knew she was the one; the one who would fill the gap, the holes in me. She was shiny black-brown and I would call her Brownie.

I stood beside Uncle Ted. There was no sign of the boy. They must have dropped him at his home, wherever that was. I was sorry, for I wanted him to see. I wanted him to know that I too had a horse, like his, only his was white and mine was dark brown. I would be able to roam the moor like him. I would ask Mother to buy me a cap like the men wore, like the boy wore.

Uncle Ted was standing close to Brownie. I could hear him breathing gentle approval and I too found myself whispering comforting words to the animal. The words came naturally: "Come, beauty girl, sweet pony, come...come, little horse." I don't remember exactly which words I used, but they were the same tone as Uncle Ted's words in the cowshed and when lambing the sheep.

I felt it would not do to put my hand out to Brownie, but stood there quietly in that silent September evening. Everything had grown still, just a faint whine from Jumble and the down-the-nose breathing of Brownie. It was that time of evening when the world is holding its breath. For a few seconds there is a stone silence before the held-back evening breath is ready to let go into the big sigh of nighttimes, as though all creation is honouring the last vibrant moments of the setting sun.

The silence was broken, for Brownie sneezed, wetting me, making me laugh. Everyone was laughing, even Mother. Uncle Ted and Bert let go of the rope ends and I walked beside her. For a moment she pulled back, but determined, I walked towards the orchard. Bert held the gate open and I marched through, Brownie following me into the lush sweet meadow where wasps had so recently been sucking at the fallen apples.

In no time Brownie became calm and biddable. Uncle Ted and I worked with her every day, despite my mother's disapproval. She said she was afraid for me, afraid I'd be hurt. I could not understand her fear. Brownie was something I could not possibly fear. She was my friend, my almost constant companion.

It was as though we were made for each other. Even after a short time she would follow me around. Sometimes I stole out of the house in the dead of night just to be near her. On moonlit nights I would drag a blanket to the orchard, feeling joyful just seeing her there in the moon-washed landscape. Brownie would nicker a welcome to me through her soft nose and come to my side. I would nestle my head against her warm flanks, intoxicated by her horse smell; or lie beside her with my blanket over me as she cropped the grass close to my face. I loved the sound of her teeth pulling at the grass and the smell of her breath caressing my cheeks as I lay watching her dark shape shifting around me, gently, carefully, tight to my prone body yet never stepping on me.

Returning to London was going to be even more painful now. We were to leave at the end of the first week in October. I dreaded the very thought, trying not to let it come into my mind.

The knowledge that we would have to leave for what Mother called 'home' in London was torture, unbearable to think about. I spent every possible moment with my dream-come-true pony in the landscape that I had come to love and marvel at. Peter was happy with his head in an encyclopedia or drawing pictures of engines and aeroplanes.

I tried to dismiss worries about Mother. When she was unwell, resting in the armchair by the stove in the kitchen, I could feel her anxious eyes watching me as I cleaned Brownie's bridle. I cleaned it at every opportunity. I hated my mother's constant anxious gaze, and wished she would read, forget about me, leave me alone. Feeling her eyes on me, my stomach would twist into a knot. I felt like screaming, but I knew I mustn't. Mother was ill; I could not add to her illness, I must hold back.

Although Dad was tolerant, when we were at the farm I could not bring myself to confide in him, explain my fears to him. It was enough simply to realise my luck; that because he had painting commissions from wealthy people who had retired to the area, I could stay longer with Brownie. Dad was out all day sketching or in his studio painting and I knew he should not be disturbed.

Uncle Ted was glad to have us there longer than we had expected and Monty, although not very articulate, showed his happiness by helping Dad move his big canvases from the barn to the old dairy studio, or playing snap with Peter, who always won. Monty loved Brownie too, which endeared me to him. He would help me groom her or hold her head while I cleaned her hooves. I noticed how gentle and at ease Monty was with the pony and felt a sense of relief that he, as well as Uncle Ted, would be with her when I was back in London.

Mother had told Peter and me that Monty was 'half-witted'. I imagined that meant he had only half a brain but felt grateful that the half he had was sensitive to horses. She did not like it though, if I spent too much time with Monty or with Uncle Ted for that matter.

One day in the kitchen as she was drying dishes and I was cleaning Brownie's tack, she said, "You mustn't spend so much time with Uncle

Ted, dear." When Mother said 'dear' I knew from earliest days that she was trying to soften the effect of her will against mine, and alarm bells rang in my head.

"Why not?" I asked, rubbing the leather of the reins harder.

"It's not good for you," she said darkly. "Not good for your great uncle either." She paused. "He has work to do. You mustn't interrupt him so much. It's a nuisance for him."

I gazed at my mother, speechless. I knew she was making it up. Uncle Ted liked me being there beside him helping and now, with Brownie, I could help even more. Mother was wrong.

I could tell that Uncle enjoyed teaching me how to ride and school Brownie properly, because he told me so, especially when I got the lessons right. We had made a little school in one corner of the orchard and although Brownie had bucked and plunged at first when Uncle had lunged her in circles, she quickly became obedient and I could manage on my own. Even so, Uncle would stop what he was doing to come and watch me lunging Brownie or riding her in circles trotting, cantering, twisting and turning.

I could not risk upsetting my mother by showing my anger but inwardly I protested at her words, seeking solace with Brownie. I buried my face in her mane and told her about my mother's confusing lectures.

"Why can't she see Brownie? Why?" I sobbed. "Can't she see how helpful we are to Uncle?"

The pony lifted her head from the grass for a moment, as much as to say 'get on my back and don't fret so.' I smiled and vaulted on to Brownie's warm back, while she, unconcerned, continued grazing. I leaned forward and rested on her mane, my arms around her thick neck, whispering to her.

"Brownie you know Mother simply does not realise how useful we are to Uncle. Just think of all the jobs we do."

My mind went into a reverie as I made a mental list of all the useful things Brownie and I did on the farm. Out on the moor together, we had learned how to move Uncle's little band of Galloway cows, or his sheep flock, from here to there or down to the farm for inspections. Brownie and I would twist and turn while Jumble would run down the gullies to bring any stray sheep into line and my heart would sing, for this was what I wanted to do for the rest of my life. Yes, I wanted to be with Uncle Ted and he needed me and Brownie. I was perplexed by my mother's fear and dismay and felt the guilt of not trusting her. I could trust

Brownie. I could tell her anything. I knew we loved and trusted each other. Uncle Ted loved me too. It was something I felt certain about.

Once or twice we saw the boy and on one occasion my heart had almost burst with pride when he nodded his head at Brownie. "Nice little mare."

On the last day at Burrow Uncle Ted and I rode out to see the cattle. On the way home we went close to the riverbank.

"'Tis all right, maid," Uncle said. "Don't be afeared."

But I was afraid. The track we were following would lead us to the Rock. Its presence was forever lurking in my imagination.

I tightened my legs around Brownie for safety. She bridled slightly, shook her head and danced nervously.

"No good doin' that," Uncle scolded. "Relax, maid, or Brownie will catch your fear."

I tried to relax my legs against Brownie's sides and felt her soften to my will again. I did not want to feel afraid and thought about the boy. He wouldn't be afraid. He and the white pony would have ridden this track often, all by themselves, without Great Uncle Ted.

"It's all right, Brownie," I whispered patting her neck encouragingly. She walked straight again along the now narrowing track, which ran high above, but parallel to the river.

"River's 'igh," Uncle warned and I found it hard to stop my legs from squeezing my excitable little mare. Bit by bit we descended, following the diminishing sheep track through the dying bracken, until we were at river level. Uncle shouted above its rushing sound for me to keep close to him. Suddenly, as we rounded a bend, the river dropped steeply over a waterfall and we were dropping too, our ponies scrambling over some large stones.

As we came to a halt I looked in wonder past Uncle and his horse to the Rock itself. There it was, the biggest granite rock on the moor, and I was seeing it from a new perspective, closer than ever before.

We rode slowly past, stopping a few yards further down-stream where the river curved, slowing some of its waters into a pool that lapped at the bank beside us.

I stared into its calm depth, feeling in my child's heart its specialness.

Great Uncle Ted interrupted the quiet moment. "It holds many secrets," he whispered gruffly. "'Tis magic see." Then he got off his horse and picked up a small stone.

I slid from Brownie's back. Clutching the reins, I dared myself to look back up to the Rock. Its great granite flanks held the water back, forcing it to pour noisily downstream away from the magic pool. It was as though the Rock was protecting it from the violence of the river's force.

"Make a wish," Uncle was saying, "before your stone hits the water, and t'will come true," and he threw the stone, shutting his eyes tight, as it plopped into the middle of the magic pool. I picked up a small sharp-pointed stone and held it in my hand.

"Can I have two wishes, Uncle?"

He eyed me quizzically and I feared he might have guessed that I was struggling between wishing to live forever at Burrow or my mother's return to full health. "No, maid, only one," he said.

I shut my eyes tight, trying to decide. Then, throwing the stone into the magic pool, I watched it penetrate the water and found myself making both wishes, despite Uncle's words. I needed two wishes: Mother to be well, and for us all to live happily at Burrow forever.

"Is it really magic, Uncle?" I asked him as we turned away and started our ascent towards Burrow.

"Oh yes, 'tis magic all right, maid. What's more, once upon a time it was known as a place where women went to give birth. Why…I was born there myself…long time ago mind." He grinned. "People don't use it any more, but in my grandma's day it was used and if you was born by the pool you was lucky all your life, so they said."

I let Brownie's reins loose, leaning forward as she pulled up the steep slope. "Mind you," Uncle added, after Brownie had caught up with the bigger pony, "'tis mighty cold in winter so it was lucky I was born in July." Uncle was chuckling to himself as we reached the crest of the hill, and we began the downhill trot back to Burrow.

I decided not to tell Dad about the magic pool, for I guessed that if I did he would laughingly dismiss Uncle Ted's words as more of his 'wicked stories'. But I believed Uncle Ted and was glad he had taken me there.

When I said goodbye to Brownie I told her I would be back for the Christmas holidays. Dad had said we would be back then because he needed to do some winter sketches. If Dad's work is so popular here we might not have to live in London for much longer. It was a consoling thought that I shared with Brownie on that cool Dartmoor morning as I took a last look at the landscape from her warm back. I could see between her pricked ears the colours of muted purple darkening as clouds skimmed across the autumn sky, changing the sunlit bracken from bronze to brown. Then the cloud curtains were torn from the sun's face and the scene altered; the bracken became glimmering gold and the skies had changed to sapphire.

I breathed the Dartmoor air deep into my lungs as though filling myself with the very essence of the place. I would be sustained by this memory until Christmas.

"It's not for long, dear, sweet Brownie," I told her tearfully, before leaving her and walking shakily back to the house. I could feel her watching me so I turned my head for a last look. She gave a frantic whinny from over the orchard gate. I called back to her, choking with tears, "I'll be back, Brownie, I promise, I'll be back at Christmas."

But then, on that last day, I had not allowed for Mother, or her worsening illness.

CHAPTER 3

The flat, our 'home', now meant nothing to me. It felt as though it was simply a place to be, during those dark days. It wasn't a big flat. My father's studio space spilled from the kitchen to the living room, which was also home to my brother's rabbit, his toys and Mother's books and where I sat to do my homework. Here, cooped up in the flat, I could feel rather than hear the tensions between my parents.

At first Mother seemed excited to be back in Clapham. She had her hair cut and re-styled, her nails manicured and went regularly to the library, often bringing home several novels at a time. She looked better, had even stopped taking her pills.

We were only a street away from my school and the Northcott Road. I liked shopping on that street, going from one market stall to another with the list Mother gave me every Saturday morning; liked seeing the rows of colourful fruit and vegetables piled neatly on the stalls and enjoyed choosing potatoes, round and earthy they reminding me of those from Uncle Ted's garden. I would pick out a fresh plump chicken 'straight from the country...up from Kent'. I would bury my nose in bunches of parsley or thyme as I carried them back to the flat. Sniffing familiar smells, while giving me a sense of happiness, evoked a nostalgia, which I found hard to shake off.

Occasionally a horse-drawn cart carrying a few bits of scrap, household junk, would pass by, slowing down cars as it trotted past the stalls. The driver was an old man who wore a rough tweed jacket, just like Uncle Ted's. The stall keepers would call out, "'right, Jack?" and the driver would take his pipe from his mouth and raise an arm to wave in reply to their friendly greeting. All along the road he was greeted with a chirpy "'right, Jack?" or "watcha, mate." And I would scamper along the pavement, parallel with the entourage, forgetting all about shopping and home, simply soaking in the smell of horse and feasting my eyes on its flanks, as it clip-clopped along the road behind the row of stalls. The first time I saw them I kept running until at length it stopped. Breathless, I watched the driver climb stiffly down to the pavement outside the pub. He carried a nosebag made of canvas. He wore the same thick corduroy trousers as Uncle Ted, with a piece of cord tied around each of his knees. He winked at me.

"You like 'orses then?" he said, grinning. "Just givin' 'im 'is dinner." And he set the nosebag of oats in place, slipping a leather strap over the horse's ears. Standing beside the horse listening to his chewing, with my hand on his big soft shoulder, made me think of Brownie, with a deep sad longing.

I felt let down and disappointed if, as so often happened, the man and his horse were not on the street when I did the Saturday shopping. I would dawdle then, hoping they might appear before I had to go home.

I hated the endless traffic sounds outside our flat, and the bright streetlights made me long for the deep darkness of the real night which I loved at Burrow.

I immersed myself in schoolwork to take my mind off my homesickness, and longed for the Christmas holidays.

Then came the bombshell. Mother was declining. No amount of hair appointments or manicures seemed to cheer her. At first Dad was impatient with her, trying to jolly her along with bright remarks about his work or how well Peter and I were doing at school.

"At the rate my work is going," he told her, "we shall be able to afford to send Cleo to the senior convent school. Now she's eleven she can start in September." Even this news brought only a wisp of a smile to my mother's lips

Dad, I could tell, was making an effort to please Mother. He even came with us to the Catholic Church for mass, and invited Father Reagan to supper. Mother seemed not to be making an effort in return, but agreed to the supper party with the priest as guest. Dad cooked a roast chicken for the occasion, which turned out dry and hard. Mother had made an attempt at making a pudding, a creamy custard thing, which she called trifle but it was watery and the cherry on top was artificial and the sponge came from a packet. The priest was nice enough and Dad plied him with wine. I felt ashamed and awkward watching them getting drunk together, and when Dad suggested playing cards Mother said she was tired and was going to bed, and it was our bedtime too. Dad urged her to stay. "Play cards with us, darling," he pleaded. He never called her darling and his words sounded slurred.

Before leaving the room she surprisingly invited Father Reagan to give us his blessing. Dad went on dealing the cards. Peter and I obediently knelt down with Mother in front of the priest, who swayed slightly and then, speaking in Latin, made the sign of the cross over us. As we left the room he called, "Goodnight and God bless, children," and we chorused, "Goodnight, Father." I did not feel like saying goodnight to Dad, who hardly looked up as we left.

I was wakened several times during the night by the sound of their raucous laughter or a roar of triumph from one or the other of the men and, for once, felt sorry for Mother. It had been Dad who had invited the priest to cheer her up and yet it was he who was playing cards and getting drunk with him. My mother had only spoken once or twice during the meal and then received Father Reagan's blessing. What sort of cheering up was that? I asked myself.

****

The worst happened. Mother became very ill and instead of spending Christmas at Burrow, Peter and I were to spend it with a kind family whose children went to our primary school. I was unhappy of course, but wore my mask and behaved politely. We were taken to see the rock musical Jesus Christ Superstar. I knew I should have felt excited. It was nearly Christmas and this was my first visit to a theatre. But I worried that Mother would not have liked it if she knew we had gone to see a musical that suggested that Jesus and Mary Magdalene might have loved each other in an embarrassing way.

On Christmas Eve, Dad took Peter and me to see Mother in hospital. She was half asleep, only opening her eyes for a few moments. She could not speak properly and I knew she was going to die.

I felt shrivelled inside and remember opening my presents on Christmas morning as though I were made of stone, like the people in the bible who turned into statues because they looked back at the city, and I made up my mind not to look back at the happy days at the farm or think of Brownie or Uncle Ted and Monty and the heather-strewn moorland and the valley where the Rock stood. In my child's mind I knew that the Rock and my heart were made of the same granite and were inexplicably to blame for Mother's almost certain death, which I expected would happen at any moment. Even my tears refused to fall on my pillow at night; they too were solid, like lumps of lava, wedged somewhere behind my hot, dry eyes, and all that remained of my life at Burrow was in the dreaming at night. Most often nightmares — where Mother lay dead at the foot of the Rock with Betty Barton, grotesque images of their bodies lying together, drowned; and I could not distinguish one from the other.

****

Mother did not die then after all. She even recovered enough to be at home with us, though I still feared that I would wake up one morning to be told she had died suddenly, during the night. Peter was frightened too and I would reassure him by telling him not to cry at bedtime, that if he stopped then Mother would go on living. I think I felt he should share some of the responsibility with me for keeping our mother alive. It worked. He ceased his crying and feeling guilty. I sat in his room reading his favourite stories aloud until he fell asleep.

Although the drugs Mother had to take made her sleepy, she was improving. There was talk of us going to Burrow for Easter. I dared not believe it, but gradually allowed my mind, at least, to return to Dartmoor. I would lie awake at night with my eyes closed and visualise Burrow Farm. There would be Uncle Ted with Monty cutting the hedge around Top Meadow. There was Jumble lying on Uncle's jacket, nose on paws, eyes always alert, watching the sheep in the far corner, waiting to round them up at the slightest bidding from Monty or Uncle Ted. And there, looking over the gate down in the orchard was Brownie.

I watched as she wheeled around kicking her heels, snorting with exuberance, circling and bucking. I gasped at the sight of her. What was she doing now? I almost called out, for she was galloping full pelt over the orchard wall, out to the meadow where the men were working. They seemed not to notice as she sped past them. She gathered herself together and with one almighty leap rose above the sheep-wire fence, which was repaired each spring to stop the Scotty ewes from jumping into the tempting meadow grass, so different from their more sparse moorland grazing. Brownie raced across the moors and I could see the muddy water splash around her fetlocks as she leapt across the bogs and scrambled down the hillside toward the river. My heart was in my mouth for she was galloping again and sliding and slipping down the steep slope in the exact direction of the Rock. I could see it clearly, just as I had first seen it when I was small. This great edifice that frightened me in dreams and in my waking life was drawing my beloved Brownie along with its monstrous dominating power. "Be careful, Brownie!" I screamed. "Turn around, gallop home, Brownie. Brownie!" I screamed louder, putting my mind out to Brownie, forcing my will against the monster. Then I was sitting on her. I could feel her heaving flanks beneath my legs as I made her listen to my instructions. With every fibre of my body I was willing her to turn. It was as though I had become Brownie we were one now and together we struggled back up the hill, pulling against the gravity of the Rock. I felt her gather speed across the moor. We had left the fearful place, which had, I was certain, nearly consumed my treasure.

I opened my eyes and I was back in my London bedroom. I began to cry. Great tears fell like they had never fallen before. My pillow was soaked and, stuffing my mouth with the sheet to stifle my sobs, I slept.

Next morning everything had changed. For one thing when I went into the kitchen Dad and Mother were there together. What's more, Dad had his arm around Mother's waist.

Peter sat at the table gobbling cornflakes. Out of his milky mouth he spurted, "Good news, Cleo. Guess what? Guess what?"

"What?" I asked. "What's happened? Tell me."

Mother smiled up at Dad. "You tell her," she said in that cajoling way she sometimes used when she and Dad were on good terms. She even called him 'Lance', her nickname for him, instead of the usual stern Felix, when things were going well.

"You tell her, Lance, darling."

"Can I tell her Dad? Let me tell Cleo, please, please let me."

"Go ahead, son," Dad said, smiling down at Mother.

Dad never called Peter 'son' — something was afoot, something very odd. I sat on the edge of the table waiting for Peter to tell me.

"We are going to Burrow tomorrow night for Easter — and the whole of April," he announced, before thrusting another overloaded spoon full of cereal into his mouth.

I glanced at my parents' faces, unable to believe that Mother had agreed to go to Burrow for so long a stay.

"Why?" I asked. "What's changed?"

Dad explained that Mother had recovered enough to travel and he had received a very big commission, two special Dartmoor landscapes, so he could afford to take time off from his London studio. He told me that Peter and I would only be missing three weeks of school. One week before Easter and two after the holidays.

"You and Peter must do some schoolwork at the farm. Mother insists and she is quite right," he said, looking at Mother as he spoke.

Later he told me to step very carefully around Mother. It had been a terrible struggle getting her to agree to go to Burrow, and for us children to take time off school.

My heart sank a little. So that was why he had his arm around her. He had charmed her into agreeing. That meant that anything could happen even before we got to Burrow. She might easily change her mind. Mother didn't like Burrow, but the doctors told her that the fresh

Dartmoor air would do her good. Knowing that she scarcely set foot outside the house at the farm made me wonder how much Dad had twisted the doctor's arm to tell her it would be the best thing for her.

Torn by cynicism about Dad's sincerity, joy in the knowledge that I would be with Brownie, Uncle Ted and Monty for a long period, and guilt about Mother agreeing to go back to Burrow only to please Dad, meant that my delight at the prospect of our return was dampened by an uncomfortable sense of responsibility, which I found impossible to deny.

Despite those misgivings my heart soared when the taxi taking us from Exeter station to the farm reached the crest of the hill from which we would see the moor. Then as we drew closer my excitement was at bursting point. I would see Brownie, Uncle Ted, Monty, Jumble, the sheep, the cattle and perhaps — who knows, I might even see the boy on his white pony.

***

Burrow welcomed us. Meg Dodson, who used to come regularly to clean and make the cream for Uncle and Monty, was to come every morning while we were at the farm. Uncle told us that Meg was happy to oblige and had prepared our rooms and aired the beds, as well as cooking a stew for our supper.

"We don't want Mother overdoin' things, do we?" he said. I could see the relief on Dad's face. Meg being there would mean Mother could not complain about the difficult work in an old place like Burrow. It had always seemed that no matter how much Dad and all of us did to help, it was never enough for Mother when she was feeling low. Now, with Meg coming every day Mother would be happy.

Brownie had greeted me with a welcoming whinny, trotting fast to the gate as soon as we arrived. I ran to the orchard, almost throwing myself over the gate. She came to me nickering and nudging my pockets. My tears of happiness mingled with her mane as I offered her the sugar lumps I'd stuffed into my pockets before leaving London. She was losing her winter coat and she gleamed like a polished chestnut; her black mane shone in the April sunshine. Monty had groomed her for my arrival. Oh, the excitement of being back! I was happy again.

I soon settled into a routine of helping Mother, riding Brownie and working with Uncle Ted, as well as sitting diligently every day for an hour doing schoolwork with Peter. A small price to pay, I felt, for being back. It was all going smoothly and Mother seemed content, if shaky at times, but still calling my father Lance.

One day, as Uncle and I rode home across the moor after seeing the cattle, Uncle told me to "Let the horses rest a minute, Cleo." They put their heads down to nibble the new grass that was growing where Uncle and Monty had swaled in previous years, burning back the unwanted gorse and in time allowing grass to spring up. Uncle was peering across the valley to the other side of the river and I realised, following his gaze that he was looking in the direction of the Rock. Then he put his fingers in his mouth and gave a sharp whistle. I stared across to where Uncle was looking and then I saw him. It was the boy. He was on the white pony, flying down the hill on the opposite side of the river at breakneck speed. Then they vanished from our sight.

Brownie's head was up now, her ears pricked. I could see between them exactly where the boy had vanished at what must be the very spot were the Rock rose from the river. The hair on the back of my neck prickled as I visualised him and the white pony being in the shadow of the Rock, fording the river. From here our view was obscured by the lie of the land but we only needed to move a few yards along and down and we would be in full view of the Rock and the place where the boy had vanished from sight. I felt a great sense of relief when all of a sudden he and the white pony came steaming up over the rise to where we stood.

"In a 'urry, bie?" Uncle teased.

I noticed how Uncle had slipped into the vernacular calling him 'bie' instead of boy.

The boy laughed and took his cap off, briefly exposing his dark curls. I couldn't be sure if he was raising his cap to be polite or if the gesture was a habit.

My heart swelled with pride as his pony pranced beside mine and we all three set off following the track along the contour high above the river.

He told us he'd crossed below the Rock and that there was a sheep corpse in the magic pool. He was going home to fetch a rope and drag it out.

"It's not one of ours or yours," he told Uncle Ted. "I think it comes from Crediford Commons. Maybe chased by a dog or simply strayed."

I was sorry when he nodded goodbye and turned off above Burrow. I would have liked to go with him, but Uncle didn't suggest it and I knew he had promised Mother I would be back by teatime and was keeping to his word.

The sky looked dark and threatening that evening. After tea, Dad said he was going back to his studio. I had slipped out of the house quickly before Mother's disapproval prevented me from helping Uncle with the evening chores. Mother had Peter to keep her company in the kitchen.

***

Cloud gathering over Dog's Tooth Tor is not unusual. Those clouds are there much of the year. Even in summer they can be dark and threatening, thunderously heavy as they obscure the highest point of the tor. Light fluffy ones can change suddenly into a swirling mist enveloping everything: sheep, ponies, man or rock.

I felt a mixture of fear and excitement when the skies grew darker. "'Tis likely t'will turn to thunder," Uncle Ted warned. "Looks very ominous."

Usually when there was a thunderstorm at Burrow, I would choose to stay in my room watching through my bedroom window. Despite being frightened, I was mesmerised, and did not want to join my brother and the others in the kitchen's womb-like warmth and apparent safety, missing the spectacle of the grand display of light and the feel of being part of the growling, clapping thunder.

This time Uncle Ted and I watched the storm from the tallet, the loft where the hay for the cows was stored. It was always a favourite place for me. From there I could see so much — the moors, the house, the orchard — in my mind, over the hill, I could picture the river where the great Rock stood. In the summer, Uncle Ted and Dad or a neighbouring farmer would fill the tallet with hay, through the wide opening at one end. I would often climb up the ladder and simply sit there, gazing out at the landscape.

Sometimes Uncle Ted would be working with the animals below and I could hear his whistling breath as he swept the stalls or croaked gently to the horses or cows.

We sat together, now, soaked by the downpour that had sent us scurrying for shelter, staring through the framed view as thunder rumbled around the hills and lightning streaked, piercing the ground, it seemed. I clutched Uncle's jacket sleeve. It smelled of gorse.

"Don't be afraid, maid," he said. "Tidn't much good bein' afraid. See, chile, 'tis all down to fate come the finish, an' there idn't nothin' you nor anyone else can do to change it. 'Tis like it was all through the war. You

- 30 -

got it or you didn't. You ended up dead or you ended up alive, 'tis all down to fate."

I liked it when Uncle Ted talked to me like that. He didn't try to protect me from things. He told me not to stand under a tree in a storm, or do anything stupid like that, for that was tempting fate and that wasn't fair to anyone, God or yourself.

Uncle Ted held me gently, close to him. It was cosy watching the brilliant flashing from the safety of his hold, and the hay soft against us smelling sweet. Every time the thunder clapped I froze, but Great Uncle Ted tightened his arm around my shoulders, his big hand covering my ear and his rough, horny thumb stroking my cheek.

"There, chile, no need to fear."

His voice soothed me and I turned my head into his shoulder, feeling safe. A huge roll of thunder crashed above us and, for a second, the tallet was bright with light. I clung to Uncle Ted and he turned towards me, held me close against him, my legs against his. I felt a lump in his thick corduroy trousers pressing against me. The rain swept down, hammering the roof as we clung to one another; then it stopped. The rain and thunder ceased and Uncle softly kissed the top of my head.

"Tis all over, little maid, all over … the storm has gone, we can go indoors now."

Uncle Ted and I joined the others in the kitchen and stood dripping onto the flagged floor.

"Where were you, Cleo? Why did you stay out in the storm? It's dangerous." My mother, wide-eyed, stared at Uncle Ted accusingly as though he had tried to do me harm. Uncle Ted shrugged and stomped out of the room. There was a silence then, an awful silence.

I didn't know what was being thought in that silence; but it felt like yet another of those dreaded moments that would stay indelibly in my mind for ever, along with the image of my brother, pale and pinched, clutching a pencil tightly, drawing at the table. My father by the door, ready to put on his ancient sou'wester and return to his studio outside, and my mother, white and trembling, standing by the hot range wringing her hands. And me, wondering what it was that was inside Uncle Ted's trousers. It would surely be an animal, one that he had rescued from the storm.

After all, Mother was not keen on the sort of animals Uncle Ted sometimes rescued and brought into the house. One Christmas, though, he had made her laugh when he entertained us all by putting his pet ferret down his trousers. I felt so happy that he made her laugh. No one else seemed able to, especially not me.

But most of the time she scarcely acknowledged Uncle Ted. I thought it unfair that she should treat him so offhandedly. After all, we were staying in his house. He seemed genuinely glad to have us there, to have someone other than Meg Dodson to cook for him and Monty, who was simple and always wore a blank expression on his dark-skinned face.

I could not name my mother's disapproval of practically everything my father or Great Uncle Ted did or said. I thought it was something about the way Uncle spoke and the way my father would listen and drift into the same language as they talked to each other about the harvest or the price of calves.

My father had not been brought up on the farm, but he was an Endaton through and through. His father was, after all, Uncle Ted's brother, my grandfather. Unlike Ted, my grandfather Jim had won a scholarship to grammar school, and because it was miles away he had to be a boarder. This divided the brothers and Jim had gone on to University where he met my Norwegian grandmother, a fellow student.

They married and later brought their son Felix to the farm for holidays. He would follow Uncle Ted around and help with the farm chores.

When the war came the brothers both joined the army. Aunty Gwen, Uncle Ted's wife, and a land girl kept the little farm going as best they could. Dad and his mother still came for the occasional visit. Then one day Dad's father, my grandfather was killed, Dad was sent to boarding school and then there were only a few short visits to the farm.

That Uncle Ted survived the North African campaign was a miracle and when he came home it was an even bigger miracle that Monty, named after the famous general, was born just a few short months after Uncle Ted's return, though Aunty Gwen was very ill and died soon after the birth.

Uncle told me that the trouble with Monty was all because Gwen had smoked too heavily. "It turns you black," he said. "Makes the baby's brain soft."

Poor Monty, I thought, with his soft brain and smoke-blackened face. It was years before I discovered that American soldiers had been stationed in Crediford and that some of them were black.

My father laughed when I told him what Uncle had said about Monty. "He's such a rogue," he said, chuckling. "You can't believe everything Uncle Ted tells you."

But I did. Especially what he told me about the Rock.

CHAPTER 4

The Easter holiday weather continued bright and changeable. "Sunshine and showers — a bit like Mother's moods," I confided to Peter, whose face took on a look of pinched anxiety at my criticism, making me feel guilty and responsible, as though he were still a baby, not my younger brother by only eighteen months.

Mother seemed to be watching me whenever I was in her presence. She didn't like me going off for hours with Uncle, even if I were on Brownie. I learned to slip out of the house quietly or would pretend I was going to see Dad in his studio. Dad showed little interest in what I was doing when we were at the farm. I wanted him to come and watch Brownie perform her circles in the orchard, but he always said, "Not now, poppet — perhaps when I've finished this painting."

I preferred his lack of interest to Mother's over-concern. Once, she accused him of being 'emotionally lazy'. Dad had looked angry and left the room. One day on my way to the storeroom, where the horses' tack was kept, I heard them talking as I walked passed the larder window. There was wire gauze across the little opening and the window was pushed wide to allow more air to circulate around the enamel dishes of milk that stood on the cool slate shelves waiting to be clotted into cream. Mother was putting something into the larder and her anxious voice was raised higher than usual so that my father, sitting in the kitchen, would hear her.

"You know what I mean, Lance — you know very well — it's simply not healthy, this liaison. I won't stand by and watch it happening."

"Nonsense." My father sounded gruff, yet I detected that note in his voice seeming to say she may be right. I hated the way he agreed with her. I couldn't tell which side he was on.

"Perhaps Peter could go outside more, be with them too. He's always left out. There is safety in numbers," she continued persuasively.

I stood quietly beneath the window, eavesdropping and feeling guilty. I knew they were talking about me and Uncle Ted, but I could not begin to understand what the problem was. It was, I knew, a dark secret, something to do with grown-ups, and deep down I felt certain it was something to do with what had happened in the tallet with the thing in Uncle Ted's trousers.

I wondered about it and once, when Mother had hung the washing out to dry on a breezy blue-sky April morning, Great Uncle Ted's brown corduroy trousers were hanging from their huge waist on the line next to his vast long johns. I stood under them, watching the legs dancing in the wind. The long johns were made of off-white wool and I giggled when a sudden gust flipped one leg over the line. I jumped up to release it and saw the thick slit in the front, above the legs at the joint. I put my hand on it to pull the trapped leg back over the line. The brown corduroys were waving, dancing less lightly than the long johns. Nevertheless they were hopping to the sound of the wind.

The thick grain of the corduroy lines reminded me of the fresh-worked gashes in the field below the orchard, which Uncle Ted was ploughing. I could hear the chugging of the tractor, the sound wafting loud then quiet, depending on the wind and the turn at the end of each row. I liked the sound. I liked the thought of Uncle Ted going up and down all day in the open tractor, his cheeks getting redder from the constant exposure to the fickle Dartmoor air. This was all I needed. This was forever. This changing wind, this stillness, was all that mattered. It was what made me happy in my heart despite the terrors in my life, despite knowing the uncertainty of my mother's existence.

The trousers shook and rain pelted for brief seconds before a slant of sun, borne on the breeze, showed them swinging to its tune.

I laughed at the antics, saw the brown gash open and shut as the waist stretched on the line, revealing the thick double corduroy slit. I saw the buttons, brown and strong, securely sewn, and I stared into the place that I knew, and had always known, was the source of my mother's fear.

Solemn now, I tried to imagine what Uncle Ted or any man held secret behind that buttonholed place. Though I pretended that Mother was stupid to be afraid, in my heart I wondered if she might be right. I thought about asking her to tell me, but when I went indoors to find her, she was asleep, white and drawn, in a chair by the sitting room fire, with a rug over her legs. I felt a prickling behind my eyes and my heart heaved. There was a book on her knee, half held by her long manicured fingers. We had been away from London for weeks, and the varnish on her nails was slightly chipped and fading. Gently I moved the book from her hold and placed it on the table beside her. She stirred as a log shifted in the fire, sending orange sparks up the chimney. I carefully heaped more logs onto the dying flames, glanced at my mother once more before creeping from the room.

At the door I jumped, for there was a figure sitting in the dark corner. It was Peter. Wide-eyed and white, he was hunched, silent, sitting on a cushion, staring at an encyclopaedia.

"Is she dead?" he whispered.

"Course not, silly. Just resting. Leave her alone, come and help me feed Brownie." I helped him to his feet, putting my arm around his thin shoulders, closing the sitting room door quietly.

"It's all right, Peter," I said as I took his hand, "Everything is all right. We are all here together. Dad, Mum, you, me and Uncle Ted and Monty." I felt Peter's hand relax in mine and I felt the burden of it all in my heart.

Mother's illness came and went. Peter and I grew used to it. We had been drawn together in our fear about her. Usually I felt the need to comfort Peter but often we would talk about other things together. We would do our homework side by side at the table and there were times when we would get a fit of unaccountable giggles, which annoyed Mother, and made Peter and me comrades as we stifled our laughter and bent our heads over our homework.

CHAPTER 5

I was already thirteen and Peter almost twelve when we all went to Burrow for a few weeks in the winter to look after the farm for Uncle. He was recovering from bronchitis, staying with a cousin in Dorset.

Although Meg Dodson came each day to clean, make lunch and see to the dairy work, it was Mother and I who prepared the family supper each evening. Although she looked tired, she was well enough, I thought, for me to ask her a question.

"Why do you sometimes call Dad Lance"? I asked.

She stood there in that warm kitchen, looking at me, pale, thin-faced. She pushed a wisp of hair from her cheeks and pinned it carefully behind an ear. It was a cold, long winter, and we had stayed longer than I had dared to hope. Uncle Ted's doctors had said he should wait for the snow to thaw before returning to Dartmoor. So it felt like the farm was ours. Dad was enjoying being the farmer. It was a quiet enough time on the farm, just bullocks and sheep to feed, hens and horses and Jumble to look after. We fed the sheep as close to home as possible, not wanting to lose any lambs if the weather turned to snow again. Carrying the hay, burying my nose into its scent of summer, I revelled in the work with Dad. Peter wanted to be indoors helping Mother, but that day Dad had insisted on a swapping of roles. I had not objected, for was I not the luckiest girl in the world? I could afford to spend some time doing chores with my mother, knowing that most of the winter was ahead of us and I was free. Free from school, free from London, and best of all, being with my beloved pony every day, as well as living in the one place on earth that felt like real home, though I missed Uncle Ted badly.

My mother had not wanted to come, not wanted to leave London to look after Uncle Ted's farm. "There's no Catholic school," she had fretted.

"They don't need school." My father's voice had been unusually severe. "Let them run wild for a bit." He was right and I was thrilled at the prospect of the freedom of all those days on the farm and no school.

"They need the social contact," Mother had argued, "to say nothing of the lack of learning at this crucial time in their lives." But she had lost the fight, looked weary. I remember Peter's face being white while they argued.

But here we were, and Mother and I were alone in the kitchen. She had met my question with that faraway look, as though she had not heard me.

"Why Lance?" I repeated. "Why is it you sometimes call Dad Lance?" We were settled now, Mother cutting apples to stew while I washed the vegetables for supper. Big orange carrots in a bowl of water and my hands holding them, scrubbing them clean. They smelled of the earth in Uncle Ted's garden.

She answered in an offhand, detached voice. "Oh, just a habit from years ago. I christened him Lancelot." She wasn't smiling.

I scrubbed the carrots, made the orange gleam through the murky water, my mind dismissing the possibility of a connection between my father being Lancelot, making my mother into Guinevere.

I felt an indescribable anger; I could not, would not, give my mother a life. It was as though she had never really been born, was already dead. I did not want to own such a thought, did not wish her dead, though I knew she was forever on the brink. I did not hope for it, I think I just wished it was over, finished, so life could be normal, like other people's lives. Happy.

That we were an unhappy family was my blueprint. Its reality was stamped indelibly on my persona. The cleaned carrots drowned under my hands for seconds before I hauled them, splashing water noisily, out on to the table to be chopped. Vehemently, I sliced them into circles.

That night I dreamed of the Rock. My nightmares were always intense and sometimes terrifying. In this one, water engulfed me. I had climbed into the hole, the monster's eye, lost control and was submerged, drowning. I tried to scream but no sound would come. I struggled feverishly and awoke streaming with perspiration, my throat sore and dry.

CHAPTER 6

We were spending all summer at the farm. I was fourteen but the power of the Rock still held me in its grip. Although by this time I had stopped believing in a solid, real monster, I knew the Rock was the place that held luck, good and bad. It was where all our futures hung in the balance. It was the very centre of life: the beginning of things and the end. God lived there and so did the devil. To enter needed courage, but you had to go through that great mouth-eye at least once; everything depended on it. Those of us whose ancestors had sprung from this earth, this moor, this hilly domain lying between the sky and the depth of the earth's centre — hell itself — knew about the Rock.

I gathered from Uncle Ted that we were very special people, chosen like the Jews to live in this Israel. "We needn't take much notice of what governments up London says, we are masters of our own fate," he had told me once as we sat on the hillside above the Rock. Our horses munched the grasses between the clumps of heather. We had picked some whortleberries, their purple juice trickling in and around my mouth. I crammed in the last few berries and Uncle Ted handed me his huge red-spotted handkerchief to wipe my fingers.

"There aren't no big houses here with bigwigs to tell us what to do. We've lived independent all through time. We neither starve nor wallow in riches. Only God is our master," he said.

Uncle's horse moved a few yards, pulling the reins from his hands, and I jumped up and brought the horse back. Uncle was smiling

"Thank ee, maid, though I don't expect he'd have moved far from us."

I handed the reins back, noticing Uncle's hands as he took them from me. They were old, worn-looking, with ridges like the ones on his face. I suddenly felt a fear that one day Uncle might go. I had never thought of him as an old man. He was Uncle Ted. Always here, in this landscape. He was part of a world that surely could not end.

I sat down again on a boulder next to Uncle Ted. Brownie had stopped eating and was leaning her head against me, with her eyes closed. The sun shone from behind soft white clouds, and the moor around us smelled warm, earthy and fresh from recent rain. Above our heads two buzzards wheeled.

I was thinking that this place was Uncle's place of worship, his church. He must have read my mind.

"I used to be a chapel man," he mused, "but when Auntie Gwen died, leaving me with Monty, I reckoned God had forgotten about me. But then, thinking about it one day, I realised that I'd come through all that fighting in the desert, so someone must have watched over me then, and I reckoned it was the Dartmoor God, the one who lives down there, in that place." Uncle Ted pointed towards the Rock.

"He's got a proper parish down there. It stretches all over Dartmoor. Underneath, mind you. Why, this very moment we're standing on one of his rooms, dining room or something." He grinned at me and stretched forward to pick a last berry from a small plant hidden between the heather clumps.

"Auntie Gwen and I had been married just a few weeks when the call came for me to go and fight for England. Back then, I thought fighting for England meant I was saving Gwen and all the Dartmoor people."

Uncle Ted held his hand out and I took the berry. "I remember that last night before I went to war," he continued thoughtfully, "there was a full moon and I got out of bed; Auntie was fast asleep. I crept out the 'ouse and followed the track to the river. It was like something was calling me saying 'come on, Ted, come down to the Rock,' so I goes. It was like daylight, everything clear in the moonlight. As I got closer I could hear the water rushing around the Rock. It was like a thousand voices babbling."

Uncle Ted stopped talking and I, still as a mouse, longed for him to continue. I turned and looked at him, sitting there amidst the tufts of heather on the side of the hill gazing down to the Rock, the great Rock with the soft moorland waters racing around its huge flanks. Uncle Ted's face looked like granite with lichened marks and grooves. I waited.

"You see, maid," he said, "all them voices, that was ancestors shouting at me telling me not to be afraid of fighting."

"Were you afraid, Uncle?"

"Yes, maid, I was afeared to lose my Gwen," he sighed, "and all this." He held his arms out to the moor around us.

I felt tears in my eyes, thinking of Uncle Ted's sadness.

"I climbed through the 'ole," he said. "I had only climbed through once before, when I was a nipper, with my brother — your dad's father." He looked at me as though he was noticing for the first time who I was. "We Endatons have a special connection with this place," he continued. "Don't you ever forget it, maid. 'Tis our birthright. I can't pretend to understand it all, but I do know that I was saved in the war because I'd got all them people in the Rock looking after me."

I believed him, because Peter and I had heard things coming from the Rock once when we had been picnicking on a bend in the river and had wandered away from our parents. We were very close to the bend when Peter had grabbed my arm.

"I can hear people shouting," he said wildly. His fingers clutched my arm, pinching me, and I saw fear in his eyes. I pulled away.

"Stop hurting, stupid," I had said, annoyed.

"Can't you hear it?" he insisted.

"Yes," I said. I held his arm now. "Yes, it's music, I can hear music."

We stood ankle-deep in the cold water on a grainy, granite rock, stunned by the sound. It was people shouting and music filling our ears, crashing, tuneless, frantic, a crescendo of sound accompanying the shouting chorus. We turned, slipping and sliding down river away from the sounds, which I guessed had come from the Rock.

Peter had wanted to tell our parents, but I said, "No, no, no," and made him promise not to tell them, especially not our mother.

"You mustn't," I told him. "She will get more ill if she thinks there are things on the moor to frighten us. She will stop us from coming here by ourselves."

She disliked the moor enough as it was; it had been a miracle that she had agreed to a family picnic that day, and to tell her of our fears would have ruined everything. Peter, I knew, would keep our secret, not risk upsetting Mother, making her even more ill.

Now it was a relief to tell Uncle Ted about hearing the sounds from the Rock, for I knew he would understand and I knew he would keep the secret from Mother.

Uncle listened intently as I told him about that day and the voices we had heard. For a while he was silent, then: "You ask your Dad to take you through, maid. I'm too stiff for the climb now, but your Dad, he'll take you through the Rock. 'Tis important, maid."

I knew it was important, but as we rode down the hill away from the Rock, I knew somehow I should climb through on my own. If I asked Dad he might say no or somehow involve my mother. No, I thought, I shall do it alone. I shall ride there alone on Brownie and climb through the Rock and everything will get better after that. We will have good luck, Mother will get better and everything will be all right.

As Uncle Ted and I rode homeward, my heart sang with the hope of the success of what I would do.

'Climb through and you'll never get rheumatism. You'll dream of your true love too — if you're lucky.' My father's words rang in my head. Uncle Ted's warning tones repeatedly went around my brain that 'If you climb through and get your feet wet you're in for bad luck for a whole year.'

I considered all these possibilities the next day as Brownie took me there. She was fit now, hardly noticing the long pull up the hill above Burrow. She cantered, tossing her head as we made our way, the gorse crisp in the heat. The heather in full late August bloom, dry and crackly, swishing against Brownie's legs.

I heard the water as we drew close, rushing around the Rock. The river was lower after the warm summer days but it swirled around the foot of the Rock, dark like a whirlpool, before flowing back into the main stream. The river was wide here, strewn with whale-like boulders, hump-backed, now smooth and dry.

I sat on Brownie, staring at the Rock, letting her graze. I was scared. Perhaps I should have heeded Uncle's warning not to climb through alone after all. My resolve was draining from me. Looking down towards the magic pool it looked dark and I fancied that its magic was somehow warning me. Leaving Brownie's reins dangling in the heather, I went gingerly to the river's edge. Brownie, I knew, would not leave without me. She followed me down to the bank by the water's edge, cropping the short sheep-grazed grasses. I sat on the bank, removed my boots and socks and dabbled my feet nervously in the shallows, while sizing up what I would do next and how I might achieve this terrifying deed. The water was icy cold and already my feet felt numb. There was no way I could cross over to the Rock without getting my feet wet, whatever Uncle said; but his words of warning — 'bad luck for a year' — seemed to keep a rhythm in my head, in tune with the rushing river.

Ignoring my fear I stood up, took a deep breath, told Brownie to wait for me and stepped down to the first humpy stone. Being close to the bank it was dry and felt warm, but there were at least ten more between me and the Rock itself. Some were almost completely submerged and others were just wet enough to have developed a slippery slimy algae that was unnerving to stand on.

Breathlessly I leaped from one to the next, not giving myself time to fall when I felt myself slipping. I had not expected the water dashing around the Rock to be so deafening as I got near to the base. It raged around my legs as I jumped onto the final submerged boulder, throwing me off balance and hard against the great base of the Rock. There was no time to think. Instinctively I hauled myself onto a narrow shelf, which skirted a few inches of the Rock. With my feet so placed I was bound to lose my balance and could fall back into the deep water.

To regain my equilibrium seemed impossible and, in the panic of a few seconds, I threw my arms out as though to grab the smooth wall of rock. To my surprise I found my fingers grasping onto tiny handholds of granite, which gave me split seconds of time to gather my wits and move my feet upwards. They too found footholds, which I had not seen from below. I had to move quickly to avoid falling and each move gave me a foot or handhold. So I clambered up its side and, with a sense of exhilaration and terror, pulled myself up to the relative safety of the brim of the great hole, worn smooth by a million winters.

I lay there for several moments, breathing hard before realising that by crawling forward a few inches I would be looking down into the depths of the Rock. Trembling now, I eased myself into a sitting position on the very edge of this monster mouth. Peering through the misty spray sent up by the force of water, I could see that the Rock was three-sided, for on the side that faced away from me there was a large oval opening, a doorway, through which water was gushing in and out. It was through that opening I would have to pass, where the water swirled around a smaller rock. I sat with my legs hanging down toward the rushing waters below.

If I eased myself down the side, through the hole, and balanced myself, keeping my hands flat on the gigantic brim, I might, just might, be able to touch that small shelf with my feet. Then if I leaned against the side and far enough towards where the water raced past the Rock, I could possibly place a foot in that crack and heave myself onto the shelf that jutted from the other side. From there I might be able to swing out through that door, that opening, and then…then what? Would it be possible to ease my way around the Rock to where I had entered the river, to where Brownie was waiting? I shook with fear at what I would attempt. Suppose I slid down inside this cave-like Rock, landing safely on the little ledge, managed to let go of the brim while at the same time saving myself from over-balancing, by leaning on the smooth wall? Suppose I got that far, would I be able to heave myself around to that shelf without falling, without knocking my head and drowning, without getting wetter, without bringing bad luck for a year?

Leaning forward and over the edge, the water's gush almost obliterated the sound of the buzzard's call above. Looking up again I saw it hovering, searching for its prey. It was as though I could be that prey, as though I had already plunged into the confusion of the deafening dark waters below — was already drowned.

"No! No! I can't," I shouted as I pulled myself back. Shaking uncontrollably I crawled to the place where I had climbed up. I must get down again. I must get back to Brownie. I would go down the way I had come. It was the only way. Sobbing I turned my body to face the Rock, then, gripping it for a brief second, my body began to slide. Slowly at first, then gaining momentum, I slithered down the granite wall, feeling its roughness tearing at my clothes, my arms flailing in their desperate search for something to hang on to. My face grated as my hands tore at the now non-existent holds.

I had crashed to the base of the Rock, bounced onto a rounded boulder and was lying there letting water wash over me. Gradually it dawned on me that I was safe and could move. Cautiously I stood up and saw Brownie on the bank watching anxiously and nickering her usual welcome. With tears of relief streaming down my face I stepped over the safe innocent whaleback stones to the safety and comfort of Brownie.

I washed the grazes on my arms and face, leaning over the magic pool, shakily splashing its healing waters over them, and then pulled on a jumper to hide my torn shirt. I realised how lucky had been my escape. Apart from the grazes on my face and arms, which felt sore, I was not in pain physically; but I rode back to Burrow with a heavy heart.

To my relief Mother was resting by the time I got back. I allowed my hair to hang over my hurt cheeks. The men and Peter seemed not to notice; they were already having tea. Meg Dodson had left the table spread with cake and scones and I was hungry. My hands were still shaking though as I lifted the big blue-and-white jug of milk and poured myself a mug full of its creamy liquid, relishing its comforting taste. I ate a third scone, plastered with yellow clotted cream, topped with strawberry jam, made by Meg Dodson and full of real strawberries, whole from Uncle's garden.

Wiping my mouth with the back of my hand, I asked, "What happens, Uncle, if a person looks down into the hole but doesn't climb through the Rock?"

Uncle Ted looked up from the table, put his cup down carefully and looked me squarely in the eyes. "Oh, you mustn't never do that, chile," he said. "If you do that you lose what you most want to keep." My father winked at me.

"Take no notice, Cleo," he said. "Uncle Ted's teasing you." But I was devastated by what Great Uncle Ted had said.

I had failed and hated myself for my cowardice, and felt so miserable that later I tried to tell Dad about it. He was in his studio and seemed preoccupied, uninterested in my dreadful adventure and hardly listened. Dismayed I left him to his work and went to seek comfort with Brownie.

All the same, Dad did come to my room to say goodnight. He found me sitting on the broad window seat, wrapped in a blanket, staring out at the cold moonlit moor. My room was a back one; 'dingy' my brother said, but I loved it.

"It's the best room in the house," I had declared at first.

"You don't even get morning sunshine," Peter had taunted.

I didn't care. I liked the way the morning stole into my room quietly, not blaring with great strong rays of sunlight. I could sit on my windowsill and watch the stealthy rays of sunshine creep across the landscape, light up the trees, the moors, the granite rocks, bringing the mornings to life slowly.

Dull drizzly days were no less important. It was the essence of the landscape that penetrated my being, gave me something secret, something perfect, which no other place in all the world could ever have given me. Later it would be unbearable to think about.

"We'll go and climb through early in the morning," my father promised. He was sitting beside me on the windowsill. "I'll help you, then you can forget what wicked old Uncle Ted said."

My father persuaded me to sleep now, for we must get up early for our adventure. I snuggled down into bed, relieved and tired. I wound my arms around his neck like I used to when I was small, and kissed him. "Thank you, Daddy." He stroked my head and I closed my eyes. He tiptoed to the door and as he turned the handle I opened my eyes.

"Dad," I whispered, "you'll never ever leave me, will you?"

He came back to my bedside, leaned over me and I could see a perplexed look, a concerned look as he kissed my forehead. "I'll never, never, never leave you, my little princess," he whispered.

He did, of course, but I believed him then and fell asleep.

***

The rain wakened me. It was still dark. A car's lights swished across my ceiling. I sprang out of bed. The car had stopped. What was happening? I listened to the noises coming from the kitchen, Mother's voice, high-pitched and angry.

My door was opening slowly and Peter's figure appeared. He clutched a teddy bear. Peter was almost thirteen, nearly my age, but I thought of him as little, a baby almost. He was small, then, for his age and needed protection, I thought.

His eyes were round.

"It's Mother," he said. "She's been screaming. Dad has called the doctor."

"How do you know?" I asked.

"I heard everything," he said. "Dad came into my room — I pretended to be asleep but I could hear everything."

I wondered why Dad hadn't come to me. Perhaps he had and I had been so fast asleep I didn't hear him. I was so wrapped up in my dreams, my own fears. It was all my fault; I should have climbed the Rock.

"Cleo, I'm scared."

"There's no need to be, Peter," I reassured him, but my heart was beating wildly. I knew I should have climbed through the Rock. I knew I should have put aside my silly fears. I should have done more to help Mother and now maybe it was too late. Maybe Mother was going to die this time.

Peter and I stood shivering looking through the window, holding hands. We watched as the doctor hurried through the grey dawn from the kitchen door, below my window, to his car outside the garden gate. He was reaching into the back of the car, taking something out; we craned our necks to see. The rain was increasing and he was running back up the garden path, his jacket pulled up over his head. Then we heard the back door open and close.

"No, I won't," we heard our mother shout.

Peter squeezed my hand until it hurt but I let him, for it was nothing to what might be happening to our mother.

At breakfast, Mother looked pale, but her eyes were bright and dark circles hung under them. I hardly recognised her.

Uncle Ted was nowhere to be seen. Dad gave Peter some porridge and I helped myself to toast. I was wearing jodhpurs, ready to ride to the Rock. Hail, rain or snow I was determined to climb the Rock today. Then I saw them — Mother's suitcases, two, smart blue, standing by the back door.

I looked at my father, then at the cases. He shrugged.

"What's happening?" I asked him. "Is Mother going somewhere?" I tried to sound normal. Mother looked as though she hadn't seen us, Peter and me. I buttered my toast, the scraping sound grating in the silence of that bleak breakfast.

"We are going back to London, Cleo," my father said quietly. "All of us, going home. The taxi will be here in an hour."

"But why?" I was stunned. "Why?" I asked. "Why? I don't want to go."

"I do," said Peter "if it will make Mother better."

Mother sat sleeping now, her head lolling forward. I noticed her hair, greying at the roots, looked greasy. She looked ugly, I thought guiltily.

"But what about Brownie? Uncle Ted? Monty? The Rock . . .?" My voice trailed as the awful truth dawned on me. We were leaving early. We should have had two more weeks. This was awful.

"But, Dad," I pleaded, "Please, please let's stay. You promised to come with me. I can't bear the thought of going back. I want to stay. Stay with Uncle Ted and Brownie. I could do that," I said animatedly. "I could stay here. I'll look after Uncle Ted and Monty."

"Nonsense," Dad was unusually irritated. "How can you be so selfish, Cleo? Look at your mother, she's ill. Stop thinking about yourself."

Shamed, I quietened down; crumbled up the toast and gave it to Jumble, who banged his tail gratefully from table leg to chair, licking my hands. Silent now, I washed the breakfast things and went upstairs to change and pack.

The taxi waited as Mother was helped into the back seat. Her eyes looked very bright now, she seemed almost happy. Peter too looked keen and content to cuddle up to her and be cuddled up to.

I had scarcely had time to give Brownie a carrot. "I'll be back soon, Brownie," I told her. But when? And how? The grey Dartmoor day had changed from dimpsey dawn to daytime and Uncle Ted had said, "Goodbye, little queen, don't fret. Monty and me'll take good care of her," as I climbed the orchard gate.

He meant it, I knew, but the words hung heavily around me just like the black skies hung over the land.

The old Humber car from Crediford, burdened with our family baggage, squeaked and rolled away, down our rough lane with me squeezed between Herbert the taxi man and my father. I was rigid. No tears came; they stayed inside me, deep down inside me. My stomach ached and my neck strained as I turned my head to catch a last glimpse of Great Uncle Ted staring after us, standing in front of Burrow. I held the sight for less than seconds, for suddenly the whole picture was blotted out. A heavy mist had dropped like a grey wet curtain, blanking out the sight of my beloved Burrow and Great Uncle Ted.

A feeling of loss enveloped me, pangs about having failed in my attempt to climb through the Rock. Why had I not climbed through yesterday? Now it was too late. Now I would lose what I most wanted to keep. Would that be Mother? Burrow? Brownie? Uncle Ted? Which was worse? I felt a deep and terrible guilt at the thought that losing Burrow and Brownie along with Uncle Ted would be worse than even Mother dying.

Mother was holding Peter close. Father stared out of the passenger window. He must still be very angry with me for being so selfish. He had said he would never leave me. Without him there was no one. London life held no joy for me. I was lost without Brownie and Uncle Ted and a terrible instinct warned me that I had already lost them.

My head was swimming, aching. Words chanted in my head repeatedly to the thud thud thud of the windscreen wipers. Shall I ever see Burrow again? Shall I ever see Burrow again?

CHAPTER 7

My worst fears were being realised. Not only was Mother back in the hospital, Uncle Ted was taken seriously ill. I begged to be allowed to visit him in Exeter, where he was in intensive care. Dad went but was adamant that I stayed at the flat to keep Peter company.

Nell, the good-natured Welsh woman who used to care for us when we were small and Mother too ill to look after us, was coming to stay. It was a relief to know she would be with us. She was fond of Peter and me, had been a strong support in our lives. What I liked about her was that she never pried, and when we were little would tuck us up at night and croon in a deep Welsh voice songs sad, and yet reassuring, for they were always about mountain streams and vales, reminding me of Dartmoor.

I was glad she was going to be there for Peter and me while Dad was away and Mother so ill in hospital. She would cook and keep the flat going while we were at school, and have a meal ready for when we got home. I loved the homely atmosphere she created for us. Her bustling, round shape in a grey apron, and white shirtsleeves rolled above her elbow, was a comforting presence. Yet nothing, not even Nell could make up for what might happen to Uncle Ted. The dread that lingered in my heart was so intense that I was scarcely able to move properly. Dad was to be away for only two nights, but the time seemed interminable.

"It's not good news, Cleo," he told me when he returned from seeing Uncle Ted. Although it was evening Peter was still at school; he often stayed late doing homework or playing football. It was a private school and he was doing well there and would beg Dad to let him be a boarder. We were sitting having supper, Nell had gone home again, and there was just me and Dad. I felt cold and afraid. Dad was silent and for a horrible moment or two I believed I was back in time, in my younger childhood, in those days when I used to sense the monster lurking. The room was shadowy dark, neither of us moving to switch on a light. I stared down at my open homework book and snapped the pages closed, as though to stem the gloom. Dad looked up startled, then he suddenly thumped the table with his fist, making me jump.

"First it's your mother and now it's Ted." Dad's voice was raised. "And the farm will have to go," he blurted angrily, before dropping his head in his hands, elbows on the table. I sat rigid with the shock of his words.

"What do you mean, the farm must go?" But Dad seemed not to hear me and I realised that my voice had been little more than a whisper. The front door banged and I knew Peter was back. He was whistling. Dad didn't move. I heard my brother open his bedroom door, the thud of his school bag being dumped on the floor. Dad got up quickly, switched on the light and then the radio. Radio Two: Petula Clark's clear voice: 'Downtown...' It was one of Mother's favourites and I realised that I had not thought about her all evening. Had not asked Dad if he had telephoned the hospital. I could think only of the terrible news, which Dad had still not explained properly.

Peter burst into the kitchen. "Hi, Dad, Cleo." His team, I guessed, had won. "What's up?" He was about to open the fridge door, but stopped when he saw our serious faces.

"I'm afraid Uncle Ted is on the critical list in hospital. He may not survive," Dad said. His voice sounded steadier now.

Peter frowned. He took a bottle of milk from the fridge and a cup from the sink. "Any news of Mum?" he asked, looking hard at Dad before pouring himself a mug full of milk. He came to my side of the table, opposite Dad, rucking up the green linen tablecloth as he squeezed in beside me. Some milk spilled in the process and I watched the stain grow on the clean cloth.

"Mum's a bit better today," Dad said. "She wants you both to go and see her at the weekend."

It was not until late that night, after Peter had gone to bed, that I plucked up courage and asked Dad to tell me more about Uncle Ted. I had washed and was ready for bed. Dad was still in the kitchen when I went to him. There was a bottle of whisky open on the table and he was writing something. It looked like a letter. I told myself that it was my imagination that he covered it with his hand when he saw me.

Dad got up and steered me back to my bedroom. "Come on, love," he said, gently persuading me into bed and tucking me in like he used to when I was little. Then he sat on the bed and took my hand.

"Uncle Ted," he said, "is pretty ill, and Monty has moved into Crediford with his mother's younger sister, Aunty Phyllis."

I had met Aunty Gwen's sister and liked her so felt relieved for Monty. "How long for, Dad?" I asked.

"Maybe for a very long time, Cleo. You see Uncle is too old now to farm and is too ill to return to Burrow — ever."

Waiting for Dad to tell me more, I stared at the mural on my bedroom wall, the one I had painted after we had left Burrow so suddenly. In a passion of longing for my real homeland and pony, I had covered the high wall, facing my bed, with a vibrant vision of Dartmoor hills and, in the background, the Rock. And there, with her head high and her mane blowing in the wind, was Brownie. My eyes stung, listening to Dad.

"Uncle will need to go to a residential home. There's a very nice one in Crediford," he told me. "And," he added, "I'm afraid he was in quite a lot of debt. The farm has to be sold so that Monty and Ted can be looked after."

"But what about Brownie, Dad? What's happening to my pony?"

"We'll just have to wait and see, Cleo, wait and see what happens." He kissed me goodnight, saying, "It could be worse, Cleo, at least Mum's getting better."

But I lay awake for hours, going over and over all that he had told me. He had promised I could go with him to see Uncle Ted as soon as he was a bit better. I would see him and he would be able to tell us what would be happening to the animals. At the moment, Dad had told me, they were all being looked after by Monty and his Aunt Phyllis. I was relieved to hear that Monty was still able to look after things, but I was afraid of the future. I could not possibly keep Brownie in London and I wondered what would become of her once the farm was sold. Perhaps in two years' time when I had my sixteenth birthday, Dad would let me leave school. I could find Brownie, get a job on a farm, live on the moor, be like the boy, and work with sheep and cattle on the moor. Such thoughts were a comfort but it was impossible to sleep with so much to worry about.

To make matters worse I felt sure that Dad was keeping something from me. He had been even more preoccupied since Mother had begun talking of coming home to the flat. Peter was glad but I felt desperate at the prospect. Dad, despite having gently tucked me into bed and made promises about visiting Uncle, seemed vague; there was something new about him that I could not understand.

Lying in the silence of my room, my mind full of anxieties, I went over in my head the times, lately, that I had felt Dad's distance from all that was happening. Hard to pinpoint, yet I knew I was right, he had in a sense 'moved away'. It was as though he was vanishing, wasn't present. Those moments of intimacy when he tried to be honest with me about Uncle and the farm were rare, and anyway I could not be sure of the truth in them.

Sleepless, lying in my bed, the vision of the Rock and my failure to trust myself to climb through its open mouth was again haunting me. The threat of 'losing what I most wanted to keep' was perhaps happening now, just as Uncle had warned. My heart raced and my thoughts with it…Dad would be lost to me, as well as Uncle Ted. But how? An illness? Perhaps Dad was getting ill, like Mother, and I would have to look after him, be responsible for him too. Yes, that was it; perhaps that is why he'd hidden the letter from me. A letter to his doctor perhaps? I must prepare for the shock and be responsible. After all it was my fault this had all come about. The separation from my beloved Brownie and Uncle Ted was all my fault too.

***

I slept fitfully, dozing off and on for what seemed hours, until the traffic had dulled, just a few cars and taxis thrumming along the road past the flat. The room was dark, darker than usual. Perhaps the street lamp outside had blown a bulb.

I thought I saw something in the blackness. Something moving in the room, a shape. I sat up, gasped at what was transpiring. It was Uncle Ted.

Uncle Ted was in my room, standing at the foot of my bed. I smelled his familiar scent: a mingling of heather and grain and cows in midsummer. At first he was simply a shadow moving slowly, then I heard his wheezing breath.

I held my arms out to him — tried to speak — but no words came, no sound from my throat, though I made a huge effort shouting his name. But Uncle Ted was vanishing from view.

"Don't go, Uncle. Please, please don't go." But my voice was silent and my words fell nowhere and Uncle Ted was nowhere.

It was a nightmare, just a dream, I told myself in the morning. I was hanging out of bed, the bedclothes strewn on the floor. I felt feverish and thirsty and got up to go to the kitchen for some water.

The clock on the wall said eleven. I had slept long and late. Dad was standing by the table with a teapot in his hand, which he was about to pour from. He looked up and I saw his face. White and drawn.

"What's happened, Dad?" I asked.

Dad told me to sit down, and handed me a cup of tea.

"Cleo, it's sad news I'm afraid."

"It's Uncle Ted, isn't it?"

"Yes, darling, I'm afraid so. Uncle Ted has gone. He died this morning in the early hours."

I knew it was true and I knew that Uncle had gone, for I had seen him in my room. He had come to say goodbye, and I had been unable to stop him leaving. Now the reality of it all was sinking into me and I knew that nothing would ever be the same again. Although I put on my mask, I could feel tears rolling down my face.

CHAPTER 8

Peter, at least, was happy. Dad had given in and arranged for him to board at his school. The day before he started I had confided to him how responsible I felt for all the bad things that were happening.

"Don't be daft, Cleo," Peter had said and later had given me his camera 'to cheer me up'. I knew I was going to miss him, though it felt as if he was years and years younger than me. But nothing was going to dissuade me from believing that it had been my failure to face the Rock that had made bad things happen — causing me to be on the downward spiral of 'losing what I most wanted to keep'.

***

The farm and animals were sold. Dad did not go to the sale. "There's no point," he said.

He told me that Uncle had not been keeping up with all the paperwork that modern farming entailed. He owed money to the bank, which had persuaded him to borrow in the first place, and he was charged compound interest on the money he had to borrow to pay the debt. He had been farming in the same way his grandfather had farmed, because it was all he knew. As for Brownie, to my intense sorrow she had been sold along with all the other animals at Burrow, to meet the death duties and various creditors.

I felt pulverised by this news. Had my father taken a knife and thrust it into my heart I could not have suffered more than this. The thought of not knowing where Brownie had gone and whether she was all right dominated my waking thoughts and at night she was forever appearing and disappearing in clouds of mist, which hung around the slopes of the moor surrounding the Rock. I was frightened for her. Yet sometimes in my dreams, I saw her standing near the Rock, facing it with her head held high, as though gaining strength from its protection; in the same way that I had sensed, that day with Uncle Ted, that the Rock protected the magic pool, keeping it calm, not threatened by the rage of the river's turbulence.

This thought comforted and confused me in turn. I found myself praying to the Rock, to guard Brownie from being unhappy, as though it was God, all-powerful and therefore capable of anything. At other times it seemed the Rock was deaf to me, and my nightmares gave me visions of Brownie rearing to escape from some unidentified evil.

I think I wore my mask permanently after losing my Dartmoor family. It was unbearable to think of Uncle Ted as gone from Burrow. Where was he? If I could go to Burrow perhaps I'd know if his spirit really had joined the ancestors. I wanted to climb the Rock, to be there and find Brownie.

"Dad," I asked, "could we spend a holiday down there — stay in Crediford?"

It was Saturday. I was doing my homework. Dad was cleaning the kitchen sink. Mother was in bed, tired, weary, not well.

"Look, Cleo ... " Dad turned around, sat down at the kitchen table. "I'm sorry love there's no chance of holidaying anywhere at the moment. Mum's treatment is costing a fortune. I'm not painting, let alone selling any paintings. It's a struggle, Cleo, keeping Peter at his school. At least the poor chap's happy now. It can't have been easy for him watching Mum getting iller and iller."

I gazed across the table at my father. That it might be just as hard for me seemed not to have crossed his mind. A terrible feeling of loneliness crept into me. Dad was talking again. He leaned across the table. "Cleo," he said gently, "you are all right; you are strong, and so brave. Not emotional like your brother. He takes after your mother."

Dad looked thoughtful, far away. His hand was touching mine, on the table, but I couldn't feel him, couldn't feel anything. I knew what he was saying, I could hear the words. They came to me clearly.

"You know, Cleo, don't you, that great Uncle Ted was in debt and what was left from the sale of Burrow has gone to the place where Monty is being cared for? It seems he will never progress beyond the mental age of ten or twelve. He's always been like that."

"Poor Monty," I whispered.

"I don't think he realises anything. It's just good that he's being cared for at the Centre in Plymouth. He can spend all his life there." Dad went on talking. "Cleo, you are a marvel. It's such a relief to know you are so capable — doing well at school; at this rate you'll have no trouble getting to Oxbridge. The nuns tell me you are the cleverest and most diligent pupil they have ever had. I'm very proud of you, Cleo. Glad you don't feel things like poor old Peter or Mother."

I listened to my father speaking and felt the mask not just on my face but liquid, like clay, pouring over me. He walked around the table, stroked my head and smoothed my hair down. I felt his hand stroking me, as though I had become clay. It felt as though I was being re-formed.

I sat stock-still. My father is shaping me, I thought, and I am Cleo, sliding into the person he wants me to be. I felt the weight of his hand on my shoulder. My body was heavy. He patted me, patted the clay. It was cooling now. I was made. I was the cool, clever, unemotional, distant daughter that I was required to be.

"Cheer up, Cleo," he smiled. He seemed satisfied with the fine work he had done and the speech he had made to me.

I smiled faintly back, feeling as I did so the tautness of the mask around my mouth.

"That's better," he said. "Keep an eye on things won't you? I'm off to see a potential client, someone who is interested in buying one of my paintings."

When he'd gone I switched on the TV.

I wore the mask more frequently. It was like a friend who came like magic and covered my face, making me invisible. When the mask was in place, people ignored me. Behind it I could stay silent, mute, show no emotion, stop tears, stem laughter with no effort at all. .It was like clicking a switch in my head. Somewhere between my brain and my throat was the switch, which I clicked on more and more often, and it saved me again and again.

Mother was in hospital the night I woke up, hearing laughter from my parents' room. I had been dreaming about Burrow and Uncle Ted. I was on Brownie, cantering over the moors, when something woke me. As usual my heart sank. There was no Uncle Ted, no Burrow, and no Brownie. But I could swear I had heard my father's laughter. I crept from my room and walked across the hallway. The light shone under his door and I put my hand on the handle. I wanted to cry. I longed to tell Dad about my dream, about the feelings of loss without Brownie and Burrow. He would listen to me. He would help me. Now with Mother gone into hospital and Peter at boarding school there was only me and him. I would be his queen, like I had been for Uncle Ted. Dad would surely now listen and help me.

Quietly I opened the door. Dad was standing in the full light of the room. I stared with disbelief at what I saw. Dad, Felix, was naked; unashamedly standing near my parents' bed and on the bed lay a young woman, also naked. She lay on her side, her head propped up on her hands. A smile faded from her face when she saw me.

I turned and walked away, silently closing the door behind me. I crept back to my room, closed and locked my door and got back into bed. I lay still, wide awake, my heart weighed down, drenched with disappointment and disbelief, overwhelmed by an indescribable feeling of dread. My eyes wide open, I lay awake until dawn when sleep finally overcame me.

***

I had never seen a naked body before, not even Mother's. She had made certain that Peter and I would have no opportunity to view each other's nakedness. It seemed natural that even when we were small we would bath separately.

When she was away in the hospital, Nellie looked after us. She was kind and sang as she worked around the house, hummed and sang. She did things as Mother had ordained. Separate bath times for Peter and me, strict bed times. Lights out at 7.30.

We saw little of Dad then. I don't know where he was; visiting Mother perhaps or talking to his numerous friends about his work. Just occasionally the friends came to the flat. They drank a lot and smoked. I would sit on Dad's lap feeling excited. We stayed up late then and Peter bounced around with red cheeks and bright eyes as the grown-ups played games with us.

On those evenings Nellie didn't sing when she put us to bed. "It's late for you poor children," she would say in her lilting Welsh voice. "Your poor mother would be mortified, yes mortified."

I wondered what 'mortified' was, and asked Nellie.

"I don't know, Cleo, really. I don't know just what it means, but I know your mother would be it if she were here."

I was mystified about everything: about 'mortified', about Mother, about what Peter would look like without clothes, about Dad smoking in the flat when mother wasn't there; I thought maybe he liked her not being there. It worried me. It was always such a relief when, home again, Mother took charge. Dad visited his friends less and they never came to the flat. Nellie only came to clean and cook and Mother put us to bed, still sighing as she found our pyjamas, brushed our hair. She would lead me to my little room where she tucked me into bed and swept a hand gently across my forehead before clicking off the light and saying, "Night, Cleo. God bless."

"Night-night, Mother." I did not want her to go. Once I cried, "Please stay with me, Mother, please stay," I sobbed. She came back to my bedside.

"Whatever is it, Cleo?" she asked.

I could not tell her what it was. I only knew I was unhappy.

"Don't be naughty, Cleo. Go to sleep now, you always cry when you're tired."

She sounded irritated, I stifled my sobs and she left the room. But I felt liquid pouring warm down my legs, wetting my long nightie, swamping the sheet under me. The warmth of my urine was somehow comforting and I fell asleep wet, warm and empty in my heart. That was when I first learned about wearing the mask.

Now I was fourteen and too grown up to cry or wet myself. I wore the mask though, more and more.

***

The woman I'd seen in my parents' bedroom was not there in the morning. Dad looked at me sheepishly and gave me his lopsided smile. I could not look at him. I don't think I ever really looked at him again after that. He tried to talk, even said sorry. I felt uncomfortable, didn't want him to talk to me about anything.

Mother seemed to be better and the routine of schoolwork absorbed me. I lost myself in it, and sailed through examinations. The convent school was something of a haven for me, but even there I would escape to the library, away from the other girls, with their noisy giggling and endless chattering about boys, sex and films. Not that I was one of the good ones, constantly rushing to open doors for the Mother Superior or a priest. Being alone in the library was what I wanted, safely hidden from the world. My mask became a permanent fixture. Behind this invisible façade I could pretend to like what I was doing, immersed in maths and science — not that the subjects fascinated me, but they stretched my brain without the dangers of having to delve into my imagination. It was then I stopped painting and drawing.

I felt a mixture of relief and terror when Dad left us. I began referring to him as Felix. Dad had gone and now I looked after Mother. She seemed to perk up and take an interest in Peter. She even went to watch him play cricket at school.

So it was a shock when I realised that her illness was no longer to do with her mind but her body. She was dying of cancer.

CHAPTER 9

It didn't happen until I was nearly nineteen, living in a bed-sit and working in a department store. Having deferred my place at university I suppose I was waiting for my mother to die.

To be near her during her last weeks, I had moved into her flat in London, which was close to the hospice. I remember being numb, feeling nothing in a conscious way. So much happened between us in those weeks — my mother and me.

My father came over from Spain and stayed in Dorset with his girlfriend's sister. I had never liked the girlfriend. Prue was her name, but she was far from being prudent, I thought, or prudish for that matter. She had literally thrown herself at Felix's feet and I despised him for falling for it. He had promised never to leave me, but simply forgot his promise when this female Prudence came to one of his art lectures and dug her claws into him.

That my mother had suffered over it was not something I wanted to think about. After all, it was, in my view, her fault in the first place. She was so frail and far away and unaccommodating all the time. I didn't blame Felix for leaving her — but for him to leave me was more than I could bear. Of course Felix came back to see Peter and me after the separation. We even went down to Dorset for a weekend with him and Prudence, to her sister and her husband and their three horrible brats of kids. I prayed that Dad would not give this old bag a baby. Prudence was a drip and Dad must have realised this by the time Mother lay dying and he came to visit her.

He had got off the ferry from Santander in Plymouth and driven straight to London and the hospice, his hands full of flowers. Perfect, scentless winter greenhouse flowers bought from some motorway service station en route. The room was mostly pink. My mother was sleeping when he whispered to me, "Prue and I have split up."

"Bit late, isn't it?" I hissed back, glaring at him. He looked grey, not just his hair, but his face was putty-coloured.

My mother's eyes filled with tears when he left. I stayed on, till the drugs held her in their grip so she could sleep for a few night hours.

I would be back early the next morning. Be with her all the time. We talked a bit. She slept a lot. One day she asked me to find her old rosary. It was in a jar on her dressing table in her flat. There were two. One with big beads and a small wooden cross attached, and another broken one, which I mended and took to her the next day.

"Look, there are two," I said brightly. "We can say the rosary together."

She gave a wan sort of smile and turned her head away from me.

I felt ashamed. It was too late, I told myself, too late to make up for all the years we had not said the rosary, certainly not together. We had not said much together in fact, and now she was dying and I felt her disappointment and blamed myself.

I didn't cry until I was back at the flat and then only a sort of sob, quickly stifled, as I briskly prepared myself for tomorrow and another day at her bedside.

My brother Peter was there on that last day. I had met the overnight train from Scotland early in the morning and watched the passengers walking along the cold, wet Monday platform. He stood out, being so tall and thin. I was faintly shocked to see him looking even more like our mother than when I had last seen him at Christmas. He looked serious and pale, though his first year at university was suiting him, I could tell. There was an air of confidence about him that I had not seen before.

We went straight to the hospice and walked along the corridor towards her room. I found myself thinking about the first time my brother and I had visited our mother in hospital. We must have been about four and five years old and I remembered thinking it strange that all those ill people were not in bed. It was a mental hospital, and we, Peter and me, holding Felix's hands, walked quietly along the corridors to the large room where my mother was sitting. Except for chairs and a table or two, the room seemed empty, though full of people, all slumped and dozy or shuffling about slowly.

"We are not allowed to go to bed in the daytime," Mother had told us. Her voice was sad and she clutched her handbag. "The priest visits me," she added.

"Good," my father nodded. Then silence. There was an old man, long and skinny, who waved his arms around. His eyes bulged and his tongue fell out of his mouth. He dragged it in again with his teeth, muttering strange sounds, frighteningly.

My father must have seen my terror. "The kids could go outside. The sun's shining and there's a bench on the grass." I looked through the French windows. They were closed. The garden was dead, just a green space with a bench seat. It was empty and no one was out there.

"No." My mother's voice was loud and snapping. I jumped, surprised. "There are men there." She was twisting her hands around the handle of her bag. My father sighed and took peppermints from his pocket. I watched him handing one to the man with the tongue. Sucking my peppermint I thought about Edie, my friend at kindergarten. She told me that if a man wants you to have a baby he puts his tongue in your mouth. I had said, "That's disgusting." "It's all up to the man," Edie had said. Although impressed by her knowledge I had also felt sickened by it. I stared under my eyelids at the man with his tongue falling out of his frothy mouth, hating the thought that he might put it into my mother's mouth.

"I feel sick."

"You shouldn't have brought them. Cleo is always car sick," my mother scolded, and I began to cry.

Dad sounded gentle but I saw the look he held in his words — despair and frustration. "We'll go now. Say goodbye to Mummy." I stopped crying, but I remember Peter sobbing loudly as we left our mother in that awful room.

I ran down the corridor in front of them both, longing to escape.

***

This hospice was so different. There were warm glowing carpets and our feet were soundless as we walked. There was a fresh smell of lavender.

Mother's eyes were wide with hope as she gazed at my brother. He stroked my mother's head. I couldn't stand it and left the room. Down the corridor I found a loo reeking of disinfectant. I washed my hands.

"I'm like Pontius Pilate," I told myself. "I wash my hands of him, and her." I pinched my cheeks hard to bring some colour to them. "These two hurting people. It's too pathetic," I told the reflection in the mirror. Silently, of course, for there were two other women in there, crying, perhaps their mother was dying too, or dead.

Later, in McDonalds, I wondered how my brother would react if he knew how hard my edges were.

"You look tired." He sounded gentle.

"I'm fine," I quipped, with a quick smile. I stirred my coffee.

Peter leaned towards me, wearing a serious expression. "Sis, there's something I want to talk about." That's when I learned the awful truth — which would change me, change my thoughts, my feelings

"Fancy her telling you all that, Peter." I was genuinely shocked. "Did her father really do that to her?"

My brother glanced across the room as though expecting everyone nearby to be listening enthralled. His face had pinkened with, I guessed, a mixture of embarrassment and the effort of telling something so secret, which had been confided to him.

"I thought you would have known, that she would have told you. After all, you're a girl, her daughter."

"Tell me more." I could feel sweat gathering under my armpits. We must have sat there for almost two hours. The waitress came twice and walked away again seeing that I had not touched my burger. It lay there congealing, cold. The smell had cooled off too. The coffee, not sipped, had gone slate grey in its cardboard cup.

"Disgusting," I said, looking at the coffee.

"Yes, I'm afraid so," my brother said sadly. He too stared at the coffee cup. Perhaps we both wished that the coffee were all we need feel so revolted about, not what he had told me concerning our mother's experiences with her own father, our grandfather. I was more upset than I wanted to be. It was time to go, to return to the hospice, to our mother's warm room and the pink, red and blue flowers that stood on the windowsill. Perhaps there would be time to tell her how sorry I was feeling for all that she had borne when she was only in her teens, a year and a half younger than I was then. I was angry for not having known about her pain.

The lift took us to her floor. The journey seemed endless. I tried not to think about what Peter had told me, about the awful background that she, our mother, had known. They weren't poor or anything simple like that. They were what used to be known as lower middle class, he a chemist's assistant. He had failed his exams to be a full-blown chemist because of having to work to keep his mother and father from poverty. The opportunity to retake the exams never came, for he was married with a family of his own. Our grandmother had married him when she was seventeen and died at twenty-five. Our grandfather reared the four children, of whom our mother was the oldest. The others were boys. Our mother became second mother to them and, from the age of twelve, had to bear the advances of her poor frustrated father, who had turned to the bottle as well as to his daughter for comfort. When at fifteen she became pregnant, he performed an abortion on her. She ran away then, vowing never to return to her Liverpool Irish background. She found jobs where she could, making her way towards London. Eventually she met my father when she worked in a café in Oxford. He, an art student, drank coffee there with his friends. She was quiet and pretty. Her sadness touched his romantic artist's heart. She was eighteen when they married. She never told him her story.

"Are you the only one who knows?" I asked Peter, aghast.

"Apart from you, now, Cleo — as far as I know it's never been told." He hesitated for a moment and touched my arm. "I thought it might help — er, help you understand her better."

We stepped out of the lift. What my brother didn't realise was that it made me understand her less. Why hadn't she told our father, I wondered.

"Apparently," said my brother, as though reading my thoughts, "she couldn't tell Dad because she feared he would leave her."

"He left her anyway," I reminded him sarcastically.

Peter sighed. "She hated sex, you know," he said, "and Dad must have been quite demanding."

I thought of my father, his big body wanting my thin mother in that way. Somehow it was hard to imagine them coupled.

"Are they really our parents?" I asked, before opening the door to my mother's room.

My brother gave a faint smile. "'Fraid so, Sis, that's our luck, to have the parents we have."

By the time we stood beside her bed, our mother was too close to leaving us to be conscious of my hand or Peter's on hers. We stayed with her, quietly, and watched as she breathed in and out. My throat was dry as I tried to say, "I'm sorry, Mother." It sounded meaningless. Guilt for not having made our parents happy clung to my gut. I held an image of a clean, white gull struggling on a blackened, oil-polluted beach as I looked down at the face of my dying mother.

"There is nothing to do but pray," my brother said; and I hated myself for being irritated by his words.

The night seemed endless. Nurses came silently in and out from time to time, made us tea. "It won't be long now," they told us in hushed voices.

Peter had dropped asleep, his mouth open, leaning back in the chair when I noticed the change in her, the slight struggle as she fought for air.

"Peter," I whispered hoarsely, "something's wrong. I think she's going."

Peter sprang from his chair. "Shall I get a doctor, or press the alarm?"

The hospice was quiet. It was three o'clock in the morning, the time of lowest ebb, before the rhythms of the night had changed.

"No, please let her be with us," I replied. It felt strange, being here at the moment in my mother's life I'd always dreaded and feeling different because of what Peter had told me about her. She looked whiter than the whitest paint. She stirred slightly and we, Peter and I, leaned over her and held her hands. How small they were. I had always seen her as small, but had never before registered how utterly tiny were the nails on her fingers.

Gently I held them, touched them, feeling the smoothness of the skin, the perfect oval nails. My mind was awash with all that Peter had told me. I looked down, my heart wrenched from me in my longing to comfort this torn-apart, sad, unhinged, brave woman — my mother — who I had always so callously dismissed as feeble until now. And now my feelings for her overflowed, full of regret and fury about her life. Her eyes opened briefly. She gave me a long look, as though surprised that I was there, and then, with a characteristically deep sigh, she shut them as she breathed her final breath. A sad peacefulness filled the room.

After a while: "That's it," I said, hoarsely. "It's over now. No more worry about what to do about her. She's gone Peter, really gone now."

"I'll phone the priest," my brother whispered, moving to the door. He opened it quietly and left, clicking it shut again.

I always remember the click of that door. At that moment there was a click inside me, somewhere near my heart. It restricted my breathing for a moment or two and my heart began to beat unevenly.

That really is it, I thought, it's truly the end. Now I am an orphan, really an orphan. I leaned closely over my mother, my face near to hers.

"Mum, I wish it had been different. I wish I'd really loved you. I never thought you loved me. Are we incapable of love, you and me? Is this what happens to some women? This mother-daughter thing going on and on for ever, hating each other. I don't think I'll ever want children, certainly not a daughter. It's all been spoilt for me — all the normal things. Why couldn't you and Dad have been normal?"

I was sobbing and put a paper hanky to my face, for the room was suddenly filling up. The priest, doctors, nurses jostled around the bed. I left, closing the door tightly behind me.

***

After the funeral it had been a relief to escape from England. A relief to leave my homeland for Canada. Peter had decided to go to Australia to finish his degree. We cleared Mother's flat together. There were few possessions. We shared her books between us and took her few good clothes to Oxfam. Peter wanted to have her rosary and I chose the only piece of jewellery worthy of the name, a gold cross and crucifix which she used to let me put on, when I was small.

We were quiet all through the process of sorting her things. The funeral was a modest affair attended by some nurses from the hospice and a couple of people from the neighbouring flats. The only familiar figure was Nelly, who sobbed copiously all through the service. The priest agreed to us using the church hall for tea and biscuits afterwards, and Nellie had made a cake. I half expected Felix to turn up, though he had written to say that he could not return again because of painting commitments, in Southern Spain. I could tell that Nellie was disapproving about his not being there for the funeral. I felt disquieted too, for minding his absence. I was resentful of his lack of support, although by then I should have been used to it. Certainly there would have been another woman involved, taking his attention from Peter and me. I had begun to hate him for this neglect. Peter was non-committal about it, but I wondered if deep down he minded more than he let on.

I knew I had to move on and, when the letter from an old friend of my mother's living in Canada came, I accepted her offer to live with her. She was sure I would get a place at the university there. Peter and I hugged goodbye at the airport, both of us leaving. His plane was departing before mine. His "Don't let's lose touch, Sis", before shouldering his travel bag and striding toward the departure gate, was the last unbearable moment of that era. At least I hoped it was, as I saw his tall swinging figure vanish from view.

Typically he hadn't looked back for one more glimpse of me. I stood for minutes, half expecting, perhaps hoping, he might reappear, change his mind, come with me to Canada. Such thoughts were fantasies. In reality I was more alone than ever. I was truly and absolutely alone and my eyes were overflowing as I forced myself to move, to trek with the other passengers towards the gate from where I would join my plane.

Mine was a window seat next to a middle-aged woman reading a Jilly Cooper novel. I turned to look out of the window and when the plane began to move closed my eyes, my mask well clamped to my face. As the jet climbed more steeply, pointing its nose into the late evening skies, towards Canada, away from England away from Dartmoor, it felt as though my life's blood was being drained from me.

CHAPTER 10

My host met me at the airport, greeting me kindly and, to my relief, unemotionally. Her name was Carol Perfect; she was headmistress of a girls' school in Toronto. Her house was as drab as the clothes she wore, sombre red brick with ivy climbing the walls. My room looked out onto a shared garden. All the houses bore the same smug, private expression.

Miss Perfect's house suited me and so did Toronto. Toronto the good, they called it.

"Toronto the dull!" my new friend Lucy said.

We met on a bus. Every day I would leave my quiet Victorian enclave of dignity for the university. A bus ride took me there in twenty minutes. Lucy, in the green uniform of Miss Perfect's school, was always on the bus. Often we sat next to each other. She was less than a year younger than me.

"You actually live in the same house as Miss Perfect?" She raised her eyebrows and whistled a disbelieving sigh of sympathy.

"It's nice there," I said, not defensively, for I knew that had I been like Lucy or any normal person of my age I would not have wanted to live there with the dry Miss Perfect. "I like it. It gives me a chance to think. It's undemanding."

Lucy laughed and said, "Rather you than me, kiddo."

She got off the bus near Miss Perfect's school, at the stop before mine. I would feel a small pang. A sort of envy. She would wave, a cheerful wave that told me Lucy was the very image of everything I would never be. She was what people in England still called 'a bonny girl', exuding health from every pore of her smooth skin; with a sprinkling of freckles scattered across her nose and upper cheeks, enhancing her broad smile and blue fearless eyes. She looked somehow cared-about and I imagined her with her family of younger brothers and sisters, and doctor parents, living in the security of a normal family.

We travelled to and fro on the same bus every day for a year. Once, coming home, she got off the bus at my stop. It was snowing and the bus had broken down. She phoned her father from Miss Perfect's house and he said he would pick her up on his way home. Miss Perfect was not yet back from school and I made hot chocolate for us. We took it up to my room.

"Gee, this is a big bedroom," Lucy exclaimed. She cast an eye around the place and I knew she was comparing it in her mind with her own room, which would be bright with posters of horses and film stars.

"I haven't got around to organising it yet," I said. "I mean the walls and so on. I intend painting them and putting up a few pictures — it's just that I spend most of my time with my head in that lot." I was referring to the big desk. It was covered with books and files. "Science essays and maths take up a lot of it." We supped our drinks,

"I guess you're not only beautiful," Lucy said suddenly, "but clever too." I felt myself blushing with surprise. "I wish I was," she added. Her words fell around the room like hail on a summer's day — unexpected and hard hitting.

"What do you mean, 'beautiful'?" I asked quietly.

"You must know you're a stunner." Lucy was laughing again. "Gee, are all English girls like you? Sort of in a fog about themselves?" I blushed again. She said kindly, "I'm so dumb, I'm really sorry, I didn't mean it that way. I meant that you're somehow so unaware of your looks. It's nice — if I looked like you, I'd flaunt it."

"Flaunt?"

"Yes. Get the guys I fancy instead of always getting the spotty one." Lucy chuckled. "Oh well, I'm leaving school this term and have no intentions of going to university. No," she was grinning at me, "I have every intention of disappointing my beloved parents and going straight into training as an air hostess."

"You seem so sure of yourself," I told her.

"Yep, it says 'over confident' in my reports from school. Funny old world, isn't it, Cleo? There's you with your amazing good looks, like a Scandinavian princess, with hardly any confidence, and me the plump Irish girl with a snub nose who doesn't give a damn."

Lucy was good for me and we met as often as my studies and her home life allowed. I enjoyed meeting her family and thought how different my own childhood had been. It was a great relief to have a friend I could trust and confide in; though even with Lucy I found it hard to describe my guilt surrounding my parents: Mother's death, Father's unfaithfulness. She would listen sympathetically and reassure me in her cheerful way. Her warm friendship helped but she soon left to be an airline hostess and was away for long periods. We met when we could. Snatched lunch or coffee. I was studying for my finals and Lucy was already flying, so there was little chance to meet properly.

When the time came, I had gained a first in Maths and Sciences. To Miss Perfect's horror I went straight to the Canadian airlines and became a trainee stewardess. The airline life suited Lucy — I would make it suit me too. We were able to grab the occasional evening together but she was already doing trips to the States and I was busy learning the ropes so we saw less of each other. Yet I knew she would be a friend for life, my first real friend. She made no bones about what she really wanted out of life and why she had not gone to University.

"I want a family and a gorgeous husband," she told me one evening. We were dining in a quiet Italian restaurant, celebrating Lucy's first flight across the States to California. Her eyes were shining as, sipping red wine, she told me of her real ambition.

"I know you'll think I'm mad, Cleo" she grinned "but being an airline hostess is only a passing thing. It's exciting and all that, but what I really want is a man!" I laughed aloud and told her I thought she would find one easily enough. For indeed, even without her pretty face, her personality drew people to her. Everyone liked Lucy

"I really mean it, Cleo. I mean I want a good husband and lots of kids. It's kind of like a career for me. It's the only thing I want to do." I believed her, wishing I could be the same.

CHAPTER 11

As it turned out, Lucy had two disastrous and childless marriages and was already thirty-one before she met and fell in love with her dream man, Patrick, a doctor.

Though we had seen little of each other I missed Lucy when they moved to California to live. As for me, my lifestyle on the airline gave me every excuse to keep aloof and in control of my time.

By this time Dad had married a French woman and seemed desperate to be in touch with me. I ignored his letters at first but when he wrote to say he and Nadine were having a child I relented and with strange mixed feelings I penned a short note to him.

'Dear Felix,
It seems odd to be in touch after more than ten years and even stranger for me to contemplate the idea of having a baby brother or sister at this stage in my life. I wish you and Nadine well.'

I started writing copious letters to Peter pouring out my resentment about Felix having another child when Peter and I were already in our thirties. He replied cheerfully and briefly, unconcerned it seemed about having a father like ours. He sent snapshots of himself with friends on Malibu Beach. They all looked so healthy and happy but I was not tempted to take up Peter's invitation to join him there, though I wished I could be that brave. We had grown up so differently, and I knew I would be incapable of following his lifestyle. No, I was better off here in Canada where I could wear my mask and be private.

Once we met up in Vancouver, when my flight coincided with a conference he was attending. We had little time for I was flying early next day, and he was tied up with seeing delegates from all over the world.

"How important you've become" I teased.

We were making the most of our time together, dinner at a quiet Restaurant. It had been raining and we had dashed from the taxi laughing as we shook our summery jackets. "Just like England this weather," Peter had observed, as we took our seats and settled down at our table.

Peter grinned at me, "No, Cleo I'm not that important. Just lucky to be able to pursue a career in something I've always liked doing."

As a design engineer my brother was indeed following his childhood interest and I felt a sudden surge of nostalgia seeing him, while remembering how he used to spend hours drawing planes, wasting time I had thought, when we were at Burrow, where he could have been doing what I did and ride a pony across the Dartmoor hills.

"It is strange that you and I are all that's left of the family," I said.

"Nonsense, Cleo." Peter, pouring wine into my glass; stopped abruptly. "Mum and Uncle Ted may have gone, but it was a long time ago. And remember Dad's still alive and married again, and then there's Kate."

I hadn't forgotten. How could I? Especially sitting there opposite Peter. For he had that same lopsided grin as Dad, was like him, despite the slightly darker hair. And since we now had baby sister Kate I had to admit I was curious to see her. I felt apprehensive but determined to meet my new stepmother and little half sister when my job next took me to Paris. Peter said he would try and do the same, but saying goodbye to him, something told me not to get my hopes up of us ever being a real family again.

CHAPTER 12

Boyfriends were an embarrassment to me, even though I was well into my thirties. They seemed to want me in a way that made me feel I was being eaten alive. What they wanted was my body. So I had never had a sustained relationship with a man. I did not like being the cynic I had become by the time I met Vince.

At first I was, as always, cool, careful, ready to wear the mask at short notice. By then I had learned better how to manage the mask; taught myself to avoid men without being overtly rude. Mostly I would lie if they became seriously interested in me, pretend that I had a fiancé or husband to go home to when my flight touched down. I had, I knew, a reputation for being cold.

Lucy, whom I saw infrequently, had asked me to be godmother to her third child, one of twin boys. Vince, one of Patrick's old college friends was to be godfather to the same twin. We had both flown from Toronto to the ceremony on different flights, but by the time the weekend was over I was glad we were both booked on the same flight back.

I had been relieved to find, after arriving in California, that Lucy and I were still close, despite the infrequency of our meetings. She had always accepted me as I was. Even after sixteen years of knowing one another we were still the same loving friends. She admitted that she and Patrick had hoped that Vince and I would like each other.

Vince was so different from other men I had known. For one thing he had been married and had a child. He was in no hurry to make another mistake. His wife and child lived on the other side of Canada and he would go there every two months to see his little son. He was the first of my men friends not to mind that I didn't like sex.

At forty he had not lost his good looks. We suited each other to perfection. He was taller than my five foot nine, well over six feet. We shared a mutual sense of relief when we came together at Lucy and Patrick's house in the hills above San Francisco. It was a happy household and the atmosphere rubbed off on Vince and me. We played with the children and admired our new godson, Jamie. I surprised myself by telling Vince about Kate, and I could tell from the way he listened that he understood my reticence to say much about my father. To my relief he did not ply me with questions about him or Nadine.

On the evening of our flight back to Toronto the family were gathered in the garden watching the sunset. Vince was standing close to me as we looked across the bay, surrounded by the bright wild geraniums that grew in abundance around their property. We watched the sun as it dipped from sight, leaving a reflection of golden light trailing for seconds across the sea.

Vince gently reached for my hand as we watched the night sky enveloping us and I felt a deep sense of relief, reminding me of moments with Uncle Ted. I felt safe for the first time since being with Uncle Ted at Burrow.

CHAPTER 13

It was a Sunday and we were driving back to Toronto from the cottage on the shores of Lake Huron, where Vince's little son and ex-wife were on vacation with her new husband.

The son of wealthy bankers, Vince had revelled in a youth of powerboats and fast cars, but there was a Puritanism about him that he inherited from his parents and grandparents, who were well respected. He bore the name of the bank they had founded.

The day at the cottage had been surprisingly pleasant. Susie was pregnant, looked pretty and content. I wondered how she and Vince had managed to have such a ghastly marriage, Vince being so even-tempered and she so girlishly honest and patient looking.

Clearly they both adored their son, who ran amok amongst the adults, flinging his chubby three-year-old body again and again into the lake. We took it in turns leaping in after him from the little pier where Susie and Mike kept their boat. I enjoyed wallowing in the water. It was warm, hard to imagine its ice covering all winter. The child stood on my shoulders and shouted as he jumped time after time into the water. His little legs felt smooth and strong and I was again reminded of Kate and the times I had spent with her when I flew to Paris.

It was Kate who made Paris exciting to me, not all the wonders of the place, and certainly not because of it being my father's home, or mine for that matter. Dad was always telling me it was my home too and I wished he wouldn't. The suggestion made me feel uncomfortably angry. It was as if nothing of the past had happened, as though none of his blatant unfaithfulness mattered any more. How he could expect me to forgive him was beyond comprehension and had it not been for Kate I would have avoided contact with him. It had been out of curiosity that I plucked up courage to visit them and meet little Kate, who captivated me from the very moment I set eyes on her in the hospital where she was born.

From then on, going to see my new sister when I had a stopover in Paris became the norm, and I revelled in being with this delicious child. Deep down, I went on resenting my father, made little effort to communicate with him or Nadine who as mother of my father's young daughter was somehow, in my eyes, another of his accomplices. Her seeming adoration of him showed me how, yet again, he had used his charm to get what he wanted from a woman, confirming my view that his faithlessness was forever to blame for everything wrong in my mother's existence, let alone my own. It was ironic, I knew, that I had become so attached to little Kate; I tried not to believe that my feelings for her were born from any maternal longings — but out of sisterly affection

As Freddie leapt from my shoulders I wondered if I would have a child like this one, who was every inch like his father. The thought of it was incredibly rewarding, a thought, which gave me a feeling of happy anticipation, something, I had not experienced since childhood days at Burrow.

"He really is a dear little chap, your Freddie," I said as we were driving back to the city that evening.

"Yep," Vince replied, "I know, honey, he's the one reason I almost didn't give up on the marriage."

I put my hand on Vince's knee. It felt warm, big boned, strong. His pale blue shorts complemented his tanned legs. He pressed the accelerator and the Mercedes shot forward past the line of traffic streaming home from the Ontario Lakes after the weekend.

Turning my head slightly I looked at Vince: blond, serious, hard-working Vince. I felt a warmth for the man, sadness for his suffering. We had sometimes tentatively talked of marriage and children. I knew it was getting late for me to put it off for much longer.

We both had our reasons for delaying things. Vince because he was afraid. For him marriage spelt hurt and misery. My reasons were different, for I had never been married — had only had a couple of lovers and each time it was disastrous, for I was never prepared to be the woman that the sort of man I attracted seemed to need. Each time I became involved I felt this iron sheet, like armour, clanging around me. It rendered me virtually impotent, certainly held me in an icy grip of fear, stirring my memory circuits with something unfathomable.

I had, early on in my life, decided that marital commitment was virtually unthinkable, in the light of my parents' unhinged marriage, which had caused so much grief all round. My own part in its gloomy ending was always there lurking, hanging like a heavy aircraft droning its way across the sky of my seemingly unending heavy-hearted existence. Sometimes I felt frightened by the gloom that pressed down on me and stayed, unless there was something to take my mind off it. This is why I went on working so much longer in the air than other cabin staff. I welcomed the droning of the plane despite the realisation that I was tired of the years of travel. It was being with Vince that had wakened me from hanging on the thread of this unreal life. Vince had gradually brought me back down to earth. At last I had someone who understood and tolerated me. We were two damaged people brought together by chance who had fallen into a safe, solid pattern of living.

"You should be doing something creative, not flying still," he told me once. I knew he was right. Flying was exhausting. He hadn't said 'You're too old for flying,' but I knew that was what he meant, and indeed I felt too old. Being chief stewardess and sometimes being on the ground teaching youngsters was well paid, but I was more than tired of it.

We were nearing Toronto. Vince suggested eating at the Granite Club. It was then I told him about the letter from my father with the momentous news that he had bought Burrow Farm: it was in the family again. He was there with his French wife and young daughter.

"That's great," Vince enthused. "What you've always wanted, Cleo. I bet you'd like to go back there, wouldn't you?"

"Yes, I suppose I would." In my heart I found it almost impossible to visualise. It was all so long ago — Burrow, Brownie, Uncle Ted.

"You would see Kate again, and kind of touch base, as it were."

We were silent as Vince drove the Mercedes into a gas station.

"Time to fill up, honey," Vince said. He turned to reach for his leather bag with his wallet inside, before getting out to fill the tank. "You somehow don't look all that pleased about the good news. Is there something wrong, Cleo? Something you haven't told me about?"

"No, it's just such a surprise, that's all, Vince."

He squeezed my hand. "Was it surprise that prevented you from telling me about it before?" he asked gently.

"No, Vince, it was just we had so much fun today I forgot about it," I lied.

He kissed me lightly on the nose before getting out of the car.

As the petrol surged into the tank I tried to assemble my thoughts. It had been one thing dreaming about Dartmoor, dreaming about Burrow, about Uncle Ted, now long dead. One thing telling Vince about my passion for Brownie, the landscape, how perfect the place was and how happy I had been there. But another thing contemplating a return to that place with its Rock and memories. I had never mentioned the Rock to Vince. I shivered.

"You cold?" Vince asked as he got back into the car. He took my hand.

"No. Someone walked over my grave." I smiled at him.

"I'm glad your Dad has bought the farm back, Cleo," Vince was saying. "I know it's what you've always wanted. I'm looking forward to seeing it too."

I sat silent, feeling the shock of his words. Somehow I could not imagine Vince at Burrow farm. He belonged here. The Mercedes' quiet hum as we glided down the highway was like an anaesthetic, and a feeling of sleepiness almost overwhelmed me. I pulled myself awake. Vince was speaking.

"Your dreams are coming true now, honey." We were turning into the car park at the club and I shuddered at the thought. An image of the Rock flashed through my mind, with water gushing around it and me terrified.

I felt unsteady as we walked through the large clubhouse doors. Heads turned as usual, some I recognised; and I nodded back with a quiet smile. We were an impressive couple, I knew. But I felt a fraud, like a gorgeous chocolate cake, which when cut open has no substance, only the icing and a thin shell under it.

I stared half-heartedly at the menu: it was the size of a newspaper with a choice that almost sickened me. I ordered a modest salad with fish, protesting that I was not very hungry while Vince was ready to tuck into a large steak. After ordering the food he leaned forward, smiled encouragingly.

"You'll want to go back there for a visit, Cleo."

"Dad wants me to," I said. "Wants me to help. The whole place is in a bit of a state. The people never farmed it. For the last few years the house has been used for rearing chickens. There'll be an awful lot of work to do."

"Cleo, honey, I reckon a trip to see your folks would do you a power of good."

I felt more than just the table's width away from Vince. I was a lifetime away from him, a whole world away and wearing my invisible mask again. It felt tight around my head and stopped me thinking about anything more than what was needed to appear functional.

How could I explain the thought of being with Felix again, the father I had detached myself from for so long? I would find it hard to take the plunge, accept my father's invitation to join him and Nadine and Kate. The occasional meal or stopover with him and his family in Paris when my flights landed had been easy enough. Then I was always able to pretend — though it did not necessarily feel like pretence — more a way of being as comfortable as was possible in his presence.

Nadine presented no problems. I used to think she might be someone I would have quite liked to be close to, had she not been my father's wife.

There was Kate of course. No need to pretend with Kate. That I loved her and she loved me seemed so natural. We were sisters and too disparate in age to quarrel or be catty as sisters so often are.

Sometimes on those occasions in Paris I would put my little sister to bed, bath her and tell her stories. I loved those gentle times together. I would tuck her in and she would hug and kiss me.

"Please, Cleo, dîtes-moi about Burrow Farm when you were a little girl."

It became a habit, this repetition of what it was like at Burrow Farm.

"The little farmhouse is thatched with straw from another county called Norfolk, which is a long, long way from Dartmoor," I would say to start the story. Then I would describe to her the way the walls of the farmhouse were solid granite, the thatch was heavy and at one end, if you stood on a big plant pot and stretched up, you could touch the edge of the thatch with the tips of your fingers. I would describe how the front garden had a granite dry stone wall hemming in the lawn, the borders of flowers on one side of the pathway from the gate to the front door, and the vegetable border on the other side. How in some places great Uncle Ted had grown onions amongst the carrots to keep the carrot fly away.

I told her about Brownie, the pony, which Uncle Ted got from the sales in Tavistock for me to ride. I told her that in summer the purple heather smelled like honey, and the gorse, all buttery yellow smelled like the sweetest nuts, and how the seed cases popped like fairy balloons pop pop pop when the sun shines hot on them and the flowers open their petals to the heat.

I never told her about the dark skies that sometimes threatened life on the moor with a blanket of cloud, which meant you could not see landmarks or find your direction in the thick mist; or the heavy rains that could whip you until tears of pain would join the rivers of water, dripping down your face. I didn't mention the big Rock, the way it stands sentinel high up on the moor where two streams meet to make a river that rages around its feet. Nor did I explain that the Rock held powerful secrets, which sometimes caused grief.

Now, Vince was touching my arm across the table. "Come on, Cleo, where are you? Dreaming of Burrow?" He poured a glass of wine for me.

"I'm sorry, Vince," I stammered. "It's all a bit sudden you know. It's just that I never really thought Dad would buy the farm back. It's all so long ago, I'm not sure I want to go back. In fact I'm certain I don't want to go back."

"Nonsense," Vince said. "You need an early night. Come on, honey, let's go. I'll take you home."

We had separate apartments. I could look from my twelfth-storey balcony across the lit-up houses and streets to where Vince's apartment block stood. Sometimes he stayed with me, or I with him. That night we were in my apartment. I showed him Dad's letter. While Vince read I kicked my shoes off, walked across the thick carpet, opened the balcony doors and stepped out into the cool evening and stared down to the flickering lights below. For a moment I was back in Devon. I remembered how it used to be on a crisp winter morning at Burrow Farm. Me, the child, alone in a shadowy dawn, creeping outside, sidling past sleepy dogs on my way to Higher Strap Meadow. The slow-rising sun striking the rimy ground. The short stiff grasses twinkling in the sunlight. I, like a giant, standing mesmerised by the gleaming vista of tiny lights — some bigger than others — no sound of traffic, just the magic of a gleaming, frosted meadow on the slopes of Dartmoor.

I turned back into the room. Vince held the letter.

"Gee, it's hard to read, Cleo. His writing is impossible." He laughed.

"Here, give it to me. I'll read it to you."

"Dear Cleo,

I know you will be as amazed and pleased as I am with the news I am giving you in this letter.

Burrow Farm is back in the Endaton family again. Yes, it's true. I didn't mention it when you last came to Paris because it was not at all definite. Now it is absolutely certain that it really is ours again. I have bought it. I have seen the farm a few times and I can tell you it is in a mess. We intend more or less camping in the sitting room, which is the least messy room, while we do some basic renovation. Nadine is longing to get her hands on the kitchen; she has great plans for it. At least the roof's all right and by the time you read this letter we should be there working our socks off.

So many years have gone since our days at Burrow, and, believe me Cleo, I feel pretty wretched about everything."

Vince was listening intently. I looked up from the letter — stopped reading. Vince said, "Jeez, your Dad sounds really guilty about his past."

"He deserves to feel guilty," I answered, surprised at the aggression in my tone, which I could tell was a shock to Vince too. I read on:

"I want you to realise just how bad I feel about having left you all those years ago.

I want you to know that with Nadine and Kate in my life I am truly a changed man.

I know that the past was painful for you and what I did was absolutely unforgivable; but you are a grown woman now and I am getting old. I long for a proper reconciliation between us. Oh yes, I know we have seen something of each other in Paris. You missed our wedding and I don't blame you for that, and I am really grateful for the interest you have taken in young Kate. She and Nadine and I have always loved seeing you, albeit only briefly, when you touched down in Paris. How are we to see you, even briefly, now that you have given up flying and we have moved, unless you come and stay at Burrow?

I think of you often. I remember how much Burrow meant to you. Now that you have finished with flying, can you envisage taking a few months off to come back — dare I say come home? Could it be home again for you? It is easier for me to feel happy about returning, I have Nadine who is as excited by this as anything she and I have attempted before.

As for Kate, well you know her a bit and she really is as she appears. Happy wherever she is and thriving. All she needs is love and food, like a puppy. She would love to see you. Please come. We need to go over things perhaps. I need to make amends for the past. Please, Cleo, before it is too late. I'm nearly seventy and you are already older than I was when it all happened. I cannot forgive myself unless you forgive me.

All your father's love, Felix.

P.S. The place is pretty shabby, needs paint and a lot of reorganising. Will you help? Please, Cleo."

After I had finished reading, Vince was quiet. He sat forward in the deep armchair. His head was bent down, looking at the carpet.

I walked to my desk; put my father's letter in a drawer. I could tell that Vince had something serious that he was struggling to put into words. I felt nervous, wondering why he was being this way. I couldn't blame him for thinking me too complicated a person to contend with. Panic was setting in as I waited for him to say something, my imagination running away with me. I feared that Vince, whom I had known for nearly a year, was finding out just how unstable my relationship with my father was. I convinced myself in those moments that it was impossible for him ever to become my husband, for the instability in my family relationships was too great a contrast to his own family — his good, constant parents who lived in Ottawa in staid luxury and were so different to mine.

- 77 -

I guessed Vince must have been thinking this now. I had briefly told him about the Rock as we drove home from the club, and the significance of climbing through its vast hole — "for luck," I told him. He hadn't laughed at me, and I had tried to make the Rock sound like something as light as the Irish Blarney Stone. I dared not let him know that somewhere inside I still held the belief that had I been strong and climbed the Rock all those years ago, my life, and probably my parents' lives, would have been totally different.

Vince spoke at last. "Cleo, I hope you won't mind what I'm going to say." I noticed as he spoke how his right eyebrow, with its thick golden hairs, was raised higher than the left. This phenomenon, this quizzical gesture of his face now turned towards me, was one of his charms. It always roused in me a deep affection, and now, was no exception. I wanted to touch his eyebrow. I felt the familiar mask closing in on me.

"What is it, Vince — what are you going to say?" A desert stretched down to my windpipe. My voice cracked.

"I was thinking, Cleo, and forgive me, but," Vince hesitated and I was rooted to the ground, unable to move. "I just have to ask you — about your dad — about his way of asking for forgiveness and all that."

I waited for Vince to continue. "Well, honey, did he ever — you know — do something he shouldn't? You know — was there any abuse — sexual abuse?"

His words came like gunshot, peppering me with shock. For a few seconds we stared at each other. Vince had touched on a fear, which, though it had absolutely nothing at all to do with my father, had nevertheless always lurked around me. When my brother had explained our mother's reasons for being the way she was, it had not then dawned on me that, as her daughter, a girl, a woman, I carried somewhere in my genetic memory a terrible pattern: a knowledge that lay hidden, had never been unearthed, though the possibility of its emerging in my own life had always existed. A secret threat.

Now, with Vince's question, I recognised the horror of my own girlhood. Its significance had dogged my life and was still growling within me, even now. This terrible conflict deep inside had, I now saw, always been part of my life. I realised how the confusion of it had come from the mixture of feelings I had known with Uncle Ted, the safety I had felt with his arm around me, the trust of his strength, the knowledge he had shared with me about the world in which he lived and which I had loved more than anything else. He had allowed me to see his understanding of the nature of our world, and he was, for me, the centre of that world. His corduroy smell had haunted me always and the mystery of his embrace that day after the storm, when we lay in the tallet, had never left me.

As a grown woman I had dismissed the memory, but now, while Vince waited for my answer in the quiet of my sitting room, I allowed the recollection to come alive in my mind.

"No, Vince, no," I said reassuringly. "I was never abused as a child by my father or anyone else."

I could not tell him about Uncle Ted, for nothing had come of his innocent longing for me. Neither did I tell Vince about the incestuous history I had inherited from my mother, which I knew was at the root of her problems, and mine, for that matter.

"No," I repeated. "Why do you ask such a thing?" I knew why, of course. I knew he sensed my total lack of passion when we made love. I was affectionate with him. It was all I could be, and he was the only man I had ever had such affection for.

"I don't know why I asked that, honey, just something in the letter I guess. But I just want you to know I care about you, whatever has happened."

I felt a surge of relief that he had not been thinking of giving up on me.

That night, while Vince slept, I lay in his warm arms, wide awake, thinking of my mother and wondering how it was that a residue of her past should show so vividly through me, her daughter, and not for the first time in my life I wished wholeheartedly that I was different, more like other women. I wished that I could really feel the love I wanted to have for Vince.

Vince helped me to decide to go to England — to Burrow — to 'home'. At the airport he teased me. "Cleo, you look like you're going into the lion's den." He grinned. "A few months in the country will do you good, and I'll phone often and then as soon as I can I shall come like a knight in armour to claim my bride — you will be my bride, won't you, Cleo?"

My eyes filled with tears.

"Oh, Vince, yes, yes of course I will. But let's do it now. I don't want to go back now. Let's cancel — get married instead. I want a baby. I want to stay here."

Vince held me close, kissed me gently. "As you like, honey. But I get the feeling there's something special at Burrow with your Dad, and you may regret not going now."

My flight number was being called and I clung to Vince.

"You're probably right, Vince. You usually are. But it's hard to leave."

"I promise I'll be there soon, honey. I'll be there and whisk you back to Canada."

I left his arms, turned to wave that last goodbye before joining the other passengers already leaving the departure lounge for the plane. My feet felt heavy, my heart like lead. My return to Burrow was not going to be anything like I'd always imagined. I was not looking forward to it. I was dreading it.

CHAPTER 14

We walk, my sister and I. Well, I walk. She runs in front or trots behind, humming. She is only six years old. Me, I'm thirty-six. We are so different. She's a dear little creature, with thick fine fair hair tumbling down in curls. Her little body is slender, yet well covered and sturdy.

When I was away working I thought about her all the time. On flights to Europe or long hauls to the Far East or Australia, helping passengers with kids, I was reminded of Kate. My dream was to be here, by the banks of the River Teign, walking my little half-sister home from school.

This is the third time I have collected her. It's only a week since I got here, but Kate insists it's me who picks her up. Mothers and a father or two hang about waiting at the school gates. The women don't notice me, for they are so involved with each other, and I long for Kate's arrival. The men glance my way and I cringe at the thought of being noticed by them.

Today I time it right. Too late to stand there not being part of anything; the group of women, or the solemn-faced men. Just right, for I can see Kate running up the track to the gates. She's in front and a smile lights her face. The sight of her stabs me. I feel myself reeling.

In the second it takes for Kate to hurl herself, puppy-like, at my midriff, I acknowledge with a slight sense of joy that perhaps I am feeling real at last. For this is what I came back to find. It's just that I didn't expect it so soon — if ever.

I cast a brief smile towards the parents, while Kate skips around me, tugs my hand, shows me her painting. Her face shining with eagerness hard to remember in my own childhood.

"Thees one is for you." Once again, I smile charmed as always by her French accent. She hands me a brightly coloured page of quiet landscape. "Thees one is for Mama." Another bright drawing with a little house in the hills and a person holding a fistful of multicoloured flowers. "And thees one," she holds up a picture of a man with a huge smile and a big round face, again with the yellow sunshine pouring down on him, "is for Papa."

It's strange, now, to think of Felix as Papa.

Kate runs along the path, which snakes in and out of tall beech trees beside the river. In some places willowy alder hangs over the banks and here and there the rowans lean their scarlet-berried branches to the low September waters.

I take in a deep breath, down into my solar plexus, smell the leaf mould, the damp air, pungent with earthy fungus. I almost shout aloud, "Yes, I have come home at last!" No more flights and turnarounds in strange foreign lands. I grew to hate all that travel. Waking up in some tall, hot building. Wondering, in those brief seconds before full morning consciousness, which country I was in: Hong Kong, Venezuela, Kuwait, or North America. Of course there had been the Paris turnarounds when I had spent a night, or breakfast or an evening at Felix and Nadine's flat; sometimes bathing my little sister or reading to her and singing her to sleep, before returning for my next flight.

"Chase me, Cleo," Kate laughs and I run behind her darting figure. The leaves crunch beneath our feet. Their yellowy bronze is the same colour as Kate's hair. Like Dad's was, years ago. In every other way she takes after her French mother, Nadine, who is dark, petite and only seven years older than me.

I catch Kate and hand-in-hand we skip to the river's edge and stare down into the moorland waters. It is deep here, dark and peaty. I remember as a child being fascinated by the bronze on my body when I stood in the water. Even in summer the cold would grip me as I lowered myself into it. I would stand quite still, gasping, staring at my arms. Looking down at my legs, with the rusty-coloured water swirling around them. How marvellous it had felt to change the colour of my body by immersing it in the coppery Dartmoor stream. I always hoped that when I jumped back onto the bank the colour would have stayed. Instead I had to bear the ordinariness of my white flesh.

I look upstream in the direction of Dog's Tooth Tor, remembering how, up there, the water tumbles and dashes against stones and boulders. It swirls and sucks at the huge Rock, before it edges around the great clitter-strewn apron that sweeps down from the tor. From there it falls steeply into the valley, where we see it now in its more sedate woodland valley mood.

It is on the slopes of this 'would be' mountain that our farm sits, clinging to its mother, the hill. It's good to have made the break.

Tonight I'll write to Vince. Vince — as I think his name I realise that he has not featured in my thoughts, not since he rang to see if I had arrived safely.

Kate pulls my arm. "What are you looking at, Cleo?"

"I was remembering something, Kate." My arm goes around her and I squat at her level. "Somewhere up there beyond the woods," I tell her, "there is a little place beside the river where I used to hide away from everyone. It's in between the banks of the river and the trees and it's secret." Kate's hand squeezes mine.

"Why did you hide from everyone?" She looks up at me. "Were you playing hide-and-seek?" Kate looks puzzled when I tell her that I had not been playing hide-and-seek, but that I had simply liked being by myself.

When we reach the bridge and open the gate onto the lane, we see the ancient Land Rover, one that Great Uncle Ted bought after the war. It faces up the hill away from Crediford. Felix is there in faded corduroys and muddy black wellies, leaning against the back of it, with his pipe in his mouth, waiting. Kate lets go of my hand and rushes to him.

"Papa! Papa!" she screeches, throwing herself at him. He lifts her into his outstretched arms. I feel a sudden pain in my gut. Kate chats all the way in her high-pitched voice and the Land Rover soon turns off the road to bump over the mile of rough track leading to Burrow Farm. Kate sits in front next to our father, not waiting for him to say anything as she describes her school day. She giggles enthusiastically, recounting each event. I can see in the driver's mirror my father's gentle smile.

"Daisy said that her Mama is the prettiest mama in the whole world and I told her it is not so, for my Mama is the prettiest lady in the whole world and France. It's true, Papa, do you not think so, Papa?" Kate tugs his sleeve and Dad, laughing, tousles her head with his free hand. "Yes, my darling, you are right. Your Mama is the prettiest mama in all the world — including France." He catches my eye in the mirror and smiles conspiratorially, full of adult indulgence for his little one, expecting me to share it with him. I half smile back to him then turn away.

I think about Nadine. She is indeed pretty, with her dark short-cropped hair, deep brown eyes and Mediterranean olive skin. She is efficient and quick at everything she does. I know she will be waiting for us, busy in the kitchen; though not too busy to flash her glorious smile at Felix and Kate. She adores them. There's nothing she wouldn't do for them. Even leaving Paris for this entire wilderness. That's what I want to be for Vince — a wife, like Nadine is to my father — a loving happy wife. In Canada.

For the rest of the way I sit quietly on the back seat, hearing Kate's voice and watching the sky. Clouds move slowly, lowering around the hill. Grey, then black, they brighten briefly as a shaft of sunlight glances through them: then darken again as though the sky itself is unsure whether to open the cold floodgates and give vent to a preview of winter, or hold back for yet more time to contemplate the serenity of autumn.

CHAPTER 15

Still I had not been to the Rock, the hours being taken up working on the house and clearing the garden.

Yesterday, while Dad and I were putting new wallpaper on the sitting room walls, he asked me how I was feeling about being back at Burrow. I could tell that his real intention was to get me talking about the past, and felt my stomach muscles contract. I answered him briefly, almost flippantly, as though the past was finished, disposed of. Though something told me that my father knew it wasn't.

My father hadn't pursued the subject, and I felt the chasm between us widening instead of narrowing, as I was hoping when I came back here. I wrote to Vince:

'Sometimes my father looks so tired. Nadine looks after him with tenderness and affection. My mind tussles with the anger I still feel towards him — my father — Dad — Felix, I am still unsure how to address him. I feel frustrated with myself, realising my obduracy about him, my inability to forgive the past; the way he ran roughshod over me. I'm shocked by my thoughts. I think I still despise him, more than I once despised my Mother. If he'd been different everything might have turned out well — even for Mother.'

I found myself talking to Vince in letters in a way I never did when we were together in Canada. Although he wrote often he never referred to my soul-searching. I did not mind this; indeed it was one of the reasons I had allowed him into my life. He was trustworthy and I had sensed his probity from the very beginning. It was his air of constancy; the way he spoke and behaved towards me that had given me that special sense of security I had not felt since childhood, with Uncle Ted.

Felix and Nadine had asked me to stay on after Christmas, until the end of January. Nadine's mother was to have an operation and they wanted to be with her in Paris. They asked if I would look after Kate. I liked the idea and Kate seemed as delighted in my company as I in hers. She loved it when a mother at the school gate mistook me for her mother. My heart missed a beat when I heard it, making me realise just how much I longed for motherhood and marriage to Vince. I wrote to him:

'You won't mind, will you, Vince, if I stay on to help out? Looking after Kate is always a joy and it's a great opportunity for me to explore my childhood haunts at leisure, when she's at school. You won't mind too much, will you? Perhaps you could stay on after Christmas also? We could look after Kate and explore

together. Oh yes! That would be wonderful. Please, Vince, do say you can manage that.'

CHAPTER 16

I tried waking myself from a dream, a nightmare:

The boy on his white horse is galloping fast across the moor. I am standing on the hillside above the Rock. Brownie is not there. I have lost her. I call to the boy. He looks back towards me, waves an arm and is gone. I cry out. It is then I see Uncle Ted walking towards me. Mother is there. I stretch out my arms towards them. Mother is turning away. 'Don't go, please don't go,' I call but she is floating beyond my reach and Uncle Ted is nowhere to be seen. I struggle to follow them — be with them.

After the dream I lay awake numbed and empty until the quiet light of morning.

All that day I felt unnerved, edgy and sad. When I first returned to Burrow I had expected to sense my Mother's presence around the place. It was a relief to find no trace of her frailty anywhere. Not a vestige remained, nothing dark or gloomy in any part of the house. In fact there was a lightness, which shone around the kitchen with its dark blue modern Aga and herbs growing amidst scarlet geraniums on the windowsill. A new South window letting in the morning sun and soft, blue gingham curtains diffusing the glare at midday in the white-walled room.

No, there was no feel or sign of Mother in the house and as she had rarely set foot outside I would not expect to find her ghost there anyway. But Uncle Ted — I could smell him, smell his earthy, moorland smell. Sometimes I felt a sense of him in the tallet, or cow house, now a garden tool store. It was occasionally so strong that when I stepped over the cobbles I quite expected to see him sitting on a sack or in one of the stalls with his cows. I would peep into the darkness, hoping to catch a glimpse, wanting to believe him there.

The man who emerged from the cow house with my father that morning was clearly not Uncle Ted. Though only about my age, he looked somehow old-fashioned enough to be Uncle Ted, I told myself in the brief moment before our eyes met. He raised his cap to me. I saw the dark, curly head and knew I was looking at the boy, my childhood idol, the boy I had wanted to emulate.

"This is Cleo," my father said, "my daughter home from Canada."

The boy's hand shook mine.

"You may remember each other. Will used to help Uncle Ted a lot," he explained.

The boy smiled and our eyes locked for a brief few seconds. Recognition and memory were bursting inside me. I controlled the wave of remembering, stopped myself drowning in it enough to smile faintly, return the strong handshake.

"Yes, I think I remember Will," I said to my father in a voice that I hoped sounded perfectly ordinary. "I was coming over for a rake, Felix. Is there another one? The handle has broken on this one."

"I'm afraid not, Cleo. We must see about getting a handle in Crediford.""I could get one today," Will said, "I'm going to Crediford. I'll come back this way and drop it in, if you like."

I told myself that nothing extraordinary was happening, as though seeing the boy, now grown up, was a perfectly natural occurrence. After all, I should have known that he, the boy, would still be around somewhere and that, like me, he too would have grown up. It was the dream, the nightmare about him, with Mother and Uncle Ted, him, the boy, on his white pony. What was he doing, growing up like this, leaving my dreams and memories to become part of everyday life, even connected with my father?

It was clear that they were on familiar terms, Felix and the boy. My thoughts whirred around in my head making me dizzy. I heard Felix's voice. "Thanks, Will," he said, "it's kind of you. How was your stay away? Bit of a working holiday I daresay, being up there on your Uncle's farm"

Dad gave Will no time to answer but continued, "Look, Nadine's waving." We all turned around, looked towards Nadine who was standing by the back door, then started to walk towards her.

"Will!" she called as we drew near, "you are just in time for coffee."
We walked up the garden path together. Will leaned forward, to return Nadine's kisses, one on each cheek. I envied her easiness with the boy.

"You've been away too long, Will!" she scolded, as we removed our wellies in the stone hallway and stepped down into the kitchen.

"I've lost some ewes." Will pronounced it 'yows'. "Been looking since early this morning up over the moor. You haven't seen them, have you?"

My father shook his head as he scraped his chair back over the stone floor and sat down at one end of the table.

"There are two down the hill on the other side of the orchard wall," I told them, seating myself opposite the boy.

"We brought the ewes down for dipping," Will said, nodding his thanks to me. "About half a dozen's missing. I thought they might have strayed over this end of the commons. I'll take a look, but not till after I've drunk this coffee." He closed his eyes, feigning bliss, making Nadine laugh. "It smells fantastic," he added. "It's true, Nadine, this coffee is nothing like anything I've tasted before, and as for the croissants — mmm, they're lovely, too. Can I have another?"

"But of course, Will. There are plenty."

How does she do it? I wondered. All the polish, and flowers everywhere, and the cooker alive with the smell of rising bread and thick autumn soup. Nadine poured four mugs of coffee, and pulled fresh croissants from the oven. She lifted the lid of the domed pottery dish with a quiet flourish exposing the farm butter, yellow as buttercups. She had laid plates on the table and a jar of blackberry and apple jelly, red-handled knives and a jug of hot milk.

There we all were sitting around the table, talking about Will's sheep. I was conscious of the rolled-up sleeves of his faded blue shirt and the sweat patches, the brownness of his muscled arms as he removed his jacket, and an unfamiliar feeling gripped me. My hand was shaky as I lifted the mug of coffee to my lips.

Will flashed a smile towards me, then turning to Felix said, "We'll be cub hunting next week up this way. OK if we meet up here Tuesday? There'll only be four or five of us. Need to give the hounds a bit of practice and stir up the young foxes."

A cold feeling ran over me. I watched my father, waited for him to say something.

"Yes, of course, Will."

How could he! I wondered. How could he agree to Will coming here with his hounds to frighten the foxes! Had he forgotten? Forgotten that day, when I was a child and the fox had appeared at the very spot we were standing and nearly run into us.

I left the table with my mask closing over me and walked across the room to the sink, ran my sticky hands under the cold tap. The voices around the table continued. I looked out of the new south window as I dried my hands. Saw Kate's white socks fluttering on the line next to some sheets billowing alongside Nadine's dainty bra, pants and denim skirt, and Felix's Viyella boxer shorts.

Turning around again my father's eye caught mine. "Your coffee's going to be cold," he admonished.

I walked back to the table, picked up the cooling mug. "Thanks, Nadine. I am so sorry, I'm afraid I have things to do," I said feeling the boy's eyes on me, but avoided looking in his direction. "See you later." Leaving the room, stumbling over the pile of wellies where Jumble used to lie, I saw Will's dog was there. He jumped up wagging his tail and followed me across the yard to the cowhouse.

"Go back, boy," I snapped, "go back." Then I climbed the ladder to the loft, carrying my mug of coffee, and sat on a hay bale, feeling disappointed and wretched. My heart pounded. I did not want to feel angry with Felix but I was shaking. An immense feeling of loneliness washed over me. I was homesick for Vince, longed to have his calm, faithful arm around me, longed to go back to the world we both knew. I wished I had not promised to stay on and look after things for Felix and Nadine when they went away. I didn't want to disappoint Kate, who looked forward to being with me, but I desperately wanted to go home to Canada. But doing so would jeopardise this opportunity of reconciliation with Felix.

CHAPTER 17

It was Tuesday. I had calmed down since the episode with Will, but to avoid bumping into him hunting here I joined Nadine for a shopping trip to Exeter.

We were silent at first, as she negotiated the narrow lanes, and I allowed myself to visualise Will on his horse. They were jumping the orchard walls, galloping up to the moor with the hounds streaming behind them. When we reached the duel-carriageway Nadine relaxed, chattering endlessly all the way to Exeter, I only half listened until she mentioned Will. I turned my head to look out of the window, not wanting to hear about the man, but as a captive audience I had no choice. I was gazing absently at the tiny, by-passed villages, with their church towers and clusters of houses, when I realised that Nadine was talking about Will and someone called Maria.

"I really think poor Will's getting over it now," she was saying.

"Getting over what?" I found myself asking.

"You don't know, Cleo? No, of course, why should you? It was ages before your father and I knew that Will's wife, Maria, died four years ago. Or is it three? I'm not sure exactly, nor how it happened; only that it was a hunting accident."

Nadine and I lunched at 'Le Café' in the town centre. I tried not to dwell on what she had told me about Will's wife's death. It all seemed so shocking, I felt unnerved by the story. We ordered a glass of wine and some food. It was the first time since my arrival that we were on our own and I feared she may talk about Will again. I tried to keep the conversation light, guessing that she wanted us to be cosy, confidential even. I did not want that closeness — made trivial conversation.

"I shall go back to Marks for that skirt, those shoes, perhaps," I said, but it was no use she was determined to be personal. The waitress brought our food. Nadine sipped her wine and then spoke in a low, serious tone. "Cleo, my dear," she started. "You know how much your Papa cares about you."

My mask was well and truly in place. First it has been about Will and his dead wife and now she wants to bring Dad into it, I was thinking angrily. I looked hard at her across the table

. "What about it? What are you trying to say Nadine?" My voice, I knew, sounded brittle and hard and for a moment I felt sorry for her; she would clearly do anything to make my father happy.

We were sitting at a small table, amongst huge-leaved potted fig trees, beneath paintings by Felix. They were some of his earlier work, smaller than recent pictures. The exhibition in the popular, intimate café had been going only a week and already I could see from the little red stickers that four of the ten pictures were sold. My eyes moved towards the pictures, but Nadine was relentless in her attempt to draw me into a confidential tête-à-tête.

"Your Papa is anxious — thinks perhaps you do not like him." Nadine flashed her smile at me; put her hand across the table. Her neat, tanned, beautifully manicured hand touched mine.

"Don't worry, Cleo," she almost laughed. "I tell him 'come, come, Felix, of course Cleo loves her Papa. It is just your crazy imagination.' Is it not so, Cleo? I know you love your Papa!"

"Of course," I snapped, "I don't know what's wrong with the old man." I saw how Nadine flinched at the words, but did not apologise. Anyway, I excused myself, he really is an old man now, and if Nadine has married an old man then she must take the consequences. We were eating prawn salad. I stabbed at the pink flesh with my fork.

"What Dad doesn't realise," I blurted despising my own childish petulant tone and meaning of course what they both didn't realise, "is that he can't expect me to be like a child. Like Kate."

Nadine surprised me by agreeing emphatically; then spoiled the effect by patting my wrist, a tactless gesture, an attempt to show that we were really somehow comrades, but which seemed to me patronising,

"Don't think I don't understand, ma chérie, for I do. Now, how about some dessert? See, they have delicious gateaux."

The moment of tension had passed but my stomach rebelled at the dessert.

We listened to the radio on our drive home, and even shared laughter at some trivial comment. By the time we reached Burrow it was after five o'clock and there was no sign of the hounds or Will. Kate dashed down the garden path to greet us and Dad stood smiling his lopsided smile, content to see his women returned safely home.

***

I decided to tell Vince more about the Rock: it was so much easier writing things down. I needed someone to encourage me, to understand what I had come here to do. It was as though I didn't know why I had come, or what I should do in this place of my dreams. Perhaps, if I wrote it down Vince would be able to help me. I hardly knew how to address him when I wrote. 'Dear,' no, 'dearest,' or should I say 'darling?' 'Dear' is too distant, 'darling' too gushy. Usually I started: 'Vince, my love...

'My father and I avoid talking about things other than what is happening now,' I told him. 'Perhaps it's right, like you so often tell me, Vince, to let go of the past — forget and forgive. I can feel the importance of getting things straight with Dad, but somehow can't reconcile the past, and him with the here and now. It's something I have to face, the past and my father, something I need to deal with, but I don't quite know how. When I look up at the moor in the mornings it's as if a veil is hanging over the tors. The mist has scarcely been absent since I arrived. I need courage to walk through that misty veil and visit the Rock. I am ashamed of my fear and cannot bring myself to tell my father. Please come soon, dear Vince. I know you intend being here for Christmas, but I wish you could also make an interim visit. What chance is there that your work will allow that?

It's very quiet here most of the time. Apart from working on the house Felix spends a lot of time in his studio. He works on large canvasses these days, sells a lot and has several commissions. He rents the fields to a local farmer, but still intends keeping the vegetable plot, Uncle Ted's old garden.

We have picked up the apples from the orchard, there are dozens strewn about. I'd forgotten how many old trees there were. This is where Brownie used to be. While we picked yesterday I fancied I heard her neighing— even looked up, sure she was there. Something else I'd forgotten about this place is that at night the landscape lies in total blackness. This darkness is so natural, so real. As well as being in touch with the light, I long also to be in touch with the secrecy of the dark night. When I stay too long in artificial light my soul gets thirsty for darkness'.

I didn't know if Vince understood what I was trying to say. He mentioned the Rock as though I had been merely thinking of doing some particularly tricky climb. He seemed not to realise that it was the Rock's magical qualities that were calling me, that my ancestors were part of it and the surrounding moor. He would think me crazy if I told him that the Rock had something to do with my inability to forgive my father.

'Of course we can climb it together, darling', he wrote, 'don't do it without me. It sounds dangerous, but it can wait till I am with you.'

His letter was disappointing for he could not come early. I was touched by his concern for his parents: 'I must not leave before Christmas because of father's retirement and the handover. It is a tricky enough time, in the present financial climate. I want to make it all as smooth as possible for Dad. I am sad you can't be here for the handing over ceremony but I know that what we are both doing in helping our parents is absolutely the right and proper thing.

'Freddy is excited about his new baby brother or sister arriving around Christmas time. Won't it be exciting when our turn comes to tell him that he will have another one by next Christmas perhaps? What do you say, Cleo? I know it's what you want too, my darling.'

CHAPTER 18

I lie in bed. I have moved it closer to the window. Snug under my duvet I can see the darkness of the sky. Tonight, moonless, it envelops the whole house, fills my room. No stars show beneath the mist, which itself is blackened by the bituminous night. In this varnished pitch of dark I am in prison. A prison of comfort, for here I can release the mask which lately I never fully put away from me. I can let it go, feel my features relaxing in the secrecy of night. It is in these moments of dark solitude that I can allow my mind to make sense of the day. Especially this day, this confusing day, with all that happened. I go over what I saw again and again. I cannot stop myself from remembering how he looked — Will — the boy — today, by the river.

I had braced myself this morning to go at last to the Rock; had left behind the gardening, bonfires, apple jelly making, painting and decorating. It was a cloudless day, except for seeing the boy, seeing Will, just when I had pulled myself together, taken the plunge, walked up the hill beyond the orchard, intending to drop down to the pool below the Rock.

I saw him by the water's edge and dived sideways behind a clump of gorse. I must have made some sound for I could see through the dark green spikes with their golden halo of petals, Will turning around, aware, like the hunter he is, that something had moved on the hillside above him. I sat very quiet, controlling my breath, my heart racing. He stared for what seemed ages at my hiding place. Then, to my relief, he turned and walked away. Gradually I began to relax. The air was quite warm and I lay down on the tufty ground. I could forget about Will. I looked up at the sky. A buzzard hovered high above. A sense of peace came over me and I felt myself letting go of the mask.

Lying in the Indian summer sunshine, I must have slept for when I woke it was growing cool and the sun was sliding down the western sky, its orange sunset streaked across the heavens, the moorland around me growing shadowy quiet in the stillness of the oncoming evening.

Soon it would be dark. I headed towards Burrow, the longest way, across the side of the hill and down to the far side of the orchard. In the yard I saw — Will's Land Rover, his dog sitting up in the driver's seat looking expectantly towards the farmhouse. I entered the back door, heard voices, laughter: Will and Dad. Then Nadine's coquettish voice persuading Will to have supper, Kate joining in: "Yes, Will, please, please stay," she begged.

As I slipped off my wellies I hesitated, wondering if I could make some excuse and not have supper, all of us together. I did not want to be involved with Will. Even though Nadine had told me a bit about him. He was as mysterious for me as he was when I was a child. Then I had admired, hero-worshipped him. Now I wanted to hate him; but I realised that he still held a fascination for me, similar to then, and despised myself for being so affected by him.

All through supper I wore my mask, felt glad when Kate insisted it was I who put her to bed. She kissed Will goodnight. He held her in his arms, turning her upside down on to his shoulders. She screamed with delight, her little hands clutching the dark curls and he ran around the room, pretending to be her horse, galloped around the kitchen, twice; then playfully, gently the horse bucked her to the floor. She landed giggling into my arms. I hurried Kate from the room, playing a pretend game of who could be first upstairs, but my heart was leaping unevenly as I bathed the child, read her stories and tucked her into bed. I stayed with her until she slept, then went silently to my own room. I heard Will leaving, Felix calling at my door. "Gone to bed have you, Cleo?" he asked in a hoarse whisper. I pretended to be asleep.

***

This morning there was a letter from Vince. I longed for his warm, loving words. I was missing him so much. Again he wrote how sad he was that he couldn't come, even for a few days, before Christmas. But he would be with us on December twenty-second. 'Only seven more weeks, Cleo darling,' he wrote.

There was a letter from Lucy, too, from London. Patrick had a six-month contract there and they were to bring the children to Burrow before going back. It would be exciting having them here.

CHAPTER 19

This has been the strangest of all days since I arrived. I go over the events again and again in my mind. In the quiet of the night, unable to sleep, I try to make sense of my feelings. I can hear the rain pelting against the house, and a faint moaning wind, a warning perhaps that winter is truly setting in.

It had rained heavily all the previous night and everyone slept late. Kate, too late to catch the school bus at the end of our lane, needed to be driven to school. It was my favourite job taking Kate to school. She was good company and so observant. As we bumped along our rough track, she leaned out of the window to watch two buzzards hovering above us. Then, when we stopped before joining the deep, high-hedged lane to Crediford, she wanted to get out to see where, the day before, she had seen a rabbit vanish into the hedgerow. "Not now, Kate," I admonished. "You don't want to be late, do you?"

"OK," she agreed, but she watched everything through the open window as we drove the four miles to Crediford. The hills are steep and the hedges high and it is hard to believe that one drops so quickly from the wildness of the moorland into the gentle grass and woodland slopes of the valley, the 'in' country as it is known. At the school gates Kate jumped out of the car but not before she had wound her arms around my neck and hugged me goodbye. She trotted away down the short school drive, eager to get on with her day. As usual I marvelled at her confidence, so unlike the way I was at her age and reminding me of Lucy — the bounciness, the way she believed in herself.

After leaving Kate I was in no hurry to return to Burrow. It was pleasant to do the shopping in the village and I took my time. Dad had given me a list: nails, screws, sandpaper, connections for the garden hosepipe. Nadine also had asked for numerous items from the one food shop: butter, cheese, flour and bread from the bakery.

It was well after eleven by the time I'd finished, so I went into the pub, the White Duck, for some coffee. I had been there several times before, with Felix. At lunchtime it's quiet and the fire flickers warmly, a real comfort on cold days.

The last time I was there with Dad, Will had come in. He had gone straight up to the bar, without noticing us sitting in the corner, and spoken to Gloria, the blonde girl who works there most days. He held a piece of paper and I watched as Gloria leant across the bar to read whatever was on it, their heads almost touching. They seemed totally engrossed for several seconds while they shared the contents, then, flashing a smile at him, I noticed how she had folded the note, and stuck it into her shirt pocket. She was laughing agreeably, said something like: 'Of course I'll do it, Will. Don't worry'. But I couldn't really hear because Felix was telling me about one of his paintings that he'd sold and could not believe someone would have bought.

"It was by far the most expensive in the whole exhibition," he was saying, "and I liked it the least. It was Nadine persuaded me to ask that much, and she was right. It sold at once to some television presenter. More money than sense, if you ask me." Felix had been so happy about the sale and had said loudly, "Look Cleo, there's Will!"

Will, turning from the bar, was still in some way sharing a secret with Gloria, for he playfully pulled her hair before moving towards the door. "Thanks, Gloria, you're an angel," I heard him say, and then he strode across the room to us smiling.

"Have a drink, Will," Felix had invited. To my relief Will refused.

"No thanks can't stop, only dropped in to see Gee." So, she had a nickname too, I thought. "I'm off collecting sheep, the horse is waiting outside. There are still a hundred or so up on Higher Moor to bring down for the winter." He had included me in his smile. "Next time though, Felix, I'd love to stop for a drink. Perhaps you'll come and join the darts team? Every Wednesday night, now that it's nearly winter again. It's just started. We need a few reserves." He was looking at us both.

"Okay," Felix said, "you're on, Will."

"You too?" Will asked me

"Oh, no, not me. I don't really like the game." I stumbled over the words. "I've never played darts."

"Gloria had never played before she came here," Will said, "now she's a star. Often gets our team out of trouble. She's one of our best, in fact."

Looking back to that day, I could remember feeling more than a tinge of envy for Gloria. But today the bar was empty and I put my shopping down on the floor near the fireplace, waited to order coffee. Instead of Gloria, a man appeared behind the bar. I hadn't seen him before. I asked for my coffee.

"Gloria not working this morning?" I asked when the man brought it to me.

"'Fraid not," he said ruefully. "Had a bit of an accident in her car, head-on in one of the lanes. You know what it's like around here."

"Oh, dear," I said, "I hope she's not hurt."

"Only a few bruises and shock. She'll be okay; she's tough. Her car was a bit squashed in front, but it's not a write-off, she can still drive it. She'll be back to work tonight. Good old Gloria, takes more than that to put her off darts night." He laughed.

I decided to drive home the longest way — the back way Felix called it. I was unsure of the exact route, but it was interesting to explore and I found my way surprisingly easily. In some places grass grew down the middle of the road, very little traffic used this back lane.

I accelerated. Nadine's little Fiat was nippy, and I enjoyed the fast pace down the hill, then realised that the bend at the bottom would be hard to negotiate at this speed and put my foot on the brake. I had been driving too fast for the narrowness of the lane, which wriggled and bent, bend after bend, for what seemed forever.

Despite knowing the dangers, especially since hearing about Gloria's accident, I was risking life and limb negotiating the road. The car was sliding on the wet leaves, ripping the hedges of dying Goose-Grass that wound around the wing mirror. I caught glimpses of late summer's scarlet-mouthed Campion as I sailed along the narrow roadway. Then, veering around a bend too fast, and too close to the hedge — honeysuckle berries spattered the windows as I slammed on the brakes — skidding to a slithering halt in front of the bent-down figure of none other than Will.

He scarcely looked up. The car stalled. For a moment I was too horrified to move, shaken by the surprise of seeing someone on this quiet lane; shocked at skidding uncontrollably on the wet leaves, and furious because Will was staring at something in the middle of the lane seemingly unmoved by the danger he had put us both in by being there.

Suppose I had killed him? The idiot, I thought as I scrambled from the driver's seat and strode towards Will, more bravely than I felt, and wondered what on earth had been the focus of his attention.

I stood beside him, looked down at the road where he was kneeling. "What!" I gasped. "You risked your life and mine for that?"

"It's a stoat," he said, quietly, as though that explained everything.

"A stoat?" I questioned.

"Yes, you know, a stoat. Look."

I looked, crouched down beside him. There in Will's hand was the furry animal, floppy, and lifeless.

My anger melted at the sight of the long, snake-like bronze beast, the colour of autumn bracken. Will turned the little creature in his hand, its front was white, its tail long and black-tipped.

"Is he dead?" I managed to ask.

"Yep, he is now. I just wrung his neck, had to finish him off."

Will stood up and carried the stoat to the side of the lane and laid his furry body in the hedge amongst the wild flowers and grasses. I felt very cold.

"What happened?" I asked.

"Don't know really." Will pushed his cap back and scratched his head. "Someone driving too fast for the lane." He eyed me as he said it. He must have heard me racing along before screeching to a halt in front of him.

"It's unusual for a stoat to be struck, though," he added, "they are such fast movers — must have been carrying a weight, a rabbit perhaps."

I watched as Will glanced about, and then he saw it.

"There it is, the rabbit. He must have been dragging it across the lane when something walloped into him. Poor old stoat lost his life and his dinner. The rabbit must have tried to drag itself to the side of the road before breathing his last."

I was appalled at the sight, looked away quickly. "Poor, poor creature," I said. "What a way to die."

"Yes," agreed Will, "a pretty awful karma, poor thing." He pushed the rabbit, what was left of it, into the hedge.

"Karma? What do you mean karma? Are you saying it was its destiny?" Really this man was so contradictory. On the one hand hunting and killing and on the other thinking in terms of destiny. I felt my anger rising again. Just an excuse, I thought, to say killing is OK: it's all part of destiny.

Will interrupted my disturbed thoughts. "Not exactly destiny. No, that's not what I mean. More like something that would happen somehow — it's a question of when and how."

"You're being ridiculous," I said, challenging him. He shrugged.

"Do you mean to say that these animals would die exactly this way sometime and that a car would dash around the corner and slam into them to fulfil some plan made by — who? God?" I sounded cynical, almost laughing at Will.

"No," he said firmly. "It's about synchronicity, about something happening to the rabbit, the stoat and the person who drove into them, all at the same time. An opportunity, you could call it."

"And I suppose," I said sarcastically, "it's synchronistic that you arrived in time to put the poor thing out of its misery? You can't really believe that. If so, I'd like to know what my part is in this charade." I was aware of the patronising tone of my rhetorical question.

"I don't know," Will answered with unexpected sincerity. "Perhaps your coming along was just to cheer me up after a bad morning at market followed by this tragedy." He gestured towards the hedge, which was now a secret graveyard. We both stood quietly, then he said, "Got time to come in for a cup of tea? We live just around the next bend."

I hesitated, and Will said dryly, "Not that I want to divert you from your destiny. I could tell by the way you were driving that you were in a hurry." He was smiling now and I felt my face flushing.

I did not know how to justify my fast driving, so I said "OK, just a quick cuppa, thanks." I wondered whom he had meant when he had said 'we'. Of course, he would have a girlfriend, or a wife, though I had heard no mention of either from my father. I climbed back into the car and Will got in beside me. He told me he had been taking a few unsold bullocks along the lane to new grazing and had come across the stoat on his way back. We drove the short distance to the farm gate, then down a lane nearly as rough as the one at Burrow.

The farmhouse looked like a picture postcard. One of those heavy, thatched Devon longhouses, a bit like Burrow, only this one was bigger. It looked out onto a rectangular yard with stables all around. Horses' heads peered over the doors and a young woman came out of one of them. It was Gloria! I was surprised to see her there and with a strange pang wondered if she and Will were together.

She waved a friendly hand, calling to me: "Hi, Cleo, how are things?" Then she disappeared into one of the loose boxes. I hardly knew her, but liked her friendliness. I noticed the bruises on her face where she had hit the windscreen in the crash; felt relieved that my speeding had not resulted in anything more dramatic than it had.

"I'm giving Cleo a cuppa, come and join us, Gloria," called Will before he pushed open the back door. Gloria's head appeared above a stable door.

"No thanks, Will — must dash — working at the pub this evening. See you later, though."

Will and I entered the house. The door opened straight into the kitchen. I was reminded of Uncle Ted's kitchen at Burrow in the old days, when everything happened as it should and there was bread and jam for tea and work to do. It was a safe and secret place, out of reach from outsiders. I felt a sudden urge to cry, tears of nostalgia.

"Well, don't just stand there," Will was laughing at me, "you look horrified. I know it's a mess, but Mum's away and I'm a bit untidy when she's not around."

"No, no, it's not that," I tried to explain, "I like it, it's warm. It reminds me of Uncle Ted's kitchen when I was a kid."

Will filled the kettle and put it on the stove. Bending down, he opened the fire door and threw in some logs, picked the cat off the armchair and gestured to me to sit there.

"Tea? Coffee? Sandwich?" he asked. "Don't know about you but I'm starving."

"I ought to go," I said, sinking into the armchair.

"Why?" Will asked.

"I've got Dad's shopping, Nadine's too, and I have things to do."

"You could phone Felix, tell him I'm giving you lunch. It's the least I can do, making you skid the way you did." Will's eyes were on me and I felt my resolve melting.

"Okay," I said, getting to my feet. "Where's the phone?"

"I'm glad you're having lunch over at Kessel," Nadine said when she answered. "Felix and I are going out. Could you pick Kate up after school?" I agreed.

In the kitchen Will was slicing thick portions of ham. "I'm boiling some eggs too," he said, "are you vegetarian?"

"No," I told him. "I'm just fussy about where food comes from."

"Well, you don't need to worry. These animals are off my own farm. They are all free range, pigs, chickens, the lot. I've never liked factory farming," he added. "It seems unnatural, disrespectful, know what I mean?"

"Yes, I do, Will. I know exactly what you mean, but it's all so confusing. How can you say you respect animals when twice a week all through the winter you charge about the countryside chasing foxes and killing them? It doesn't add up."

Will was silent. He finished slicing the ham, cut thick slabs of brown bread, and put some plates on the table. "I suppose it must be hard for you to see the sense in hunting," he said with a sigh. "I can only say I'm sorry to offend, but it's what I do, Cleo, it's part of my job. I don't actually like killing, not for the sake of it. I don't wake up on hunting days and say 'hooray, I can kill a fox today'. It simply isn't the way we do things. We aren't out to kill for pleasure. The hunting's a pleasure; I have to admit that. It's tricky sometimes, challenging in fact. The healthy fox gets away most of the time; it's the mangy weak ones we want to cull; but the hounds are on him in a flash and he is dead before he knows it. I carry a gun too, in case of having to put the poor beast out of his misery, or an injured hound, or a horse for that matter. Things do go wrong sometimes, Cleo. Nothing's perfect, even in nature."

"I simply can't understand anyone doing it," I said. "Why do you?"

"Because it's my life; part of everything I've always done and my father and ancestors before me. Keeping the balance with the fox population is just one of the things we Dartmoor farmers have always done. It's just part of it all. Come on, Cleo, eat up. I've got something very special to show you after lunch."

I finished eating the delicious sandwich and swallowed my cup of tea; intrigued as he described how we would have to walk down to the field he called 'Pony Meadow' to see the surprise he had in store for me. I did as he suggested, pulled on his mother's wellies and followed him across the yard.

"I thought they'd fit, you're just about the same size as Mum."

"I suppose it's more usual in the country for a man to go on living with his mother, even at your age?"

I could have bitten my tongue off. My remark was insensitive, how could I? I turned quickly around to say sorry, expecting to see hurt on his face. But it wasn't there. Either he hadn't heard or didn't care what I thought. But he must have heard, for as we walked across the yard he said quietly, "Mum lives with me. She moved in after Dad died, it seemed a sensible and natural thing to do. We get on fine; she doesn't interfere with my life at all. She's been a real brick, to tell you the truth, a good friend after Maria died." He hesitated. I saw a shadow flicker across his face. "No one really understood as well as Mum — at least I think she did. But whether she did or not, she was there for me, unassuming, yet somehow strong. She didn't walk around on eggshells like some people did for weeks. While Maria was in the coma and after the funeral. It was as though I had some disease." He grinned at me, briefly. "Do you know, Cleo, some people used to disappear into a shop if they saw me in Crediford, or even cross the street. I suppose they didn't know what to say; especially those who knew about us, about Maria and me, about the sort of marriage we had."

I wanted to ask him what sort of marriage they had had, but he was opening the gate into a small paddock. "In the summer," he said, "this place is a mass of flowers. It's never had any fertiliser other than my cows and a few sheep, and I don't cut the hay till late. I like seeing the wild flowers flourish, at least on some of the land. It seems a fitting place for my special friends when they come to the end of their lives."

We had followed the hedge to where some gorse bushes grew, and amongst them were what looked like headstones.

"What's this?" I asked, mystified. Will said nothing, but taking me by the arm gently led me to where I could see clearly what had been written on one of the granite stones. I was stunned as I read the words in big, capital letters. 'Brownie.'

Incredulous, I stared at the gravestone, and then at Will.

"My Brownie?"

"Yes." Will spoke almost in a whisper. "She was very special, your Uncle Ted gave her to me just before he died — made me promise to look after her and give her back if I saw you." He put his hand on my shoulder. "I'm sorry Cleo, but she did live to a good old age."

Tears crept down my face; Will drew me into his arms and kissed the top of my head, gently. "Don't worry," he said, "I've got better news now. She had several foals, your Brownie, and I have kept her great-granddaughter; she is part thoroughbred, and I'd like you to see her when she gets back from her summer grazing. "

I pulled myself together and Will handed me a red-spotted handkerchief, which reminded me of Uncle Ted.

"How old was she when she died?"

"Around thirty. I've got some pictures of her with her foals. I'll show them to you when you have time. And you can meet her great-granddaughter too."

"I have to go," I said, "because of collecting Kate from school. Thank you for showing me Brownie's resting place."

We were walking back to the house. "Where's your Mum?" I asked.

"In India, yes, India," he repeated, seeing my surprise. She goes abroad a lot, doing various works for charity. She's a Christian, you see."

"A Christian?"

"Yes. I mean a real Christian; she walks her talk. If she hears of trouble somewhere in the world she flies there, just like that, and gets involved with the agencies and gets stuck in working for them. She doesn't mind what she does — looking after people dying of poverty or Aids, or teaching, or digging water wells, helping the women with their kids."

"How long does she stay away?"

"Oh, anything up to two years. I'm expecting her back soon. She's been gone nine months this time, but she's had a virus — lost some weight, needs a rest — so she'll be back next week."

"She sounds like a bit of an unusual character."

"Could say that," Will agreed, smiling. I couldn't help thinking about my own mother and the contrast in our parentage.

"I suppose we just have to accept that everyone is different," I said. "I can't imagine anyone I know from your mother's generation still doing what she does."

Arriving at the house I took off his mother's boots putting them tidily away in the porch, wondering if I could face meeting such a formidable-sounding woman.

Will led me to the car. "Are you sure you're all right?" he asked."

"Yes, I'm fine. I'll go and get Kate. Thank's for lunch, Will. I really appreciate everything." I looked into his eyes showing that I meant what I said.

***

Now late at night still awake, memories of Brownie are washing over me, and my mind is full of all that has happened today: not least Will's gentle concern at Brownie's grave.

CHAPTER 20

Monty was back! When I woke up this morning I was surprised to hear his high-pitched laughter just as I remembered it as a child. I was never afraid of Monty, poor limping Monty. He was like a kind of shadow who came and went, one minute there and the next gone. He used to live in Crediford with Aunty Gwen's cousin Phyllis, who looked after him, loved him. Certainly he was very upset when he had to leave her to live at the centre in Plymouth, returning only for holidays. Felix had told me that, when Phyllis died, Monty had had to stay in Plymouth all the time.

Apart from feeling sorry about him occasionally back then, I had scarcely thought about him and was shocked to hear his wild laughter. He was with Felix in the kitchen. The sound of their voices rumbled in my room, though it was impossible to hear what they were saying.

Glancing at my watch I saw I had slept late. It was after nine o'clock and I guessed that Nadine would have taken Kate to the school bus. I dressed and lifted the latch on my door, walking down the short, sloping corridor to the bathroom. I wondered why Monty was here, what he would look like after so many years.

The bathroom sloped under the heavy thatch and a small window looked out onto the enclosed patch beside the yard where Uncle Ted used to keep a pig. The pig ark still stood in the corner of this walled place; grass growing where once the pig wallowed in mud. I could see the makeshift clothesline, with a stout prop lying beside it, where Nadine hung the washing. And there beside the wall was Will's Land Rover.

So, he was here again, and I wondered why.

I opened the kitchen door and saw them; Will, Felix and Monty were sitting at the table. Monty, seeing me, ran across the room, limping, arms outstretched like a child. I was trapped, felt myself tensing, going rigid.

"He hasn't forgotten you, Cleo," Will said. "Haven't forgotten anything, have you, Monty?" he teased.

"No, no. Monty never forget nothing!" Monty shouted, with an emphasis on nothing that made the cat scuttle down from the window seat and seek refuge behind the log basket next to the Aga.

I could not avoid Monty's embrace. He hugged me, saying, "Cleo, Cleo, Cleo," again and again. I returned his hug, aware of his thick short shape, his warm smell of horses and hay. As Monty clung to me I leaned forwards to accommodate his shortness and caught Will looking at me, full and square.

"Put her down," Will laughed. "Put her down, Monty." He did so. It was easier to be free from Monty's grip than it was to move my eyes from Will's steady gaze. My face, I knew, had reddened from the exertion of the hug. Now Monty put his arm around my waist in an easy fashion, like a school child would to a close friend, or a child leaning on its mother.

Will had moved around the table and was standing with a hand on Monty's shoulder. I could feel the nearness of Will's hand, close to my face. "Come and sit down, Monty," Will said, gently leading him to the table.

"Cleo come too."

"Yes, I'll come too," I said, moving around to the opposite side of the table. Felix put some coffee in front of me. I thanked him.

Monty looked exactly as I remembered him when I was thirteen. Although nearly fifty, his hair had not gone grey and his face, unlined, held a youthful innocent expression. I knew he was not my real cousin, not really Uncle Ted's son, yet seeing him brought me closer to those childhood days.

I gathered that Monty stayed with Will and his mother for occasional weekends and special times like harvest and Christmas. I walked with them both to the Land Rover. As Monty climbed in, Will turned to me. "Come over this afternoon to Kessel?" he asked. "I'd like to show you Brownie's great-granddaughter. I've just got her back from where she's been turned out all summer. She's looking quite rough, but you'll be able to see what great lines she has."

I drove to Kessel that afternoon in the Land Rover. It was cold and the air was still, under a pale grey sky.

Monty was in the yard. He carried a bridle and grinned, nodding his head excitedly when he saw me.

Will appeared from the house. "I'm just helping Monty," he said. I joined him and watched, over a loosebox door, Monty grooming a big chestnut gelding.

"Benjy, Benjy," Monty said, "this is Cleo." I went inside the box and stroked Benjy's neck. Monty worked deftly, crooning to the horse, cleaning out his feet, grooming his coat, and bridling him. I watched as he led him outside, taking him to the mounting block. Will stood beside me as Monty vaulted lightly on to Benjy's back.

The horse immediately put his head up and danced forward. Monty held his hands still and quiet, hissing gently to the gelding. He looked magnificent up there on Will's best hunter, the shining-coated liver-chestnut gelding. Monty was no longer Monty. As Benjy pranced around the yard I saw him transformed from the slow-witted, dark-faced, lame human being to a proud Delacroix figure, a mixture of Attila the Hun stamping proudly over civilisation itself and a passionate Jacob ready to wrestle with an angel. Monty, like his namesake, had suddenly become a force to be taken seriously, to be respected.

The horse pawed the ground, reared slightly, and Monty laughed. Benjy tossed his mane, which fell around his ears like a gleaming waterfall after a moorland storm. I was mesmerised by what I saw.

"He hasn't lost his touch," Will murmured as we watched the rider take Benjy over a low pole across a gateway and canter down the field. "He's the only one I trust with Benjy," Will added.

"I can see," I said, amazed by Will's trust in Monty on his favourite hunter. "But is he okay, flying along like that without a saddle?" I did not need to have an answer, for I could see that Monty and Benjy were one, that under Monty's careful directions the horse would not make a mistake.

"He's the best horseman I know," Will said. "When he's here he spends all his time with the animals, especially the horses. He loves them. It's a shame he's not allowed to live here. He stays in the caravan when he comes and looks after himself. We just give him whatever meals he turns up for, otherwise he cooks for himself — mostly chips," Will laughed.

They were circling the field now, Monty's hands were low, his legs close to the horse's side, and he sat deep into the animal's back.

"They are beautiful," I said, softly, as Monty set the horse at some jumps, clearing them effortlessly. Benjy slowed to a walk, a swinging confident walk towards the far gate. We watched as Monty dismounted and led Benjy into an adjoining paddock, where, set free, he galloped away from us, to be joined by three other horses. They wheeled around each other, playfully kicking and squealing before galloping out of sight into the woodland beyond.

"He's being clipped this evening," Will said. "Gloria's done the other hunters. I try to leave Benjy till last, let him gallop about without a rug for as long as possible. His coat is getting long now, so he needs clipping. That means lots of work." Will grimaced at me. "Winter chores starting — exercising every day and keeping him in the stable rugged up a lot more once he's had a hair cut."

"It's a shame," I said. "Why do you do it?"

"He needs to be fit," Will said, "and with his natural thick coat he'll sweat too much and lose condition. He's a hunter, Cleo. It's his job," he said, looking at me in a way that made me realise he was expecting me to object. I said nothing. Then, losing that rather anxious expression in his eyes, Will said, "It's time for you to see her, to see Brownie's granddaughter."

He put his hand under my elbow and gently steered me back across the yard. Will's hand on my arm was making my whole body tingle and I was glad when we reached the big barn and he let go of me and opened the vast double doors of the old granite building. I followed him through the barn to another door at the far end that opened into a smaller yard and an orchard beyond.

There she was! Cropping the grass contentedly. She raised her head and gave a quiet nickering whinny when she saw us. In a corner of the orchard was a field shelter, one side stuffed with sweet-smelling hay and the other a space for the horse and her companion, a small donkey.

Will opened the gate and the mare came up to us. Dark bay, with a kind intelligent eye, the mare breathed into my face, and I knew that I had found Brownie again. Speechless, I put my hand on her neck, felt the warm soft place under her mane that I had loved to stroke on Brownie's neck.

"She's bigger than I thought she would be," Will was saying, "though her dam was over fourteen hands, the stallion was sixteen hands. She won't make more than fifteen — just right for you." I couldn't tell if he was teasing. "Like her? She's called Skylark."

"Oh yes, she's absolutely beautiful, Will, and the name is perfect."

"I've backed her a few times. She's a dream," he said. "You can ride her when she's ready."

"When do you think that will be?" I asked.

"She's three now, so she will be perfect in the summer next year. But you could ride her sooner of course," he added hurriedly. I hoped he hadn't said that because he had detected the disappointment I felt. Next summer I was going to be far, far away from Brownie's descendants, and from Will, for by then Vince and I would be married, living in Canada. I might even be pregnant.

"I'm not sure I'm up to riding her, Will, I'm not very experienced. Perhaps I'll leave that to you and Monty." I smiled. "Thank you for letting me see her. I really must go, it's getting late and I promised to meet Kate." Will walked me to the car, explaining that he and Monty were planning to work with the mare over the next week and inviting me to watch the schooling sessions.

"Then you can ride her quietly out with me when I'm exercising Benjy."

My heart was thudding. "Thanks Will." I tried to sound casual as I climbed into Nadine's Fiat, but the invitation had rendered me almost speechless.

Driving to Crediford I asked myself why I found it so hard to tell Will I wouldn't be here to ride Brownie's offspring next summer. Somehow I found it impossible to talk about Vince to Will. I'm being very childish, I told myself, I must explain to him that I'm going to marry Vince and leave Burrow. After all, it's not going to make any difference to him. It's not as if we are in any way alike, or in any possible way is he attracted to me. I am certainly not attracted to a man who is such a brutal killer.

But, yet again, I found myself thinking about the feel of his touch, and the sensation it had evoked in me. I must stop these feelings, I told myself fiercely as I drew up at the school gates, but I feared that I might not resist if I accepted the opportunity to ride Brownie's young filly with him.

CHAPTER 21

I was closer to Lucy than anyone in the world, and seeing her again reminded me of the last time we were together, at the twins' christening, when Vince and I had first met. We greeted each other warmly. I could sense Nadine's surprise at my uncharacteristic enthusiasm. I have always been able to relax more in Lucy's company than with most people.

Patrick was to come later, with six-year-old Tom, the eldest. Lucy was tugged along by the four-year-old twins, Jamie and Sophie. They came from the station in a taxi, tumbling out, the twins and Lucy, all golden-haired and freckled, with laughing eyes and smiles as big as melon slices. Kate had been excited all day about their arrival. Taking them under her wing, showing them around the garden and farm. They came running indoors at teatime with pink cheeks from the chill blustery autumn wind and played with Kate's farmyard toys all evening, by the fire in the sitting room. That night, in my room, the twins slept end to end in the single bed. I had put a big mattress on the floor for Lucy and Patrick, but he wouldn't be here till tomorrow, so tonight Lucy and I would sleep in the same bed — and talk.

"You're pregnant!" I exclaimed when she told me. "Again?" I was incredulous, searched her face for a shadow, even a flicker of regret. But there was none. She was grinning.

"Don't look so shocked, Cleo. We both love kids, and after all Patrick's one hell of a Catholic." Her giggle was catching. Briefly I thought about my own mother, also a Catholic, who had seemed not to like children, or sex. I, too, was a Catholic for the first few years of my life, and I didn't like sex either, and I said as much to Lucy.

"Do you really still feel like that, Cleo?" Lucy sounded more serious. "What about Vince, you must be in love with him?" I was silent for a while.

"Yes, of course, I am. He's the nicest man in the world. I suppose it's what you'd call being in love."

Lucy lit a cigarette. "Don't mind, do you, Cleo? We could open the window." Alarmed, I opened the window wide.

"What about the kids, passive smoking and all that?" Lucy gave me a wry look. "It's only the one," she said, moving a plant pot from the windowsill to the bedside. "This can be the ashtray, and I'll puff the other way, away from the kids."

I looked across to where they slept, rosy-cheeked cherubs, healthy and golden. Somehow I knew that, with Lucy as their mother, they would grow up bouncing, like her; unafraid, un-neurotic, natural, unaffected by their mother's smoke.

"I envy you, Lucy," I said. "I envy the way you're so unafraid of everything."

She laughed. "Oh, I'm not. I'm terrified of heights, and hate going in elevators — lifts, I mean," she said, changing her smooth Canadian accent to a false English one. It was my turn to laugh.

"Yes, but Lucy you always admit your fears, don't you? You aren't ashamed of them."

"Oh, you bet I let Paddy know if I'm scared. I refuse sometimes to go up those mountains with him. He carts Tom up, always has, on his back, and now that Tom's six he shoves him up in front of him. If the child slips, Patrick simply catches him. What's more, Tom loves it. Wants a rope for his birthday!"

"Aren't you afraid for them?"

"I've got confidence in Patrick. All the same, I think if anything happened to him I'd," she hesitated, "I'd probably die." Lucy was suddenly quiet, stubbed out the cigarette in the earthy, damp saucer. She carried it back to the windowsill.

I climbed into bed. The twins snuffled around in theirs. I watched Lucy as tenderly she shifted them around on their pillows, kissed their foreheads then climbed into bed beside me. I clicked off the light.

"I love having his kids," she whispered. "I mean, it's all part of how I feel about him."

I wondered what it must be like to have such feelings for a man.

"You still fancy each other, I guess," I said with a sigh. "Lots of people don't. I mean they get bored. How is it you and Paddy are ... " I searched for the right words. "Well, you know, okay together? What's the secret?"

"Don't know," Lucy sighed. "All I know is, I adore him, want him a lot."

"And what about him," I asked, "wanting you?"

Lucy chuckled again, whispered loudly: "Course he wants me. We want each other. Do you know, Cleo, we've made love in every room in the house as well as outside, and in the garage, and the back seat of the car. Yes, it's true. One night, when the kids kept coming into our room, that's where we ended up, in the back seat of the old station wagon, Patrick's hobby, old cars, she explained."

We were both laughing. Then she said seriously: "Surely Vince fancies you, as much as you do him?"

"Yes, he does," I answered. "You're right, he fancies me as much as I do him."

There was a silence. "You deserve better, Cleo." Lucy said, suddenly. "I mean, not better than Vince, but better in your life. Have you truly never, ever been, well, you know, been in love that way?"

"No, Lucy, I haven't, and I don't think Vince and I are the sort. You and Patrick are different, that's all, just different. It doesn't matter really."

"Oh, but it does," Lucy said. She propped herself up on one arm. "Marriage and partnerships without passion would be so boring." I did not answer. "There I go again, Cleo. I don't mean you and Vince. Neither of you is boring."

"What does it feel like, Lucy, really to love someone in that way?"

"It's not something I can describe," she whispered. "It's just something that happens, Cleo. You'll know when it does. It's unmistakable," she said, drowsily. The moon swept the bedroom briefly, as clouds parted in the night sky. "It's so beautiful here," Lucy murmured. "No wonder you've always loved it." She yawned.

"Yes, I love it, always will," I answered. But there was something else I loved. I could sense the truth of a feeling that I had never known before. It was about Will, and I longed to tell Lucy.

The clouds blotted out the moon again, and I took a deep breath — started to speak, to tell Lucy about him. Slowly, in a clear, subdued voice, for I did not want to wake the twins, I began.

"There's someone, Lucy, someone who maybe..." my voice trailed away, then, plucking up courage I continued, "He's got dark hair — it curls — he speaks with a West Country burr to his voice. He's not that tall or small, average, I suppose, but there's something about how his... how he moves — how his eyes hold me. Looking at him, I am drawn into his being, as though he is part of me, a part I have always longed to find — to love. To explore. He's awful — he kills foxes. He's kind — animals love him, kids love him. He's quiet — his wife is dead; she got killed, fell off her horse and was in a coma, for months. He sat next to her, devoted, trying to revive her, but it didn't work. Instead of letting him see how I feel, I show him how I can't make sense of some of the things he does. What I really want to be is normal with him. What I want to do is just stand there, opposite him, looking at him; if I could really look at him honestly, do you know what I'd do, Lucy? I'd lift my hand, and very, very gently touch his face. I would describe it with my fingers. I know it in my eyes and mind already — I've known it forever. But to touch his eyelids and feel the lashes, dark and long, brush my hand — to touch those creases in his forehead, the deep one in the middle that flattens when he laughs … I would stroke the curl that presses out from his cap — it's exactly the same as the one he wore when we were children. I would let my fingers follow the crookedness of his nose — I think he broke it when he fell from the white pony when he was only twelve years old.

"It's strange to think he is the same as all men, with eyes and a nose and a mouth — Oh, Lucy! His mouth! It smiles at the corners, even when he's concentrating. There's a dip on the upper lip, in the middle. I want to breathe in and put my face against his and gently bite his lip, just there. I know his taste — I can guess it — it's as though I've known it all my life. My tongue on his skin is familiar with his scent, his muskiness. If I put my fingers on his eyelids I can feel their depth, the laughter in the lines around the edges, even if he had grown older than Dad, Felix, I would want my lips to touch him and know him, to make love. If I could only feel free — free to let go. It's got nothing to do with Vince — it's me. I am somehow chained behind a mask. If I only knew how to be free of this imprisonment I could stand there with Will in a stillness of knowing, no explanations, just stillness, never again to be empty, always full. Oh! Lucy, perhaps this is just what you were saying, it's indescribable, it's for ever, it's everything, it's — I suppose it's love. Do you think its love, Lucy?" My voice was hoarse and I turned my head towards my friend. The moon lighting upon her relaxed face and closed eyes. She was out of hearing and fast asleep.

***

Lucy and family were to leave on Sunday night. I could see that everything Lucy had told me about her marriage was true. There was no hint of disharmony between them; in fact it was clear they really adored each other. I watched them with the children, playing, just being, the way they all moved together or apart, part of each other, the way Lucy allowed the twins to open her shirt and feel her breasts, making her laugh.

"I've only just stopped feeding them," she admitted, as she gently pushed them down, making them giggle as she tickled them, steered them towards some diversion — often Patrick, who seemed to delight in rescuing Lucy from his children's greed. I noticed how he looked then, how he touched her dress, brushed against her, kissing her perhaps in a way that could be mistaken for nonchalance. As though in passing, his lips happened to sweep near some part of her face, head, arm, neck. I watched her face. It was open, as Lucy always was, confident, as ever.

But there was something else, some sense of fullness, an opposite to empty, which, bursting, yet remained contained — fluent, moving, yet staying still. I envied this. This was something I wanted. Like some women might long for a child, I longed for this.

It was warm enough to have Sunday lunch on the cobbles outside the back door. We put wine and cheese and bread on the table. Kate and the twins, with Tom, were rolling around the damp lawn. Sycamore wings, brown and broken in their late autumn state, clung to their woolly jumpers. When they came to the table they smelled of the autumn leaves, which stuck to their hair.

"You must have a rest after lunch," Nadine was saying to Patrick as she poured deep red wine into his glass. "It's a long drive to London this evening."

The family were flying back to Canada the next day. The weekend had flown past and the thought of them leaving gave me an empty, sad feeling. I hardly had time to dwell upon it when I heard a clattering of horses' hooves coming up our lane. There they were, Will and Gloria on Will's hunters, both leading rider-less horses. Will waved his stick, grinning.

"Just taking a short cut," he explained. "Maestro's lost a shoe and I don't want to take him back along the road. Thought you wouldn't mind us cutting through your yard, going back by the moor instead."

"'Course," said Felix, getting to his feet. "My dear fellow, come and join us, both of you."

Will glanced in my direction. "Don't want to break up the party," he said.

"Nonsense," Dad was saying, "you're not breaking up a party. Come and meet Patrick and Lucy and their tribe."

No, no, I was thinking, I don't want Lucy to meet Will. I was glad that Lucy had slept through my soliloquy the other night, not wanting her to guess anything about Will.

I switched on my mask. Felix was at his typically hospitable best. "Put the horses in the stable or tie them up. Come on, you two, you can't miss the chance of meeting friends of Cleo's from Canada. They're leaving tonight so it's your last chance."

Will and Patrick were shaking hands, Gloria smiling at Lucy over the saddle she was carrying. She dumped it on the bench.

"I'll make coffee," I said, vanishing into the kitchen. As I left I heard Felix telling Gloria that Patrick and Lucy were "close friends of Cleo's fiancé Vince. You'll meet him when he comes over at Christmas," he added.

The cups rattled on the tray I carried, in tune with a rattling inside me. I had meant to tell Will about Vince — next time. I should have told him the other day when we had spent the afternoon together. I had not wanted to spoil anything. But now, I could feel a change in Will as he took the coffee from the tray; he looked me squarely in the eyes but, instead of being drawn into their depths, I was being repelled by a steely hardness that was totally alien to me. I almost cried out. The tray slipped as he asked, "When's the wedding, then, Cleo?"

Patrick caught my arm, straightened the tray. "All this middle-of-the-day wine drinking ain't good for you," he joked. "Here, I'll take the tray, Cleo." Gratefully I handed over to Paddy and turned to face Will. I needed to explain myself. But Will had already drained his cup and turned away.

"Come on Gee, the horses are getting restless. Thanks, Nadine, Felix — but I think we'd better go." He kissed Nadine. I watched as they clattered from the yard, my heart aching.

Later, Lucy grabbed me. "Cleo," she said, "what was all that about? He's gorgeous, and he cares about you. Pity he's got a girlfriend, Gloria whatsit — what a name" Lucy's light-heartedness cut through the solid barrier that had closed around me since Will had given me that harsh look.

We were in the bathroom, Lucy packing the twins' toothbrushes and flannels. "Nearly as good-looking as Vince, that guy. Definitely drop-dead-gorgeous," she was saying. Suddenly I was in tears — great sobs coming from inside me. Lucy dropped the wash bag, had her arms around me in an instant.

"Damn it, Cleo, there I go again stirring things up. What's the matter, honey?"

Through my sobs I said, "Please, Lucy, when you get back, tell Vince I love him, won't you? Tell him not to leave me here for too long without him. I am missing him. I'd come back now with you and Patrick and the kids if I hadn't promised Nadine."

Lucy looked worried and I extricated myself from her arms and leaned over the washbasin, slapping cold water onto my eyes. As I dried my face on the pink towel that Lucy handed to me, she said, "It's that guy, isn't it, Cleo, that Will fellow?"

"No," I answered sharply. "I don't know what you're talking about."

Lucy sighed. "Gee, Cleo, if you have fallen for him, and I wouldn't blame you, then why not say so?"

"I haven't," I snapped at her. "You're imagining things. I don't even like him. He's cruel, goes hunting – kills things. All the women fall for him, it seems. He's not my type, no, definitely not."

Lucy was scrutinising my face and I could see that she doubted my words. "Lucy," I said firmly "there is only one man in my life and that's Vince, and I'm missing him like hell. Why can't you believe me?"

"I'm sorry, Cleo, and I'm glad, and of course I'll tell Vince how much you are missing him. I'm longing for you to be married and live near Paddy and me. It's all so perfect, both our best friends marrying each other." I caught Lucy's enthusiasm. We were hugging each other. I felt a small surge of excitement at the prospect of marriage to Vince. Lucy's baby was due in seven months, and now I told her that I wanted to get pregnant the moment Vince and I were married.

She flung her arms around my neck. "How perfect," she said. "Our babies will grow up as friends." Paddy thundered up the stairs with the twins chasing him.

"We're leaving now, come on, come on," shouted the children. They bounced around, always ready for the next piece of action.

CHAPTER 22

The weather had changed very suddenly. Rain greeted each day, pouring relentlessly for hours. Felix was grumpy. "It's this sort of weather makes me want to go back to Spain or Provence," he said one morning. Kate was home from school with a bad cold sitting propped up by the stove on the armchair with a pile of picture books and the cats on her lap. When she coughed, her face went red and her bright eyes were even brighter, as though on fire. She did not complain, but simply sat there barking her dry cough over the cats. Nadine mixed a brew of dried rosemary and thyme with honey and lemon and Kate sipped it quietly whilst I sat on the arm of her seat reading stories to her.

The postman arrived late. "It's getting bad crossing the river. The water's up over the bridge, it hasn't been that high in living memory," he announced.

He was in the kitchen, water dripping down his raincoat onto the slate floor as he spoke. "They're supposed to be meeting there, Saturday," he added, "but I expect it'll have gone down by then. Hope so anyway."

I had learned that when local people said 'They' it meant the hunt, and I listened intently. The postman was sitting down sipping the hot coffee Nadine handed him. "I just saw Will driving back with Monty — come back to help Will Saturday, I daresay. They tell of it clearing."

My heart had lurched at the sound of Will's name. I had not seen him for almost two weeks, since the Sunday that Lucy and Patrick had left, had not found an opportunity to explain.

"Haven't seen Will for a couple of weeks," Felix was saying, "or Gloria for that matter."

They were talking about Monty now and Kate was yawning, nearly asleep. I stopped reading and listened to the men.

"I didn't realise Monty went hunting with Will," Felix said.

"Well, he don't really," Jack the postman retorted, taking a noisy sip of tea. "He just keeps in the background with the extra 'orse. If it's a long day Monty will be waiting — he knows some'ow where Will is and when 'ees ready to change onto a fresh 'orse then Monty rides home, quiet-like, with the tired 'orse."

"It's a shame they won't let Monty stay at Kessel permanently," Nadine said.

"He's got a section on him," said Jack.

"I never could understand why," Dad said.

"Well, see," the postman lowered his voice, "t'was that time, in Crediford, before old Phyllis died — Monty was there and he'd had a few in the pub." The postman glanced towards Kate, now asleep. I pretended to be reading.

"There were some girls there in the pub and they taunted Monty, then when they left he chased them down the street. It was late and they was screaming, so he hid behind the big tree up the churchyard. They thought he'd gone and were giggling, I expect, and hurrying back home down the hill, when suddenly Monty stepped out from behind the tree and stood in front of them; they all ran screaming and yelling back up to the village. The police were called and the girls told them he didn't have no trousers on." Jack was speaking in a whisper now. "I reckon 'ee's harmless myself, but you know what it's like. One of the girls said he'd tried to rape her, wouldn't let go of her. She had bruises, mind you, where he held her tight round the arms, so she told the police."

I felt dismayed by the story.

"In the end he was never charged, nor nothing like that," he added gravely. "He was never allowed to go in the pub again, and they ordered him to live at the home in Plymouth save for special holidays with poor old Phyllis." The postman put his cup down; enjoying the effect he had on his audience,

"After Phyllis died, that was that," he said. "No more visits for Monty. Until, that is, Will and his mum started having him. It seems to be working out all right too. He doesn't come every weekend, especially as Will's mum is away so much. But when he does he's always with Will or on one of Will's horses."

He drained his cup. "Yeah, it seems to be a good thing all round," he said, getting up from the table. "Look, the rain's stopped. I'd better get on with my round."

With the postman gone I went to leave the room, but Nadine asked me to wait a moment.

"There's a letter here I want to speak to you about." I waited as she scanned the letter. "It was hard to get a word in while Postie was here." She raised her eyebrows and smiled. "He is a great one for news even if it's decades old. But I have some news too. My Mama is a little under the weather and wants us to go and stay with her for the weekend."

Dad looked up from his letters and groaned. "Not again?"

"Well, we need not go, my darling," she said. "But if we do go, this weekend would be good because it is the anniversary of her marriage to my Papa. And well Felix, you know how she is on that day."

Felix sighed. "What about Cleo?" he asked. "We can't abandon her just like that."

"Of course you can, Dad," I protested. "I don't mind having a weekend alone, for heaven's sake. In fact I'd rather enjoy it. I could look after the cats and finish the painting in the scullery."

I meant it. I welcomed time to myself. I had not been in my own company for more that a few hours at a time ever since I got there, and the thought of three days alone pleased me. I could catch up on some reading. Above all, I could think. I needed to think. Thinking time was as important to me as sleep, and since my arrival there had been so much work indoors and out, so many trips to collect Kate from school, so little time really alone to sort out my feelings and thoughts. I had not yet been to that part of the river where the Rock stood. In all these weeks I had somehow avoided the Rock. Now, perhaps, with Dad and Nadine and Kate away I would walk out there, climb it, though the recent rain would have swollen the river. The thought of going there was uppermost on my list of things to do.

Now at last was my chance to unravel my mind. To pull together the threads of the life I remembered from the days of my childhood, with its superstitions and fears, and the Burrow of today, with the earthy normality, which surrounded the place since Dad, Nadine and Kate had settled at this ancient habitation. Where Endatons had lived and died since time was measured.

CHAPTER 23

The rain had stopped. The sun shone intermittently all next morning. Best of all, Kate had recovered and it was with some relief that, after lunch, I waved them all goodbye.

It seemed quiet, uncannily so, with just the three cats for company. I spent some time finishing the paintwork in the scullery, and then went out for some fresh air, before darkness fell. The moor looked grim, for the sky was leaden again; a heavy black lid seemed to be pressing down on the landscape. There was going to be more rain.

It held off until after I'd climbed into bed. The cats curled around me, and I was glad of their company as I lay in the darkness, listening to the rain relentlessly drumming against the window. The wind was getting up now, gathering strength, pushing the rain harder. It sounded as though slivers of glass were beating against the closed windows.

I lay snuggled in the warmth of my bed, listening to the wind increasing, before falling asleep. Then I was suddenly awake. I had heard something. It must be the middle of the night, I thought, as I sat up in bed listening hard. I heard a strange moaning sound accompanying the wind that whistled and groaned through every slit of badly fitting window frame. Dad had intended renewing all the windows one by one. I had told him to leave mine till last. "I like air coming in," I had told him.

"Yes, but when Nadine's family come to stay they won't like it at all," he had said.

"I'll be gone by then," I had replied, but now as the night hours ticked away and I listened to the wind and rain rattling the panes I wondered if I'd been right to insist on leaving my windows till last.

Again I heard the moan, or was it a whimper? It sounded like a dog mournfully howling.

I felt myself going cold at the thought of a dog out there somewhere, and wondered if it was purely my imagination. If not, then what was it? I pushed aside thoughts of the impending disasters that were said to follow the sound of a howling dog, tried not to think about Dad and the family, perhaps caught in the storm. They should be in Paris by now. They had flown on the evening flight from Exeter — unless it had been cancelled. But they would have 'phoned me if that had happened, or driven back to Burrow.

There it was again, an unmistakable howl, followed by an anguished bark. There was a dog, outside the house, not far away and maybe in trouble.

I forced myself from the bed and flicked the light switch. Nothing. A fuse must have blown. I felt feverishly around my bedside table for the small pen torch that I always kept near me. It was such a thin streak of light but brought with it an inordinate amount of comfort. The cats blinked into its beam and curled up again. They, at any rate, were not going to investigate the disturbance. For disturbance it was now, unquestionably a dog in some distress.

I crammed my feet into thick slippers and hauled my dressing gown around me. Making my way as fast as I dared down the stairs, following the pinpoint of torchlight, memories from childhood flew through my mind. Monsters and demons, which I believed had been dead for years, reared at me, and by the time I reached the kitchen I realised that my legs had turned to lead and my hands were shaking. No lights here either — damn and blast! The dog was now yowling at the front door. I could hear the scratch, scratch of its paws as it desperately tried to gain access. Frantic now, I searched for Dad's big torch. My hand brushed against a vase of dried rosemary as the pen light faded completely, I caught the aromatic herb smell, almost sobbed at its warm familiarity. Where was the torch? Where could it be? There was a terrible commotion now, for the dog, or monster, was seemingly throwing itself at the door. Here at last was the torch, its big beam filling the room then the passage as I staggered over the flagstones, past all the wellies to the door.

Shaking, I turned the great iron key. What was out there? Whatever it was had stopped scratching, had stopped howling, had perhaps given up trying to get through the door.

"Thank God for that," I muttered as I wrenched the key. It was unlocked now, yet I was unsure if it was safe to open the door.

But open it I did. And slowly peeped around its edge.

A heavy thud and a bone-jarring shudder almost took the door off its hinges as the creature made one more gigantic attempt to break into Burrow.

I screamed as I was bowled backwards. A huge black and white sheepdog thrust itself at me and I felt the full force of the storm as rain and wind rushed in with the dog — followed by the shouting, soaking, sobbing, roaring body that was Monty.

But I was still reeling backwards, falling into the wellies, pulling the umbrella stand on top of me. The torch, wrenched from my hand by the fall, went out and I lay helpless in the dark passage in a knot of fear as the form of Will's dog, Shep, and a crazy-sounding Monty sprawled over me.

"Cleo, Cleo!" Monty was shouting. "Cleo, where's Cleo?"

He was making a terrible roaring sound. I felt his saturated clothes against me and an incomprehensible stream of words spat from his dribbling mouth. His grip on my arms was painful as he poured his grief against me.

Struggling from the attack I found the torch, turned it on into Monty's face.

"Let go of me," I yelled, "Let go, Monty, let go."

Suddenly his face, which was fully visible now in the beam of the torchlight, crumpled into childish sobs.

I extricated myself from under the heap of madman and frantic dog, and stood up — pushed Monty down in front of me. I felt suddenly calm. Slammed the door closed so as to at least keep out the wind. The dog shuddered in a corner, whimpering.

"Shut up," I snapped at the dog, and he lay down on his paws, still whining. Then, "Get up, Monty," I ordered. "Go and sit by the Aga."

I was in control now. Just as I had once needed to keep a plane full of rowdy schoolchildren quiet, so I had to handle these creatures, these two mad animals, for in the terror of the moment that's what they had become. These two familiar creatures had become wild, hysterical, threatening, and I had to think hard to survive their onslaught.

Shaking still, I found matches, candles, lit them, put them on the table and took a closer look at Monty. I was aghast at what I saw. Clearly he needed immediate attention. He was shivering uncontrollably and I feared he was suffering from hypothermia.

I raced around the kitchen, the bedrooms, pulling towels, blankets and duvets, grabbed clothes from Dad's cupboard and removed Monty's clothes from him, wrapped him in a bath towel, his huge chest, covered in hairs, black and wet, heaved as he continued sobbing. I rubbed his back, arms, chest, found myself crooning to him, as though he were an abandoned baby. I put a towel around his head, wiped his face, tears poured down his cheeks, unstoppable tears. In his hand he gripped something, he would not let go, it was a length of leather — a dog lead? I tried to force his hand from its grip, but he refused to let it go.

Glancing at Shep, I saw the dog was still shaking.

"Oh, Shep, if you could only talk." I pulled Monty to his feet long enough to wrap more blankets around him, and then gently pushed him into the armchair. Hot milk with brandy and honey soon dribbled down his chin, but he swallowed some at least. Shep lapped a bowlful too as I rubbed his shivering body with a warm towel. Monty had gone quiet, sleepy, his head lolling.

"Monty!" I shouted. "Wake up! Tell me what's happened. Where's Will?"

At the mention of Will, Monty set up another moan and began sobbing again. My heart raced. "Where is he? Is he at Kessel? Monty, you must tell me."

But Monty only cried and shook. I went to the phone, dialled the Kessel number.

A woman answered, with an anxious "Hello, hello?"

"Where's Will? I must know where he is — please, I am afraid he may be hurt somewhere. Monty's here, he's incoherent. Who are you?"

"Who are you?" the woman demanded.

"This is Burrow — Burrow" then there was another sudden crackling and the line went dead.

'Oh God, it was too late. That stupid woman wouldn't listen. Now the line was dead. Oh God, what should I do?'

I tried the phone again and again, tried the police — it was no good. So that first night, when Felix, Nadine and Kate were away, I was to spend in the kitchen, in the company of mad Monty and Will's dog, praying that Monty would not die, would tell me where Will was, that nothing terrible had happened to him. The rain lashed on through the early hours of one and two o'clock, and then Shep growled a low growl, his tail thudded like a great rope against the cupboard door. He sat up, stared at the door, whined. The candles were low, there was an eerie silence, a mid-storm quiet, the tail wagging increased and then I heard it too — Will's Land Rover. Was he safe? Please, God, if you are listening, please let him be all right. I hurried to the door and saw that my prayers were answered. Whatever had happened was a mystery, but he was safe. All of them were safe. I felt the relief of this, but then as Will followed me indoors I saw in the dim light of the candlelit kitchen that his face wore a terrible expression of grief and I feared what he would tell me.

His voice shook as he told me that Benjy was missing.

They had been hunting and Will had told Monty to set off for home with Benjy, before the weather worsened, and darkness set in. Will and the whipper-in with a few diehards would collect the remaining hounds together and follow home shortly.

"I never thought," Will explained to me, "that Monty would attempt to cross the moor in this sort of weather."

Monty was asleep now, tucked into the armchair. Will had thrown his wet coat across the Aga and was sipping the drink I had made for him — hot milky coffee laced with brandy. He sighed.

"Thanks, Cleo, this is good." He looked drawn and exhausted.

"Relax, Will," I told him. "There's no point in attempting to find Benjy till morning."

"You're right," he said, putting his head in his hands, elbows on the table. "At least, thank God, Monty's okay, thanks to you, Cleo." Will looked up and put an arm out to reach my hand. I was sitting in Dad's grandfather chair at the end of the table. "I'm grateful to you, Cleo."

I said nothing, but held his hand, longing to take his head in my arms, comfort him. He explained how his mother had told him about my 'phone call, and he'd come at once. He had spent the last few hours with men from Crediford, searching for Monty and Benjy up and down the river, by the big ford where they guessed he might have attempted to cross the raging torrents on his way home. Other riders had turned back there, Will told me. They had not risked crossing, but had returned by a five-mile route through lanes to Crediford — a long ride but safer than a river crossing in that sort of weather.

Will drained his cup and Monty stirred. Will went to him, bent down. "Monty," he said, urgently, "where is Benjy? Can you remember what happened, Monty?" Will's anxiety, although less now he knew Monty was safe, was obvious.

I asked Will what he thought might have become of Benjy, and he told me that at best he was lame, struggling to hobble home, at worst — "well anything could have happened to him. The waters are raging, if he had slipped and fallen, he would hardly survive."

"Monty!" Will 's voice pleaded urgently into Monty's ear. "Come on, old fella, tell me, where's Benjy?"

Monty opened bleary eyes. He was incoherent, but I caught the words "Never let go, Will, never let go."

"What does he mean?" I asked.

"God knows." Will moved wearily from beside Monty's chair. "I reckon it could mean he didn't let go of Benjy's reins, even when they broke, he kept a grip — see, he's still clutching a piece of it — Benjy must have been on the end of that, it's part of his bridle."

I helped Will struggle back into his wet coat feeling helpless, unable to find words to comfort or reassure him.

"I'll take Monty back to Kessel," he said. "You've been a great help, thanks Cleo. Get some sleep now and I'll call in tomorrow and let you know what's happened. Perhaps the 'phones will be mended too. And maybe Benjy is back home in the yard now, while we're talking, so I won't hang around. Mother's keeping an eye out, but I don't want her to have to deal with him if he's found his way home. She isn't quite well yet, needs to rest, not go out on a night like this. I'll be out to look again at first light with the others."

It was hard to sleep after they had gone, and before dawn I was up and dressed. Although the storm had abated somewhat there was still a steady stream of rain. I made some porridge, and forced myself to eat two big helpings. I would need all my strength if I were going to search the moor for Benjy. Of course he may have got back to Kessel, but until the 'phones were mended or I went there in the Land Rover I wouldn't know. I had to do something to help — I would go mad if I stayed here worrying.

What a time to choose to walk out to the Rock — to the crossing place — I planned to walk to the clapper bridge above the Rock and follow the river upstream before striking back over the high moor that separates Kessel from Burrow.

I shut the back door behind me, wishing there had been a dog to come with me. The wind was steady now but strengthened as I climbed the orchard walls and set off towards the Rock. My boots squelched through the sodden land.

I guessed that, far below the farm, on the moorland fringes, the ponies and sheep would be huddled against the bleak shelter of granite walls; no animal would have stayed on the higher moorland in such conditions without dangerous consequences. If Benjy were there, high up on the moor, it would only be because he was unable to move. I tried not to think such thoughts but blankly trudged on, my steps automatic. I knew only that I must look for Benjy. In the half-light of that grey morning the sky hung dark and heavy. I imagined the strengthening wind scooping water from the Atlantic, and bringing it from the North West coast, across the land, intent on filling rivers to overflowing so that the moor would eventually be a morass of seething bogland, intercepted by brown, angry streams. I shuddered, tried to believe that the moor was a friendly place again, as I remembered it from my summer childhood days, but pessimism dogged me. Every breath was being grasped from me. I struggled against the buffeting wind, remembering a moment when I was very small with my mother. Someone she had known had died. "Why"? I had asked, and my mother had replied, "Because she forgot to breathe."

It seemed impossible that I might forget to breathe, but quite possible that the Dartmoor gods were trying to stop me breathing now.

By this time I could scarcely stand up in the face of the wind's pressure, and I wondered could I dare to continue? But already I was nearing the top rise. If I could persist a little longer I would be able to look down on the Rock, see the river and valley and hills beyond, maybe find Benjy.

At the summit the wind was driving rain relentlessly before it. I bent down, catching the full force of its weight, falling as I did so. My knee banged against a stone and I cried out in pain, turning myself to face down towards the river. The Rock was scarcely visible in the half-light of this dullest of dark days. With the wind behind me I half ran, limping from the crack on my knee, towards where it stood.

Above the sound of the wind I could hear the roar of water being sucked into the hole in the Rock. Despite sweating from the struggle of moving in the wind and rain I felt iciness within me. After all, this was the monster's dwelling, the place of my childish nightmares, and despite the cynicism I now owned and the pragmatism gained through the sophisticated circumstances of my life, at that moment I was terrified. I did not know really why, only that there was, surrounding the Rock and the sound coming from it, an ominous and frightening feeling that made me want to turn and run home as I had as a child. Instead I searched up and down the riverbank, not wanting to see Benjy. I had to look though, look at every inch, from the clapper bridge, across which Monty may have led the horse and from which he may have slipped, to where the Rock stood where the two now-flooding streams, met to hurtle against the granite monument. But the bridge had vanished from sight — covered by the swollen stream.

I stared across the enraged waters and it was then I saw something — a shape —, which was not a stone. It was dark and huge and it lay amongst the whale-shaped boulders that lie around the Rock, hidden now by the turbulent waters. Raging, the river poured along its banks, swirling around the half-submerged rowan trees. Gasping, not daring to guess what was there, yet knowing it was Benjy lying jammed against the rocks, I plunged into the water and struggled towards him, almost losing my footing on the slippery whale stones, reaching my arms toward him, my feet slipping on the submerged granite rocks. Pushing against a terrible pressure of water I reached him, grabbed his mane, saving myself from being swept away. A waterfall came thundering over us as it hit the Rock, swirling through the opening and bursting out again, crashing down on to us both, Benjy and me. I had my hands twisted in his mane, saw the gashes on his neck where he had been thrown against the jagged granite. I wrapped an arm around his neck — felt my feet against him — tried to stand up. It was impossible, but his head was cradled in my arm, and I struggled to hold it out of the water, as I shouted in his ear, calling his name: "Benjy, Benjy." His eyes were open and rolled with terror then they closed and his tongue hung from his mouth. If I only had the strength to drag his trapped body away downstream, down the few yards to the magic pool, perhaps he would be safe, but he was too much for me and I realised with horror that he was immovable and that I must stay and hold his head out of the water or he would certainly drown.

I don't know how long I somehow managed to hold his head above the water. It seemed like hours and I was aware of feeling I might fall asleep, still clinging to Benjy's neck, when I became conscious of someone beside me. Someone was putting a rope around me. It was Will. He was pulling me away from the horse, his arm around me, while other men swarmed around Benjy and Will dragged me to the bank. I half fainted as someone pulled me from Will's firm grip.

He untied the rope, dragging off my soaked outer clothing. Will must have removed his waterproof coat and taken his thick woollen jersey from his back, for it felt warm as he pushed it over my head, forcing my arms into the huge sleeves as though I were a helpless child. Indeed I was helpless. My body, exhausted and weakened from the exposure to the icy waters, could not move. Will held me up, calling to two of the men. I recognised Jack the postman.

"For God's sake get her back to Kessel," he told them, "as fast as you can. Mum's there, she'll know what to do."

Will's voice faded from me as I allowed Pat and another rescuer to lift me bodily between them and carry me up the hill away from the river. My teeth were chattering uncontrollably. I could hear the urgency of the men's breathing as they struggled with my weight over the rough ground.

Images of Benjy with his mouth open — eyes shut — came and went as I fell in and out of consciousness. I was aware of being put into Will's Land Rover, which was parked on the moor. One of the men wrapped a big blanket around me. It smelled doggy, and I clutched it gratefully, near to tears now.

Jack drove the Land Rover over the lumpy ground, down the road that led to Kessel. Will's mother opened the kitchen door and ushered us inside, her voice full of concern as she questioned the men, who briefly told her what had happened.

"We must go straight back," one of them said. "We'll take the tractor and some ropes," they told her as they helped me to the sofa in the warm kitchen. As they left I heard one whisper to Will's mother, "She tried hard to save him. But t'was too late I'm afraid."

"So you're Cleo, you poor wet creature," Will's mother said quietly. "What a state to be in. Come on dear, let me help you with your clothes."

I allowed her to take Will's jersey over my head and help me out of my dripping jeans. I managed a whispered, "Thank you, Mrs Foden."

"Call me Joan." She smiled, helping me into warm, dry clothes, sitting me on the old sofa near the stove.

Outside, I could hear the tractor being taken back up to the moor where Will and his helpers would pull the poor dead horse from the river and I began to cry.

CHAPTER 24

I woke from a deep, exhausted sleep. Joan was standing near where I lay on the old sofa.

"Are you all right, dear? Feeling better? No, don't move. You must stay at Kessel now until your father and the family return to Burrow."

"Just tonight," I agreed thankfully, relaxing in the comfort of the warm kitchen. "I'm all right really, Joan," I told her. "I'd like to go back to Burrow tomorrow though. There are things to do before they get back." Will's mother was tall and big boned, with a head of thick white hair that curled. Her face was lined and weathered, and her eyes, deep-set, held me in a look not unlike Will's. I felt safe.

"How's Monty?" I asked.

"The doctor's been for him," Joan told me." He's had a strong sedative. I don't like drugs of any kind," she said, "but in this case I had to agree with Dr Strang that Monty would be better if he were given something to help him sleep. He's very shocked."

"You were too foolhardy, my dear," she said gently, as she handed me a steaming mug of milky cocoa. She went to the dresser that lined one wall of the kitchen, taking from one of its shelves a wooden box, brown and polished, the size of a shoebox. She brought it to where I sat, rested it on a small table. I heard the clink and rattle of glass. She lifted the lid. Inside was an array of small bottles with droppers. Carefully she lifted one bottle after another from its small round hole, letting it drop back again, then, "Ah, here it is," she smiled at me. "Rescue Remedy."

"Rescue Remedy?" I was curious.

"Will never puts them back in order, I'm afraid, but anyway this is the stuff for you."

"What is it?" I asked as Joan filled a glass with spring water from the tap and put several drops of the liquid into it.

"Don't worry," she said, with a slight laugh, "it's perfectly harmless. It's a mixture of five different wild flowers, all chosen for their marvellous healing qualities — especially recommended for shock." She put the glass near me. "Just take a sip whenever you think about it," she said, putting the bottle back in the shiny box and replacing it on the dresser shelf. "Its wild flower essences will fortify you — ease the shock to your mind and body," she explained. "It's an old-fashioned remedy, one which we moderns have forgotten all about. It was re-introduced by a wonderful old doctor, years ago now. He worked with nature, you see."

I sipped the drink, leaned back on the old sofa, feeling sleepy, watching Will's mother as she stoked the fire with dry logs.

"Will is very like you," I said. Joan looked up and flashed a smile at me.

"Yes, I know. We are good friends too," she added, "I'm very lucky."

"So is he," I said, wondering if Will and his mother would go on living together until she died. That may not be for years yet, I thought, watching her youthful movements as she collected vegetables from a cupboard and chopped them on a board on the big kitchen table.

As though reading my mind, she told me: "It's been useful for both of us you know, my dear, both on our own. It seemed natural to support each other. But Will is his own man, and doesn't need a mother to look after him — any more than I need him to look after me." She grinned. "When I'm ninety, using a Zimmer frame, he can look after me — until then I've got a lot of living to do. I return to Africa in a month's time. I've completely recovered from the virus, and there's so much work to be done."

I must have slept, for when I woke Will's mother was chopping onions, slicing lean beef into small cubes, adding stock and carrots to the saucepan. The task completed, she sighed and sat near me.

"Feeling better?" she asked.

"I wonder how they're getting on," I murmured.

"Poor old Will," she said. "He's not going to get over Benjy in a hurry.'

"No, I expect not," I agreed quietly. The memory of seeing the horse and feeling his body in those raging waters would be difficult to erase from my mind. How Will would come to terms with the loss of his best horse was a question that neither I nor his mother could answer.

"He should be back soon," she said, more cheerfully. "He will always be indebted to you for your help." She added: "I hope this terrible accident won't spoil the rest of your time at Burrow, my dear. You mustn't let it, Cleo, though I expect the two happenings, Monty's arrival in the middle of the night at Burrow and then the awful business this morning, will be hard to put out of your mind. It's a pity Felix and Nadine are away."

"Oh, I'm glad they are," I said hastily, "especially for little Kate, though she is a very phlegmatic little girl. She would hate to have been here when Benjy was found like he was."

"You mean dead, Cleo — yes, poor, poor Benjy and poor old Will. Poor everyone," she said with a sigh. "I expect he's gone to see Gloria — tell her what's happened — she's sure to be very upset. After all, she's helped Will with the horses for years, ever since . . ." the voice trailed away.

"Ever since his wife died?" I asked.

"Yes, dear. Ever since Maria died."

We were quiet then, and again I think I slept a little. When I opened my eyes Will's mother was taking the stew from the Aga, putting it on the table. There were plates warming on the shelf above the hob. I felt sure I would not be able to eat.

"You must have at least a mouthful," she said, again guessing my thoughts. She went out of the room and I heard movements upstairs.

"Monty's coming," Joan announced when she returned to the kitchen. "He says he's hungry."

I watched, fascinated, as Monty ate a big plateful of stew, seemingly unaffected by his experience. "Caravan now," he said, getting up from the table, putting his arms around Joan. "Thank you, Joan. Monty pack now. Goodbye." He lifted his hand to me, then came and kissed me on the cheek. He smelled clean, of soap.

"All right, Monty — I'll drive you back after tea," Joan told him.

I realised that today was Sunday. Monty would be due back in Plymouth. He seemed calm now, recovered from the dreadful ordeal of the previous day. Joan made a pot of tea and we sat sipping it. I felt very sleepy, but answered Joan when she asked me when I intended going "home", as she put it, "to Canada".

"Not till after Christmas?" she exclaimed when I told her. "And your fiancé, surely he must miss you a lot?"

"Yes, yes, of course we both do," I added hurriedly, wondering if it had been Will who had told her of my engagement to Vince.

"And when are you getting married?" she asked.

"Oh, I'm not sure," I said, then added, "when I get back in the spring, I expect. Yes, that's it, it will be sometime in March." I felt slightly relieved to talk about it — about marriage. It seemed a normal, sensible, wonderfully ordinary thing to do. A simple, small church wedding in Toronto with Vince's family, Lucy and her family, Dad and Nadine. Kate could be a bridesmaid, and maybe brother Peter would fly over from Australia. Yes, it was so comforting to think about the wedding, to think about Vince. It was warming just picturing him, his big frame and clear eyes. His strong arms steering me through life. At that moment in the quiet of the kitchen in Will's farmhouse I longed for Toronto, away from the darkness of the moor on this winter Sunday. The sun's pale light had briefly lit the hills around Kessel, but had vanished again. I remembered how the strong, orange-flaming Canadian sunshine brightened the soft, deep snow in winter, white and cheerful in the parks and gardens of Toronto. It all seemed so far away, so far removed from where I was sitting with sad dark thoughts.

"I often wonder if Will might marry again." I realised with a jolt that Will's mother was speaking. I had not been listening, being so deep into my own thoughts. "You know all about Maria, of course." She was looking at me.

"Yes, I do," I replied. "Well, perhaps not all, only that she died."

Joan pulled a chair up near the stove, drawing a footstool toward her. She gave a sigh as she sat down, put her feet on the stool and spoke again. "She hurt him dreadfully, you know that too, I suppose?"

"No, I didn't know that," I said.

"Oh, I thought you'd know, my dear."

How could I have known? Who was there to tell me? "Of course I knew she'd had an accident, a hunting accident," I said.

"Yes," Joan's voice sounded tired. "But it wasn't that, you know. It was heroin — she was an addict."

"A heroin addict?" I knew I sounded amazed, perplexed. "Married to Will, of all people. I can't really believe it."

"Will is no angel, my dear," his mother was saying. "He's probably dabbled in many things he shouldn't. But one thing is certain, and that is he thought he could help Maria get over the habit."

I was wide-awake now, sitting up, the teacup in my hand untouched.

I wasn't sure I wanted to hear any more, yet I found myself listening intently as Will's mother told me the story of Maria and Will.

"She was wild, but very attractive," she said. "When she fell from her horse, she was badly cut — barbed wire — both legs injured." Joan had taken a clean tea towel from the dresser drawer and started drying the cooking pots she had washed.

"Let me help?" I struggled to my feet, but Joan came to my side and gently pushed me back on to the sofa. "None of that, my girl," she insisted. "You rest, you've done enough helping for one day."

I was glad to lean back against the cushions, for my head swam when I had tried to stand.

"Maria should never have attempted the jump," Joan continued. "It was silly of her but typical. The horse twisted in mid air." She raised an arm in a spiralling motion, demonstrating how the horse had moved. "Then she was flung into the ditch." Joan was silent for a moment, as she bent down and rattled the clean saucepans in the bottom cupboard by the cooker. When she stood up again she told me that Maria's face had been badly cut but had healed well. "But the leg wound simply didn't, and in a few days it had swollen up and was very painful. An infection had set in, you see, Cleo. No matter what the doctors did there was no saving her and she died, of blood poisoning. The doctor told Will that her immune system was not working properly — after all those years involved with drugs." Joan sat down before continuing. "She worked in London in the music world. Spent six months in a clinic to kick the habit, then her parents bought a house down here to help her start a new life, which is when she and Will met. She was a good rider, loved following the hounds. A bit wild though," she added.

Will's mother stood up and opened the top of the hob, lifted the scuttle full of boiler nuts and slid them into the hungry fire. I watched, feeling guilty about lying there doing nothing while she worked.

"Ready for some stew?" she asked.

"Just a little, thank you Joan." I longed to hear the rest of Will and Maria's story but accepted the plate of stew, realising how hungry I was as I mopped the thick gravy with a slice of Joan's warm bread.

"You'll feel a lot better now, dear." She beamed at me.

"They married not long after they met, she and Will, soon after she moved down here, you know," Joan volunteered as though guessing, once again rightly, that I was eager to hear the rest of the tragic story. "I felt a bit shaky at the wedding," she continued. "There was something not quite right, but I couldn't put my finger on it. It was a nice wedding, quite a 'do', with people from all around as well as all her London connections and relations." I detected an edginess in Joan's voice as she continued the tale.

"Maria told me she adored Will — but then she adored a lot of people. Will didn't feel very happy about the way she kept going up to London. He worried, I expect, that she might get back into drugs. She used to tell him she had to go because of her work; freelance, she was. It wasn't till her death that it transpired that the friend she stayed with was a fellow called Ray, another addict, whom she'd met at the drug clinic.

"Poor old Will. I reckon he never really knew what she was up to. He used to look a bit bleak sometimes. He's old-fashioned really, you know Cleo — married out of his class, you might say. He admired her though; was proud of the way she impressed people with her horsemanship. She was very brave — or maybe simply reckless, attempting things many a man would have baulked at cross-country. They used to argue about it. He worried about the horses; she rode them too hard, he told her. She accused him of being over-cautious, taunting him, wanting to see him take his horse over ridiculously high, sometimes impossible jumps. Will would never risk his horses more than was necessary to do a proper job out hunting. But Maria used to worry him a lot, the way she rode and risked the horse as well as herself. I suppose it was destined to end in disaster."

Joan looked at the big kitchen clock, and stood up, removing her blue striped apron.

"I don't usually tell people about Will's business," she told me as she hung the apron on the back of a chair, "but I gather from him that you and your father and family have made a big difference to him since you all came back. For some reason it feels right telling you, Cleo. I hope you don't mind. It's a relief for me to talk about it, to be honest. I don't often get the chance. He's glad there are Endatons there, you know, at Burrow." I smiled at her, not knowing what to say.

The afternoon had grown very dark now. "Come on, my dear," she said, "I'll show you where you can sleep tonight. I'll take Monty back soon. I expect he's fallen asleep in his caravan! I'd better get a move on."

I got to my feet, feeling shaky, glad now not to have to go back to Burrow and be alone.

Joan took me upstairs. The ancient floors creaked beneath our feet. "Here you are, dear." She switched on a light in a small bedroom. "This is the spare room." She busied herself turning back the bedspread. "I've put in a hot water bottle and there are plenty of books to read and a kettle and teapot and all you need in case you wake up thirsty and want a cup of tea. The bathroom is next door, and there are nice warm towels in the airing cupboard if you'd like a bath before you go to sleep."

I thanked her, this kind woman who had made me so welcome, taken me under her wing as well as into her confidence.

"Here's a nightie — a bit big, one of mine, but it's warm, and here's a dressing gown. Your own clothes will be dry by tomorrow. You'll be glad to take off my dull old things," she said, laughing. "Just leave them on the chair, dear." I felt cosseted, loved even. I wanted to put my arms around this woman and cry.

"Thank you," I managed to whisper. "It's a lovely room."

"Used to be Will's," she said, "until his father and I moved to Crediford, then he moved into our bedroom, just down the corridor. This one was his all through his childhood," she added wistfully. "Oh, Cleo, I've just remembered something," she sounded quite excited. "When we painted this room after Maria died, there were old pictures stuck on the

- 134 -

walls — pictures from his childhood — you know, posters and photos of people, horses, famous race horses and all his rosettes from gymkhanas and shows. He did a lot of that in his young days. But what I want to show you, my dear, is this. I'm sure it was taken at Burrow."

Joan had opened a cupboard and pulled a suitcase out into the middle of the floor. She opened it and revealed a pile of papers, old toys, Dinky cars and such like.

"Ah, here it is," she said. "I knew it would be here." She pushed the suitcase back in the cupboard and sat down next to me on the bed with a big scrapbook on her knee. She turned the pages. There were newspaper cuttings and pictures of horses, hounds, show jumps, sheep, pictures of 'the boy' as I remembered him, at Crediford Show holding a silver cup for the best Dartmoor ewe, the best young sheepdog handler, the best working hunter pony and rider. I was looking at the boy, the boy I had known and longed to emulate, the boy shaking hands with the judge, cap in hand, receiving the cup. As I stared into the pictures, remembering the past, Joan was shuffling the paraphernalia in the suitcase.

"Ah!" she exclaimed triumphantly, "I've got it." She took from the case a framed picture, dusting it on her denim-skirted thighs. She handed it to me. "A bit dusty, but I'm sure you'll recognise yourself."

I gazed into the picture. It was me all right, holding Brownie by her head collar, one hand on her neck, under her thick mane. Beside me stood Felix, and on the other side of Brownie was Great Uncle Ted. Next to Dad was Peter, who held Mother's hand. She looked as I remembered her, wan, ethereal, hardly there.

As I stared at the picture Joan was saying, "It was Will's prize possession, that photo. He had it hanging on the wall, next to his rosettes. I took it down when I decorated the room, after my husband died and Will was on his own again."

I looked up at her. "I don't remember this picture being taken," I said. "Dad had a camera, but I don't remember Will taking pictures then of my family."

"No, it's one he found at Burrow after your uncle died. He brought it back and put it on the wall there near his bed. He was very sad when Ted died and he lost touch with all of you. No one seemed to know what had happened to the family. We heard you'd all moved abroad."

"No, just Dad," I said quietly. "We stayed on at the flat."

Before Joan left the room, I told her I could not remember coming to Kessel as a child, nor could I remember Will's father or Joan coming to Burrow.

"No, dear," she said, with a sad note in her voice. "It was not possible, you see. Your mother was too ill, did not want people to go there — or for you to come here, for that matter — whilst she was so ill, poor woman. She needed peace and quiet."

"Yes, of course. I remember how she didn't want to do anything, except church, that is. We were Catholics, you know; at least she was," I added. Joan gave me a quiet hug and left to drive Monty back to Plymouth.

It seemed hours later that I woke hearing Joan's car return, and wondered if Will had come back too, or if dealing with Benjy had been a longer than expected business. Perhaps he was with Gloria. They would both be upset. Shared grief is easier than grieving alone. Tears wet my cheeks as I lay in the boy's room. Strange to think that this was where he had lain asleep at night all those years ago, when I had been at Burrow wishing I was him, wishing I could be that free, that happy.

CHAPTER 25

I was wakened by a gentle knock, and my door eased open.

"It's only me, Cleo," Will whispered. "Sorry to wake you up." He carried a candle. "Another power cut, the lines must be down," he explained, placing it on the table beside my bed. "I've got some news for you." He sounded excited.

Will sat on the bed.

"What's happened?" I asked, struggling to sit up. But Will pushed me gently back against the pillows.

"No, Cleo, there's no need to move. I'm sorry to wake you, but I knew you'd want to know about Benjy."

I wasn't sure I wanted to hear details about Benjy. It was all too painful. In the glow of candlelight I could make out Will's silhouette, the outline of his strong frame, but I could not see the expression on his face, and it was moments before his next words sank in. Even then I could not make sense of what he was saying.

"What did you say, Will?" I asked, not daring to believe what I thought I had heard him say about Benjy: that he was alive, not dead after all.

"It's true, Cleo. He's not dead. Benjy is alive."

I was speechless at first, and then begged Will to tell me every detail of what had happened. I clutched his arm and he took my hand and held it as he described how the horse, although he had so nearly drowned, was in fact recovering.

"The way you held him out of the water made all the difference. You saved his life, in fact."

"No, Benjy is a strong horse," I insisted. "Where is he now?"

"He's down at the hunt kennels, in the stable. It was the closest place to take him. We've been with him all night — Gloria, the vet and me. Benjy's strong all right but he would have been on the point of giving up when you got there, Cleo. Holding his head out of the water like you did saved his life."

"Is he really going to be okay, Will?"

"I think so, Cleo, though he'll be very shaky for a while. There will be scars too on his neck. They look awful, quite deep. He's been badly bashed about in the river. Cuts and bruises everywhere, but he's alive and could make a complete recovery."

"Thank God, Will." I felt a warm glow of relief. Not only was Monty all right, but Benjy, too. "Thank God," I said again.

"Thank you, Cleo," Will said. He was standing up now, leaning over the bed, bending his head to mine, breathing a whispered 'thank you' against my face. I felt the rasp of his unshaved chin as his warm lips brushed against my forehead. It was a lingering touch, causing me to draw in a sudden breath, which became one of surprise, for at that instant the light from the landing burst through the half-open door.

"Power's back on," Will said as he stood up, and we both laughed. "See you tomorrow, Cleo." He was leaving the room. "We'll go and see Benjy, if you're up to it."

Everything had suddenly changed. My heart was singing 'Benjy is alive'. The words repeated themselves in my head. Both Monty and Benjy were all right, really all right. There was something else too: the sensation of feeling Will close to me, our heads touching — his warmth — his smell. There could be no denying that at that moment, the moment Will's lips had touched my forehead, a tenderness beyond anything I had ever experienced had filled my whole being. A tenderness for Will — the boy, now the man: this hunter man who stood for so much that I despised, and who had evoked feelings in me that had become impossible to deny.

Turning in my bed, unable to sleep, I thought about how I must keep faith with who I was: my strong beliefs and my love for Vince in the face of this developing passion I felt for Will – a passion that I now had to admit had been with me since I was seven years old.

CHAPTER 26

I had taken Kate to school. Life seemed normal again. The half-term holiday was over and Kate was excited about making Christmas decorations and being an angel in the school play.

Benjy, back at Kessel, was recovering fast. When I called there on my way home from dropping Kate off, it was a joy to see him peering over his door, whinnying in his usual way.

I saw little of Will, who was busy with the hunting season starting, but Joan was always pleased to welcome me at Kessel, asking me to stay for coffee, chatting to me about her forthcoming trip back to Africa. How I admired this woman, her zest for life, her humour, and her friendliness.

"Benjy won't be fit enough to hunt this season," she told me one morning. We were standing by his stable door. He licked my hand.

"He looks magnificent," I said. Lifting his mane I saw the scars from the accident and shuddered. "They're healing so well," I said to Joan, "but I can't help remembering what they looked like that night. I really thought he might have bled to death, let alone drowned."

"Hypericum oil," Joan said. "That's the best healer; the vet gave him plenty of antibiotics too, but I am a great believer in hypericum. I still rub his neck with it and wipe him down with lavender oil, too. It calms his mind."

I put my face against the horse's neck. He smelled of sweet hay as well as the lavender that Joan had smoothed him down with. The sensation of leaning against the horse brought memories of Brownie and the sheer delight I had known, through loving her when I was still a child.

In the next stable, keeping Benjy company, was Skylark, Brownie's granddaughter. I stroked her face.

"Will intended to start riding her this autumn," Joan remarked, "but with Benjy's accident and the bad weather, also because she's a useful nursemaid for Benjy, I expect he'll leave all that till next year. Perhaps you could come back and ride her then, after your marriage — come back for a summer holiday? It would be nice to think you would come back."

For a moment I said nothing. Skylark nibbled my hand. My head was full; almost hurting with longing to speak to Joan about Will, though maybe she would be upset or disapproving. No, I could not possibly confide in Will's mother, it would be unfair. Anyway perhaps I was being totally stupid. After all Will had not made any effort to see me or renew the closeness I thought we had established when Benjy had nearly died.

"Yes, Joan," I heard myself say cheerfully. "That would be great. I am sure Vince would love to come for a holiday at Burrow as much as I would." We walked back towards the kitchen.

"I've got lots to do before Will gets back," Joan told me.

"Where is he?" I asked, as casually as I knew how. "Winter ploughing perhaps or feeding bullocks, I suppose."

"Oh, no." There was surprise in Joan's reply. "No, dear, didn't you know? He and Gloria went up to Leicester to look at a horse yesterday. He phoned last night, told me he'd bought it, a replacement for Benjy for the hunting season. They're bringing him back today — should be here by about teatime. You must come over and see the new animal. He'll have to settle in rather quickly — cub hunting's finished — it's the opening meet on Saturday."

Although the temperature was low and the air damp and cold, I felt suddenly hot — was glad to break away from Kessel.

"See you on Saturday," Joan called. "You will come to the opening meet, won't you, dear?"

"Maybe," I lied, and waved before setting off for Burrow. I knew of course, at least I thought I knew, that nothing was going to induce me to be at the opening meet in Crediford. I was wrong.

It was Kate who persuaded me to go with her and Felix and Nadine. I said I'd go only because she wanted me to, though I knew that really I needed to see Will on his new horse, wearing his scarlet jacket. I wanted to see him, hoping that seeing him surrounded by hounds and other hunters I should be able to forget those feelings of alternate tenderness and jealousy that had been overwhelming my thoughts lately. Free myself from this obsession, for that is what it had become, I told myself impatiently. I should return to normality, the proper route of my life, with Vince — Canada — home — be in control of my feelings once more. No more fantasies about Will. I needed to put all that behind me.

My thoughts were interrupted. Kate was pulling me away from the pavement where we were watching the riders as they rode into the village square, towards the hounds. She loved them licking her as she stroked and hugged them. Reluctantly I allowed her to pull me into the thick of the hounds.

"See, Cleo, look, look at this one. He's got a brown patch on his back."

"That one's called Biscuit." Will had moved his horse through the pack close to us. He beamed down at Kate, from the horse's back. Then, "Morning, Cleo." He raised his cap and I nodded in reply. He leaned forward in the saddle, took a glass from the tray that Gloria was handing around to all the hunting people.

"Hi, Cleo," Gloria called. "Isn't he gorgeous! So good-natured." For a moment I was speechless, then realised she was speaking about the new horse.

"Jumps like a stag," she continued. "He's settled in well too, hasn't he, Will?"

Will drained his glass and handed it back to Gloria. Catching my eye he said, "What do you think of him, Cleo?"

"He's beautiful," I said. Gloria touched my arm and handed me the tray of empty glasses. "Be an angel and take this back to the bar, would you, Cleo? I have to go and fetch Bonny; she's out the back going frantic." She jerked her head towards the pub. Onlookers were thronging around the entrance, several deep along the pavement. "Bob's rushed off his feet. Two of the helpers didn't turn up this morning," she added.

Gloria was dressed for hunting. "Thanks," she said, disappearing in the crowd to the back of the building from where the loud frantic whinnying of her horse could be heard.

"Good of you to come," Will said quietly, looking at me.

"Kate wanted me to," I told him. I had spoken sharply and was glad to turn and walk away as he blew the horn for the hounds to move off. With Kate following me I handed the tray of glasses to the barman at the door of the pub. We watched as the field of hunters on their prancing horses rode past us following Will and the whipper-in past the church and shop and out of sight up the hill towards the moors. Kate and I walked back the other way down the hill, passing a few stragglers, the last of the hunt followers on their excited horses. Some, who I recognised, lifted their whips, smiling a 'good morning'. I gave a faint smile in return. The horses blew steam from their nostrils. The sight of them and the clattering of their hooves on the tarmac road filled me with an unfamiliar sense of elation. This was dampened quickly as, horses now gone, we made our way to Dad and Nadine, already waiting by the car, passing a group of onlookers. Unlike most of the people who had come to watch the hunt move off, all smiling and talking, this group, dressed in baggy combat trousers, held placards telling the world not to kill anything and wore sad, grim expressions on their faces. I wanted them to know that I was like them and didn't like killing anything either. I smiled broadly at them, saying, "Hello there" but they must have seen me with Will, or watched Kate with the hounds — for they returned my friendliness with dark, glowering looks.

CHAPTER 27

It was Sunday. Will and his mother were coming to lunch. I dreaded the occasion. Dad was bringing in the wood to light the sitting room fire; its flames would bring a lightness to the room on this grey day.

In the kitchen with Nadine and Kate, I scrubbed vegetables. Kate helped for a while. She was restless and buzzed around the kitchen, her energy so strong and lively that Nadine spoke severely to her in French, which quietened her. There was a look of relief on Nadine's face when, vegetables finished, I suggested taking Kate for a walk. Excited, Kate pulled on her wellies and I wrapped her coat around her, doing up the buttons. It was cold and damp, though for once it wasn't raining.

I could hear Nadine humming in the kitchen as we left. Dad was chopping wood, so she would have the place to herself. She loved to be alone there, orchestrating the sequence of preparations for her gourmet creations. I had often seen her at work, admired her swift way, which nevertheless gave the impression that time was unimportant. Today, she would enjoy preparing the leg of lamb for our lunch: a lamb that had grown fat on the sparse hills around Burrow, one from Will's own flock. A bright Persil-white creature which, in summer, would have skipped beside its mother, jumping the heathery tussocks, keeping its little body tight against her side until, tired, it curled up in the lee of a rock — Nadine would put crushed garlic into little slits in the skin, taking down from the kitchen beam sprigs of dried rosemary, which still smelled of summer. This she would chop and mix with olive oil and sea salt, rubbing it all over the meat. She would place the joint in the big earthenware roaster on the bed of vegetables I had prepared. This was 'Devon dinner', Uncle Ted and Dad's favourite. Nadine added to this Dartmoor dish a flavour of Provence.

"Let's go somewhere completely different," Kate was saying. I agreed. As we set off I told her I would show her one of my childhood hiding places.

Just above the boundary walls of Uncle Ted's land there is a gully, an old peat track that is strewn with boulders and smaller stones, mostly hidden in summer by bracken. In the centre of this stands a thick, stunted oak tree, in amongst some rowans. Its seed must have taken root generations ago and, slightly sheltered by its position on the lower ground of the track, had thrived despite exposure to the wind.

It is tricky terrain. We struggled and clambered over the walls and fallen-down stones until we reached the shelter of the oak tree. At its foot is a natural seat where its roots mingle with the granite boulders. Laughing and puffing from our exertions, we took refuge beneath its bare branches. Down to our left, way below, we could see the river.

"It's like a house," Kate exclaimed. "We could have a tea party here." I laughed, sharing her enthusiasm and pleasure at discovering the comfort of the oak tree's roots.

"Is this were you hid when you were a little girl?" she asked.

"Yes, Kate, I did. In fact it was a very favourite place for me because it was hidden away, secret and no one else seemed to come here. But, Kate, once upon a time thousands and thousands of years ago people lived here in stone huts arranged in circles. We are sitting in the remains of one now and maybe the people who lived here were our ancestors even as far back as thousands of years BC — Beaker people or Bronze age people — long long before our great great grandfathers anyway. There are remains of hut circles and stone rows, leading to burial places in lots of places on the moor.

Kate sat close to me. We held hands and I closed my eyes, leaning my head against the tree's trunk. There was a feeling of safety, an atmosphere that reminded me of being with Uncle Ted.

"What's over there, Cleo?" I opened my eyes and looked to where Kate pointed towards a pile of stones in the distance.

"Just more rocks, I guess," I told her. Kate must have thought differently, for in her darting fashion she had already let go of my hand and was clambering over to the stones and boulders that had somehow intrigued her.

"Steady Kate, be careful," I called as she scrambled over the tumbled-down wall, dislodging a stone, which fell as she climbed. Kate had sprung deftly clear. "Ouch," she said. "My finger got a bit caught."

"Don't be in such a rush, Kate," I scolded, taking her hand and rubbing it.

"It's not hurting now, Cleo. Please let's go down there, follow that track." She pointed down to where the peat track seemed to give way to what once might have been a clearing. Taking Kate's hand in mine, we made our way towards it. I felt a strange familiarity, though I knew I had never stood at this spot before, yet it was as if I knew my way. We were standing in some sort of enclosure, and there were the remnants of an old granite animal shelter or perhaps a dwelling of some sort, for there was a row of stones in a rectangle, some half hidden in the mossy close-cropped grass. I bent down to touch one of the stones. "Help me to move it, Kate," I said. Together we forced it from its bed, seeing that underneath there was another stone, one that had been hewn into a shape. I knelt down and scraped away the peaty earth and lichen from its side, feeling certain that this was not just any old stone. At some time it had served a purpose.

Kate helped me. We swept it clean with our hands.

"Look," she cried. "Feel it, Cleo. It's got bumps in it." It was true. I scraped away the last bits of peat and crushed rock, the rough sandy substance, and followed the indents with my finger.

"I think this is an initial," I said, my finger following the natural curve of a C. "I think it's a C. Yes, that's it! It is a C! And here's another one. I can feel it. This one is an F — no it's an E. It says CE, Kate, isn't that extraordinary!"

Kate beamed at me. "It must be yours, Cleo it's got your name on it. It's yours because it's C for Cleo and E for Endaton."

***

The aroma of roasting lamb mingled with wood smoke greeted us when we reached Burrow again, making Kate screech happily "I'm starving," as she bounced through the back door into Will's arms. He lifted her high. My heart lurched as I busied myself with taking off my boots and scarf and all the paraphernalia of outer clothing that one needs to cover oneself on a winter's day on Dartmoor.

"You've got a hurt eye," Kate exclaimed.

Will put her down and faced me.

"Hi, Cleo." He smiled. Leaning forward he brushed my face on each side with a friendly kiss. My polite response was cut short as I noticed the cut above his eye.

"What on earth happened to you, Will?" I gasped, unable to hide my concern, for his eye was badly swollen. I saw there were several stitches around his eyebrow, and from what I could see of his half-closed eye it was bloodshot. "Heavens, you look as though you've been in the boxing ring. Was it the new horse?"

"No," Will said casually, "just a bit of a fight." He followed me into the sitting room where my father was pouring sherry for Will's mother. It was she who provided the details of Will's injury.

"Those darned 'antis'," she was saying to my father, "they beat him up." Will was silent. I was curious to know more, but sensing his dismay and feeling shocked at the sight of his eye, I deftly turned the subject around with Kate's help, telling them of our adventures and archaeological find. Dad told us that he remembered Uncle Ted telling him that it was the old dwelling place used before Burrow was built four hundred years ago. "C E was probably the initials of a stonecutter — there were lots of Charlie Endatons. My second name is Charles," he added. "The stone you found may have been a discarded one — maybe going to be used here at the house or as a gatepost, all those years ago." It felt strange thinking far into the past about an ancestor who shared my initials.

"We Endatons have inhabited this patch forever," he joked. "This is where we started, and I suppose this is where it will end when I go."

"I don't see why," I remonstrated. "What about Peter? He's an Endaton. Besides, both Kate and I carry the Endaton blood. It doesn't need to end with you, Dad."

"You're right, of course", he said. "But I can't see Peter coming back here."

"That's where you're wrong," I interrupted. "As a matter of fact I had a letter yesterday and he said he was coming to England for some business meetings in London." Then, seeing Felix's expression, I added hurriedly, "He didn't want to get your hopes up Dad, you see he's only in the country for a few days and may not get the chance to get down here."

"I'm an Endaton," said Kate, hugging her father. He held her to him and not for the first time I thanked fate for giving us my little sister. Kate the comforter, I named her then in my mind.

At lunch Joan mentioned Will's blow to the eye again. "I hope it will have healed in time for Suzanne's wedding or you'll spoil the photos," she joked.

After lunch everyone wanted to go for a walk. "Before it gets too dark," Dad said. I was surprised that Will said he would come too.

"What about the horses?" I asked as we strolled behind the others. Nadine and Joan were in deep conversation. Kate and Dad were ahead of us all, Kate holding his hand, wanting to be the first to show him the oak tree and the stone.

"Oh, Gloria's seeing to the horses tonight," Will told me. "She's staying at Kessel for a couple of nights." My heart sank. "She's bringing Bonny," he continued, "just till she moves into the cottage she's rented. The builders haven't finished the repairs yet. Getting rid of rats, too. It hasn't been lived in for a long time and is in a bit of a mess."

"I thought she lived with her parents."

"Yes, she did, but they've sold up, gone back to town. Couldn't stand the climate," he laughed.

For a while we walked in silence. My heart was missing beats as I tried to control my emotions. There was no denying I was feeling jealous.

Will began to tell me how he had damaged his eye. "It was my fault, really," he admitted, "I lost my rag."

"Why?" I asked

"One of the anti-hunt campaigners chucked something into a hound's face, temporarily blinding him. I was furious, jumped off the horse to help the hound and swiped the guy with my whip, intentionally, I'm afraid. Then it all started. He hit me and I hit him."

"Will, that's terrible," I said, shocked. "Is the hound all right?"

"Yes," he only threw a handful of earth. I was afraid it was something much worse, something permanently damaging. It's happened to several hounds at some hunts. Sometimes they throw acid." Seeing my expression of horror Will added, "I'm not proud of my actions, Cleo. I shouldn't have lost my temper so quickly."

He looked surprised when I told him I didn't blame him. "You must have been upset about the poor hound."

We were walking slowly, the rest of the party already out of sight beyond the wall. Will touched my arm. "Thanks, Cleo," he said. We had reached the wall, facing each other for a moment, and I longed to put my hand out to touch his face — longed to tell him how shocked I felt about his wounded eye. Instead, speaking sharply I said, "I don't like hunting. I don't approve of what you do."

"I know," Will answered seriously as he climbed onto the wall, reaching across to help me over.

Everyone was standing around the pile of stones, looking at the one with my initials carved on it. Dad remembered when he was a small boy that Uncle Ted had used this place as a makeshift shelter, when the sheep were lambing.

"He put heather over the roof and slept inside. It was just a tiny hut, a real shelter though. Do you remember it, Will?"

"Just vaguely," Will replied. "I haven't been here for years, haven't given it a thought, but it wouldn't take much to rebuild. It could be your own summer house, Cleo," he joked. "The stone with your initials on could be the lintel above the door. Cleo's very own Dartmoor hideaway."

Kate clapped her hands with pleasure at the thought. "Oh, Cleo, your very own little house!" Turning to Will she asked, "Are you going to mend it, Will? Please, Will, please, please mend it for Cleo!" Will hauled her onto his shoulders, laughing.

"We'll see, we'll see," he said as he carried her fast away down the hill towards the river.

By the time the rest of us had caught up with them he was standing on a big boulder between the magic pool and the Rock, with Kate still sitting on his broad shoulders. She clutched his head. Will's playfulness was catching. His dogs were barking, and Dad threw sticks into the waters of the pool for them. Putting Kate down, Will came and stood beside me.

"First time?" he asked.

"Yes," I whispered. "First time since Benjy." He put an arm around me. I felt his warm, understanding strength flowing into me as I stood silently looking at the great Rock and the magic pool, and the place where Benjy had nearly died.

"I still haven't climbed through, you know," I said, quietly.

The others had turned away from the river, were already making their way up the steep slope, and heading for Burrow. The light was fading now, the grey afternoon turning a darker shade by the moment.

"Does it matter?" Will asked. "Do you have to climb the Rock? It's not all that easy Cleo, and all those stories are just superstitions that maybe would be best forgotten now."

Even though I thought he might be right — surely must be right — there was still something telling me it had to be done. For moments we stood together, the rest of the party now almost out of sight.

"It isn't just 'the magic'," I told him, "when I was a little girl I thought the Rock was a monster, or at least a place where monsters lived. Then Uncle Ted told me that all our ancestors lived there. I expect some of them were monsters, who knows," I added wryly. I half expected Will to laugh at me when I told him that now I felt that the Rock itself was like a real person — that I had read how the Aboriginal people saw and felt their ancestry in nature, just as Uncle Ted had felt them here as part of the landscape. Passing through that mouth-eye in the Rock was something I must do in order to be part of the circle and really belong; then perhaps I would feel free and become part of the tribe.

I was aware that Will's arm was still around my shoulders as we stood silently for several moments. I waited for his teasing voice but instead he broke the silence slowly and deliberately:

"— 'That is not a rock. That is my Grandfather. This is a place where the dreaming comes up. Right up from under the ground' —."

When he had finished I could not speak. The moment was to be indelibly written somewhere deep within me.

"My father used to recite that to me when I was a kid, and we stopped here on our horses. He told me it was an Aboriginal poem, but he couldn't remember any more."

When we turned away from the Rock and walked through the gloaming of that winter's day, I thought I heard Uncle Ted's rich, encouraging voice and his wheezy chuckle, which faded as we topped the hill. I turned to peer back at the Rock and imagined I could see a pale shape vanishing into the darkness that now surrounded it.

Neither of us spoke, but arriving back at Burrow, with its brightly lit windows, Will leaned down and kissed me briefly on the lips as though to support my belief. That was all — the kiss told me only that he understood my feelings about the Rock, nothing more.

The kettle whistled a welcome as we crossed the threshold and I, feeling relieved, and therefore more confident in the newfound support from Will, found myself with a longing for more, coupled with the knowledge that Will and I could never be more than friends. I respected his reticence, was glad of it, because of Vince. Yet that night I found it hard to write to Vince. How could I explain when there was nothing to explain? Nothing had happened between Will and me, because Will was beyond me – obviously involved with Gloria, or was it because he respected my engagement to Vince? I turned over in my bed, unable to sleep, wondering what would happen if I set myself at Will. Could I persuade him to love me? I felt wicked, yet with my passion for him increasing I dared myself to be like other women, prepared to risk anything just to be loved. I shocked myself with my thoughts, wondering if in reality I could go that far with someone I disapproved of, while at the same time honouring my commitment to Vince.

CHAPTER 28

Peter surprised us all with a phone call from London! The household had been in turmoil, since the news of his impending arrival. I could scarcely believe I would be seeing my brother again, at Burrow, after so many years. What would he be like I wondered? And how would I feel at the sight of this grown man, who was so much part of my childhood memories? How would he be feeling about coming back to the old family place? Had he, like me, decided on an attempt at letting go of the past? As I thought about the reality of Peter being at Burrow again I saw in my mind not the confident young Australian I'd seen in Vancouver, but the pale thin little brother of long ago, frightened and clutching a teddy bear. Would he, in these surroundings, look like Mother?

At the thought of them — Mother and Peter — my whole body became strangely weak, my head reeled and my emotions surfaced like a drowned corpse coming up from the sea. I felt helpless, exposed, hollow, eaten-away. My thoughts racing from one idea to another about Peter, about the past, about what it felt like to be at Burrow again putting myself through this painful reminder — of what? Perhaps, like Mother, I was losing my grip. I had never wanted to be like her, go down that narrow, leafless, lifeless track. Feeling suddenly hot all over, not a pleasant heat from a warm sun but as in a furnace — it was roaring around me and I could feel it's fury inside — outside — and I found myself wishing angrily that Peter was not coming to Burrow. Somehow it was unseemly, out of context for him to be here. A reminder of all we had suffered and a reminder of all I felt I had lost. I hated thinking that way, hated being in such a frame of mind about Peter, or Mother. What is it about my brother's impending arrival that had thrown everyone into a fever, including me? I was ashamed that mine was so different from Kate's or Dad and Nadine's excitement. Kate was promised a day off from school and Dad was already chopping logs and filling the baskets while Nadine sat at the kitchen table writing a list.

"We shall need some extra shopping," she announced gleefully, and I, despite being appalled at my inner strictures, my despising of all the ridiculous circus in honour of my brother, felt my anger forsake me, leaving me. Instead feeling bereft, suddenly I could not tell what was happening, only that there was a tightness around my heart, my head. It was all very well for Dad and Nadine; they had seen Peter several times when he had to attend business meetings in Paris. Kate couldn't remember him well but her usual irrepressible self demonstrated her longing to meet her Uncle Peter by running from one parent to another shouting and clapping her hands. I became a statue in all this, standing rigid, rooted to the ground. Then suddenly a feeling that I would faint overcame me and perspiration gathered on my brow. I put out a hand to steady myself and heard Nadine's sharp voice telling Kate to go immediately and help her father. Then, the shopping list forgotten, she was at my side, her arms surrounding me, helping me to the armchair by the stove where the blue enamel kettle gently hissed. She wiped the sweat from my face with her hand. It felt cool and gentle and she kissed me, as though I were her little sister, with soothing words tumbling in whispers all around, falling like soft petals all over my face.

" Poor child, poor Cleo. How thoughtless of us all to be so excited about your brother; it must be so hard for you. Brings back the past eh?" She drew me close and with my head against her round warm breasts I felt the tears come pouring from a place deep down inside me, a place I could not recall as familiar, for I had never been there before or if I had it had been so long ago that the memory was covered up or buried — sealed off. But I knew that I was in the mother place and like a mother who has found her lost child or a child who has found her lost mother I sobbed my relief.

Nadine held me until at last the tears were spent and I was quiet. She admonished my apologies with a warmth that showed me why my father was so in love with her.

"You are in shock, ma petite, I can see how being here and now the thought of your brother coming, after so long, has thrown you a little."

She eased herself from the armchair telling me to stay quiet while she made us both a hot drink.

I found myself, dream-like, relaxing, as I watched Nadine reaching for the blue and white mugs. She poured hot milk into them and I was comforted by the way of her — the movement of her arm — the blueness of her shirt and sprightly collar — upright like Nadine herself. Upright yet round, she encircled her world and all that it contained. She smiled at me as the hot milk streamed into the mugs and rich dark chocolate powder was sprinkled and stirred into the creamy liquid. It was as though I was seeing Nadine and the new Burrow kitchen for the first time and was enchanted by what I saw.

The house was quiet and still. Kate and Dad were already upstairs. He would be reading her a bedtime story.

"Thank you Nadine," I whispered.

She nodded agreeably and I marvelled at her knack of being who she was, to everyone around her: Kate's mother, Dad's wife and her own mother's considerate daughter. What could she be to me now? My stepmother? I smiled to myself at the thought of this young vibrant woman being my stepmother but knew that in this woman I had found a friend who embraced all the qualities of motherly and sisterly affection.

I sipped my drink then climbed the stairs and lay in my bed where I slept in a way I could not remember.

***

Next day, refreshed, I waved Kate and Felix off on the drive to Exeter airport to meet Peter's plane. Nadine and I prepared a special meal for the reunion and when we heard Dad's car in the yard and the repeated sound of the horn, we both dashed out to meet them.

Peter was different, changed even since last seeing him in Vancouver, with his bronzed skin and hair, almost white blonde now from exposure to the Australian sunlight. He looked very handsome; Dad looked almost small next to him. Peter filled the room somehow and I wondered how that little boy from the past could have gained such a presence.

But he was still the same Peter Endaton beneath that different exterior; interested in everything, which pleased Kate, who could not stop telling him things. He was patient with her, listening intensely to all she had to tell him. She led him outside, showed him all the places she could not realise he used to know like the back of his hand, when he was her age.

When everyone else had gone to bed Peter and I stayed up in the kitchen. I told him what had happened the night before when I believed I had been on the point of breaking down, and how Nadine had been so kind.

"It was because you were coming Peter, it seemed to be opening up all sorts of things for me," I told him.

Peter leaned forward in his chair and took my hand in his. "We always were a bit odd as a family, weren't we, Cleo? You were like a Mum for me and I never stopped to think who could mother you. You seemed so, so ... "

"Go on, brother, how was I? How did you think I was?" I wanted to know something about myself. For the first time I was uncovering the mystery of myself, putting the pieces of jigsaw together — at least that was what I hoped would happen.

Without hesitation he told me: "You were self-contained, Sis. I never thought you needed anything or anyone except yourself — even Dad used to describe you as being —" Peter hesitated for a moment looked at me squarely then continued, "Dad said you were an island — unreachable and quite able to take care of yourself."

For a long time my brother and I sat in silence, then in a quiet voice I told him how I always remembered him as being the one who was most like Mother. "You were her favourite, in fact."

"You're right about me being her favourite." He grinned almost sheepishly. "But I wasn't in the least like her and I knew it — but then I never really felt that I was like Dad either."

"Perhaps that's the mistake we all make. I mean thinking we have to be like one or other parent, when in fact we are completely unique apart from a few genetic resemblances and tendencies. We are simply us ... uniquely ourselves."

It was good to share thoughts with this brother of mine and we talked far into the night remembering the past, Uncle Ted, Monty and the postman.

"Remember that boy on his white pony?" Peter asked. "I remember how he annoyed me — with his showy pony riding." He laughed, "I reckon I was pretty jealous of him and his relationship with Uncle Ted and you, Cleo, I wonder if he is still around — can't remember where he lived now but he was always thundering around the moors on that bright white horse!"

I moved hastily to put the kettle on and to hide my face. I wasn't going to let on about Will or my confusion surrounding him. Instead I told him about Vince and how he would be here for Christmas and then we talked about the Rock and its influence on us both.

"I remember being terrified of it," he agreed. "But you always seemed so grown up, Cleo, so unafraid. That's what I thought, Sis, at the time." He grinned at me.

"It wasn't like that Peter," I protested, "to be honest with you I'm still scared by it. I haven't climbed through even now."

It was good talking to my brother; it brought us closer together. It was late when we finally went to bed and I didn't wake up till late the next morning. The family were having breakfast when I went downstairs but there was no sign of Peter.

"He'll be sleeping in," I yawned. "We were talking nearly all night."

But Peter was not sleeping. He had got up early, despite the heavy drizzle of Dartmoor rain, and appeared at the kitchen door dripping wet.

"I've been to the Rock," he announced, stripping off his waterproofs and delving into the full Sunday morning breakfast that Nadine had prepared. "Bacon, eggs, and croissant!" he exclaimed. "I'd forgotten how hungry Dartmoor air makes a body." He ruffled Kate's hair and she kept him occupied with her delighted chatter.

Later, when we were alone, he said, "Hey, Sis, it's no big deal getting through that Rock of yours, I did it this mornin' — no problem — does that mean I won't get rheumatism?" he teased.

"I suppose so Peter, but seriously, how was it? Did you really climb through?"

"Yep. It's a bit of a pull up from the base, once you've splashed your way out there, that is," he said. "But once up on that lip it's easy enough to slide down to a kind of ledge — mind you, I got pretty wet!"

"Then what did you do? Did you climb through the hole — and out through the slit on the far side? Wasn't the river too deep and fast?"

"Well, yes, the river was raging and it was very fast. It seems to suck in and out through that slit like a whirlpool — makes one heck of a noise, enough to frighten anyone. Sounds like a drowning banshee," he laughed. "I can see it could be scary, but it's fine if you go with it, let the water take you through. It's the way you go that matters — you have to go with the flow. Anyway, I made it!" he said, grinning. "Does that mean I'll have good luck, Cleo? Dream of my true love?"

I knew he was joking, couldn't take it seriously, and I told him he would find a true love easily enough, for it was obvious to me that Peter had become one of those lucky people who would have a string of true loves of one sort or another. Clearly our roles had altered: he had become a free spirit, unafraid of life, so unlike the little boy I remembered protecting when we were children. But I couldn't deny he was fun to be with and part of me wished I could be that light-hearted. When he had gone I felt that a breath of fresh air had blown through the house.

He hugged me goodbye. "I'm there if you need me, Cleo," he said, looking for once deadly serious. "You can trust me if you need to."

And I knew he was telling the truth and was glad I had a brother like Peter. I envied him too his light-heartedness, so totally different from me. I wondered if, one day, I might be in need of his brotherly support. It was good to know it was there even if he did live thousands of miles away.

CHAPTER 29

"Wear something warm," Will advised. "It's like Everest where they live."

He had asked me to go with him to his Cousin Suzanne's wedding on Exmoor. Surprising myself, I had agreed. Why not? I asked myself. After all, since Benjy's near-tragedy and our walk to the Rock we were closer, friendlier now.

"Is Gloria going to the wedding?" I asked Will.

"No, she's going to be away," he told me nonchalantly.

I searched through my wardrobe. The blue pure silk dress that hung loosely over matching trousers would be smart and comfortable as well as warm. Pulling it over my head, examining myself in the long looking glass in my bedroom, I recalled that the last time I had worn the outfit was at Vince's parents' golden wedding. They had celebrated with a small party of family and close friends in their Ottawa home. Remembering the occasion — was it only eight months ago — I thought about Vince, how he had held me at arm's length when he collected me for the flight to Ottawa.

"You look fantastic," he had said. "I'm so proud of you," and put his arm out for me to hold as he escorted me to his Mercedes waiting outside the front door of my apartment block.

Remembering now in my bedroom at Burrow, I was once again homesick for Vince; the feeling swooped over me. I was homesick for the comfort of his strong arms; the way he looked at me through his horn-rimmed spectacles. I missed everything about him, his wealth, his cleanness, and his easiness with waiters, hotels, cars, taxis, journeys, flights. He is my sort, I told myself: sophisticated, able to handle all situations. Nothing fazes him. I was also horribly nostalgic for my apartment — its distance from the ground, its ethereal quality, high above the city, of not being real yet so totally functional; the gym on the ground floor; the swimming pool; Jacuzzi; my clean skin when I was there.

Now look at me, I said to myself. In this cold wet muddy place, my hands roughened from working in the garden with Nadine. We were together in not letting my father dig for long. He hurt his chest helping Will feed bullocks. It had frightened us, for we feared the pain might have indicated a heart problem. It had been a relief to find he had merely pulled a muscle. Nevertheless, we were like two nurses, strict and domineering. We didn't want anything to happen to him. We conspired — found ways to stop him exerting himself. We even put a new heater in his studio so he could work in more comfort. He complained bitterly, "I work better when I can feel the elements," but he let us put it there, eating electricity.

Dad gave a look of approval when, finally dressed, my face made up, I went into the kitchen.

"Vince is a lucky fellow. Pity he's not here to see you." He smiled admiringly as I leaned over the sink and helped myself to some of Nadine's hand cream, which I rubbed carefully into my roughened hands.

"You will wear your ring, no?" Nadine asked.

"Oh yes, of course." My ring — Vince's ring — was in my bedroom. I went upstairs, took it from the dressing table and slipped it onto the third finger of my left hand. Its three diamonds, separated by rubies, sparkled. I had scarcely worn it since my arrival.

"You look very beautiful," Nadine told me when I re-entered the kitchen wearing the ring.

Kate hugged me tight. "You smell nice, Cleo," she said. "And you look like a princess," she added.

I laughed and hugged her back — this dear little sister of mine. It would be hard to leave her when the time came for me to return to Canada.

Will picked me up in his Land Rover. "Mum's got the car. She's already up there — helping Sue get ready. She's Mum's favourite niece, and she's staying with the family for a couple of nights to prepare for the wedding."

We drove first to Crediford. It was already bustling with Saturday shoppers. "Won't be long, just going to get some cash." Will parked the Land Rover in the square. "Anything you want, Cleo?"

"No, thanks." I watched as he walked across to the bank. There were three people at the cashpoint; he would have to wait. How fine he looked in his morning suit, the grey trousers and black tailed coat suited his strong figure. Instead of his usual tweed cap he had a shiny top hat, which he had left on the seat next to me, between us. Idly I picked it up held it on my lap and putting my hand on its brim noticed Vince's ring on my finger. Without hesitation I slipped it off and put it in a pocket inside my handbag. Looking up, I realised there was someone standing by the car. It was Gloria.

Although the sun shone and the sky was a brilliant blue, the frost of the morning was still in the air. Gloria's breath steamed against my window. I slid it open.

"Hi there," she said.

"Thought you were away, Gloria," I said awkwardly.

"Yes, I know. I'm on my way, just stopped for some fags. It's not a long drive and my sister's wedding isn't till half past three. Funny all of us going to weddings today. Two weddings and a funeral!" she laughed.

I must have registered shock in my expression; certainly I felt it.

"Don't worry, Cleo, only a joke, you know," she said. "Four Weddings and a Funeral — you must have seen the film. Perhaps you didn't?"

"No, I'm afraid not." I tried to force a smile. I was feeling nervous; wishing Will would hurry back so we could drive away.

"You look stunning," Gloria said. I thanked her, tried to read her facial expression. She looked golden — healthy — her hair, tied in an untidy heap on her head, shone in the sunlight, her cheeks, rosily tanned from so much outdoor work. She reminded me of Lucy.

"When did you say your fiancé was coming?" she asked, eyeing me steadily.

"Christmas," I said. "Not till Christmas, the twenty-second, actually. The afternoon of the twenty-second," I added unnecessarily. "Just before Christmas." It was as though by repeating the details I could mask my discomfiture.

I noticed a flicker of doubt in her eyes. Again, I thought how like Lucy she was. The sort of woman who, open and honest, has few inhibitions about her feelings. At the same time intelligent enough not to allow them to dominate her actions.

"I'm sorry you couldn't come to Will's cousin's wedding," I lied, not liking myself for being glad that her sister's wedding was on the same day — that Gloria and Will would not be together.

"Yes, it's a damn shame. I like Will's cousins, all of them. It's a lovely family — lots of fun."

I felt a stab of envy at this acknowledgement of Gloria's intimacy with Will's family.

"Here he is. Hi, Will," she called. His face lit up when he saw her.

"Not gone yet then?"

"No, I've just come in to town for some cigs. I'll call in at Kessel again on my way and see Monty, make sure all is well with Benjy too."

"Thanks. Gee, you're an angel," Will was saying. "Both of them were fine when I left Kessel." He put his wallet inside his jacket, standing by the Land Rover door. "We'd better get cracking," he said. "Pity you're not coming, Gee."

Suddenly Gloria wound her arms around Will's neck and kissed him full on the mouth.

It was cold in the Land Rover and I shivered. Will responded to Gloria's kiss with a big hug, tweaking her ear before climbing into the driver's seat.

"Drive carefully, Gee," he called as he started the engine and Gloria waved an enthusiastic wave. "'Bye, Will; 'bye, Cleo."

I felt mean, cold, tight in my seat.

"God, it's bloody freezing," Will said as he turned the heater on full, and closed the window. Before driving off he stretched across the seats and took my hand for a moment. "You're cold, Cleo. Here, put this around you." He pulled a rug from the back seat and put it across my knees.

I had never been to Exmoor and was struck by the subtle differences between the two moors. Dartmoor with its rugged tors and sloping stony hillsides and Exmoor, interspersed with wooded valleys that stretched down to the sea.

"It's beautiful, Will — really lovely. I had no idea it was like this."

"Yes, I love it," Will replied. "You see, my father was born here, and my grandfather before him — for generations, in fact."

"I thought you were a native of Dartmoor," I said, surprised.

"I am, Cleo. Mum's family came from Dartmoor, but Rook Farm has been in my Dad's family for generations. My parents lived up here for a while after they married. They lived in this cottage, in fact."

Will had pulled off the road onto a piece of common land beside a woodland, the trees bare now of leaves, through which we could see down the steep slopes to the sea.

Turning off the engine Will pointed to the edge of the wood, where a narrow track led to a small stone building. "It's not used much now, but Mum told me that she had loved living there with Dad. It only had one up and one down, but they were very happy, both working for Dad's father at Rook Farm."

"What happened to make them move to Dartmoor?"

"It was when Grandfather Kessel died. Dad and Mum moved down to Dartmoor — moved into Kessel, it was left to Mum in Grandfather's will. That's where I was born. Dad's brother took over the farm up here in due course. All my cousins were born at Rook Farm."

"So you belong to Exmoor and Dartmoor."

"Yep," said Will. "I really love both moors, but my home is Kessel; that's where I love best. I've never stayed away for long, even a weekend and I'm usually longing to get home."

"I know the feeling," I said.

"Do you?" Will sounded surprised. "Is that how you feel about Canada? Are you missing your homeland?'

I stared at Will in disbelief. "You are surely joking," I said. "You must know how I feel about Burrow. That's the place I miss most. The place I dreamed about all my life when I was in London and then all those years away in Canada, which is a wonderful country, but I feel like I belong at Burrow, Will."

Will looked at me — a long, steady look and I realised how I must have sounded to him. I knew I had been emphatic. I had raised my voice too. I had even surprised myself with my vehemence and felt uncomfortable under Will's steady scrutiny. He was searching my face and with a slight frown he said, carefully and slowly, "So, Cleo — you're going back to a country which, as you say, is wonderful and yet you'll be permanently homesick for the place where you feel you really belong?" For a moment there was silence, then Will continued, "Do you never follow your dreams? Do what you really want? Get what you really want out of life?"

I said nothing. I felt suddenly hot, turned to look out of the window, away from Will. Away from this man who was suddenly pressing buttons for me — was making me think in a way I had not allowed myself to think. I wanted to open the Land Rover door and jump out, run away, hide from Will, from what he had stood for all my life.

Instead I did what I had always done, put my mask on. It did not feel right — it was loose, somehow. I felt vulnerable, tearful, but held back, went on staring through my window, though my damp eyes diffused the view.

Will broke the silence, speaking softly. "Sorry, Cleo, I didn't mean to upset you — you all right?" he asked.

"I'm fine," I said stiffly, then added: "Aren't we going to be late for the church?"

"There's plenty of time," Will assured me. "And I'd like to show you one of my childhood haunts. It will be too dark by the time we leave the party."

We drove along the narrow lane, which followed the line of the cliffs.

"So you came to stay with your cousins a lot?" I asked, trying to sound normal.

"Yes, every summer for a week or two. We kids had a great time. Look!" he said, stopping and turning off the engine again. "See that rock?" He pointed to a black shape that stuck up from the sea about a quarter of a mile from the rocky shore. "That's where we used to swim when we were kids, out to that rock. See it, Cleo?" I looked out at the sea, which was crashing against the shiny blackness of a huge rock above which gulls swooped. It had a cave-like arched entrance. From where we were, I could just make out that the rock stretched at least twenty feet seawards and Will explained that each end of the rock had the same cave-like entrance so you could swim right through it.

"Looks a bit menacing," I said. "I wouldn't want to swim to it, that's for certain."

Will laughed. "Neither would I, not in this sort of weather."

The clouds were scudding across the sky, revealing brilliant glimpses of winter sunshine that made the rock shine. "You should come here in the summer," Will said, "when the flowers on the cliffs are out and the sea is calmer. It looks more inviting then. The sea is deep and green. It doesn't seem so far to swim, and it's safe enough because, despite looking rough and frightening today, this is a safe bay. See how the land protects the inlet on both sides? We were never allowed to swim farther than the rock, and Uncle Jim, Dad's brother — you'll meet him and my Aunt Dorrie today — he put an iron ring into the rock and fixed a chain from it to the shore in case any of us got into difficulties. There were six of us here at once and we were all nearly the same ages. I used to love it — looked forward to it — it was so different from my usual life, an only child."

Will had driven only a few hundred yards before stopping once more.

"This is where we used to come pretty well every day, Cleo, when we were kids."

We were still on the narrow cliff road, the woods now behind us. We faced downhill and below us a small rocky bay was visible at the foot of a short, steep cliff. Running down to the cliff was a shallow valley where a stream tumbled its way to the cliff edge and gushed out over the bay.

"In summer," Will said, "it goes almost to a trickle, but we kids would stand on the rocks below, open our mouths to catch the water. It's from a spring up near Rook. This beach actually belongs to Rook Farm and playing down there during the summer holidays was the centre of my time here.

"We used to dare each other to swim through the rock. The thought was frightening; I remember the year I did it. Though Uncle Jim forbade us ever to attempt it, the boys, Simon and George — they're twins, a year older than me — they both did it. I was in the boat and the girls were terrified in case their brothers drowned. So was I. It was easy enough swimming through, it's only about twenty yards, but coming back again the current is so strong it nearly sweeps you back out to the open sea."

I looked down to the rock, now almost submerged by the incoming tide. "They succeeded?" I asked.

"Yes. When the boys got back we hauled them into the boat. They were jubilant and I wanted to do the same thing. 'You'd better not, Will,' they warned, 'because the tide's going out and the current is awful. We only just made it.' "But I had to do it — couldn't let my cousins beat me. It was terrifying. The tide seemed to carry me through in no time, but coming back was pretty frightening. The sky was black and I remember as I tried to turn back into the entrance for my return to the boat there was an eerie stillness, then the water seemed to gurgle like bath water does when it goes down the hole."

I watched Will's face as he described what had happened to him. His expression was serious as he remembered that day. From the way he told me, I could imagine with vivid clarity his experience — could almost feel what he must have felt — the current of water pushing against him, frightening yet having the effect of increasing his determination to succeed, not drown. I could sense the enormity of the task that Will, the boy, had faced. His determination to get to the end of the tunnel of rock — his cousins' voices calling encouragement — the water slapping him full in the face, making it hard for him to breathe. I imagined how he must have been terrified with nothing to hold on to, nowhere to rest, the sides of the tunnel being sheer and slippery black. Will told me how every stroke seemed to take him further away from the light of the tunnel's entrance; that he almost gave up, but forced himself somehow, getting there and clinging to the chain. The ordeal had not ended there, for his strength had almost gone and he could not let go of the chain to clamber into the boat, which was bucking now in the seething sea.

"If I let go," Will told me, "I thought the sea would bang me against the rock, so I clung to the chain, imprisoned, for I felt if I let go I would not survive."

I listened intently to Will's story of his boyhood; how his cousins had finally managed to get the boat close enough for them to pull him onto it. He lay on the boat's floor, glad that his face was so wet from seawater that his tears could not show.

Will laughed suddenly; looking at me he must have seen my expression of horror. "It's all right, Cleo — it all happened years ago and I survived. The girls were horrified too. They thought I was going to drown — Bella and Clare and Suzanne. They fawned all over me —

couldn't do enough for me after that. I think I probably got a bit cocky — bumptious." Will laughed again. "I liked being a hero," he admitted, "but something happened after that swim." For a moment Will was silent, then, more seriously, he continued. "That swim through the rock changed me. I felt taller, stronger. That was the year I got into all the junior teams and the year I did well at everything at school — felt free somehow. I suppose, looking back on that day, I can say that it was my rite of passage from childhood into — I suppose you could call it manhood." He laughed. "I only know I felt very different, Cleo."

At that moment I saw Will, the boy, as a Prometheus-like figure escaping his chains of grief with a Herculean strength which, it seemed to me, had renewed him, recharged his zest for life, for living in the moment. This is what I had envied most. I realised that I still wanted to be like Will. Free. Free from the continuous pull that life's horrors held me by, as though I were chained to that rock in the sea, just as I felt chained by the legends surrounding the Rock in the river at home.

How could I rise above all this I wondered as we drove slowly down the steep wooded coombe to the church. From where would I get a Herculean strength like Will's? An inner power that would free me from my mental prison. I knew it was possible for any human being — even me. I had known this all my life, at least since meeting Will when we were children. I had wanted what he had even then. Now I wanted it even more. I wanted to feel strong, be strong.

No longer could I hide away from myself. I knew that it was time for me to grasp some opportunity — allow myself to plunge into a place where I could see my reflection and recognise who I was. I could not imagine how this could be, but I must be ready for it. I was aware of that. I felt committed to finishing the task that I had come to England to do. It had felt so vague then, so self-centred.

As we drove down the short distance along steep lanes to the village church there was a queue of cars.

"Looks like lots of people are coming to the wedding," I said apprehensively. "I feel a bit of an intruder actually, Will — I don't know anyone, not the bride or groom or any of their families and friends."

"That's not true, Cleo, you know me — and I'm closer to Susie than anyone else except her immediate family. What's more," he continued as we slowed down to a crawl behind a Range Rover, "the family know who you are. I told them, you see — told them that you had come back from Canada and that you'd never been to an English country wedding. It's what you told me, Cleo — true, isn't it?"

"Yes, Will, it's true."

The Range Rover was moving now and we followed, slowly inching our way to a small field behind the church, where morning-suited men, young healthy-faced farmers, waved us into place.

"Hi there, Will," one said, peering past him through the driver's window at me.

"This is Cleo," Will said.

"Hi there — heard a lot about you over the years." Smiling, he waved us on. "See you later," he called.

"What did he mean, Will, 'over the years'?" I asked as we inched forward to park. "I think he must be mixing me up with someone else."

Will parked the Land Rover carefully, next to an elderly couple who smiled at him, giving me a look of polite curiosity.

Will raised a friendly hand to the couple and when they had moved away he told me, as he helped me down from the passenger seat. "Don't worry Cleo, all the family know who you are. They remember, you see — apart from the fact that you saved my horse's life, that is. You see I used to tell my cousins about you, years ago, when you stayed at Burrow. I always wanted sisters and brothers like my cousins, so I used to show off about you, about us doing things together, you and Peter and me. It was my fantasy. There was scarcely anything to show off about really, but I embroidered everything — like the time you went up to the Rock by yourself. I told my cousins that you were the bravest girl I knew. And that time you got Brownie — remember?"

Of course I remembered, but I had lost any ability to speak — just stared at Will in amazement.

The church bells were ringing; people had stopped arriving in the field. The last ones were hurrying down the footpath to the lych gate that led to the squat, granite church.

"Come on," Will said. "Enough of this. We can talk afterwards. We don't want to go in after the bride has arrived." Will took my hand and we walked quickly down the footpath to the church.

"This is Cleo," Will said to a tall, handsome young usher.

He grinned, "Thought you were going to be late, Will." He told us to go down the aisle to the front. Feeling strangely alone, yet suddenly unafraid and confident, I allowed Will to take my arm and guide me gently to the seat in the church that was reserved for close family.

CHAPTER 30

It was the small hours of the morning by the time we left the wedding party. Having drunk more champagne than intended, I felt uncharacteristically exuberant. Will, after the champagne toast, kept to orange juice. I surprised myself that evening, dancing with an energy I had never felt before, as though I was dancing for my life. I enjoyed the feeling of not knowing anyone, and everyone being friendly to me. Gloria had been right, when she had said they were a lovely family.

When I went to the ladies' cloakroom I hardly recognised myself in the looking glass. I was different from the me I knew, the me I was used to being; my mask was nowhere near me. Even when Will's cousins, aunts, uncles and friends talked to me about Vince, I found myself answering politely without my normal dismay, embarrassment or longing to escape.

"Next year, in the spring," I told one of Will's aunts when she asked when Vince and I would marry. "Vince is a banker," I told another relative, who wondered what my fiancé did for a living. "Yes, I like Toronto, it's a wonderful city," I told others who asked where we would live, and "Yes, I shall miss England, but we can always come to Dartmoor for holidays."

I did wonder briefly how everyone seemed to know so much about me, and supposed that Will and Joan between them must have told them. Will was quiet though. Throughout the evening I felt his eyes upon me. Unlike me, he had not been drinking champagne by the glassful. I felt strangely free of my usual inhibitions. The music moved me and I guessed that Will might be feeling confused about me. Remembering his reaction to the first mention of Vince at Burrow, when Lucy had been staying, I now could tell that he was struggling with his feelings. I knew from the way he danced, from the way he held me, that this was my opportunity to forget all the promises I had made to Vince or to myself; my opportunity to explore my feelings about Will.

I was not surprised when, after leaving Rook Farm, Will drove only a short distance before stopping the Land Rover. The night was cold. Clouds covered the moonlight, thick clouds, so it was pitch dark. Will climbed out of the car and came to the passenger side. Flinging open my door he grabbed me with an unexpected roughness, which made me cry out. He pulled me from my seat and onto my feet. I was not frightened, only surprised.

We faced each other; he had one hand on my shoulder, holding it firm. I could not see him clearly in the darkness, but I could feel his breath as he spoke.

"What are you up to, Cleo?" he asked. There was a tone of frustration in his voice. Though I could not see clearly the shape of his face, I was looking directly at him.

"I'm sorry, Will, I didn't mean to hurt you." My voice quavered, tears stung my eyes. It was then I did what I had longed to do, it seemed, all my life. I lifted my hand and very gently touched his face, allowing my fingers to follow its contours. His eyes — the scar above his eyes now healed but noticeable to my touch. His forehead — with its furrows — and above it his thick curls. My fingers explored these as though I might find secrets hidden there. Will stood silently, not moving. Carefully I felt my way, and sliding my hand down the back of his head I held his neck, pulling his face towards mine with a feverishness I had never known. It was then our lips burst together — then that I knew that at last I would have what I had longed for all my life. What was happening now was the sum total of my life's longings, my life's perplexities. All the sadness and grief and torture of my mother's madness — the inadequacy of my weak father — the isolation caused by the fragmentation of the family that I felt guilty about. All that held down life would burst, was bursting now through my expression of loving Will. I did not think of anything beyond what I was feeling. No thoughts of Vince, or Gloria, or Will's love of hunting entered my mind. That moment was something I had purposely manipulated, yet it was also beyond my conscious control. It was natural. Real.

He was carrying me now, somewhere, I did not care where, for at last something honest and real was happening to me, something I wanted, and Will was my willing accomplice. Nothing could harm either of us.

"Where are we going?" I asked. He was carrying me along the track that led to the little cottage, the one his parents had lived in, the one where his mother said she had been happy with his father despite the two tiny rooms.

I was not aware of the cold as I stood now in the rustic porch while Will moved some stones and pots, feeling for a key.

"It's a bit dusty inside. They only use it in the summer, but we can light a fire," he said, unlocking the door. He sounded happy, enthusiastic. Will led me through the door. Striking matches, he rummaged about for candles. He knew his way around — the place had been used by all of them when they went fishing or wanted to sleep out.

He had spent happy nights here with his cousins when they were children. He told me all this while, in no time, he lit a blazing fire, drawing the sofa close. There were rugs, sheepskins and blankets strewn about, with the musty smell of winter damp about them.

There was no rush now. We were together, Will and I, just the two of us, and it was the middle of the night, in winter, no one would disturb us. I could relax and show Will my true feelings, which unashamedly were of wanting the man, wanting him to the exclusion of anyone else and any other thought or promise. There was no need for talk, no need to pretend, we were equal in what we offered, what we received. I had never felt happier or more sure of myself.

It was in that state of mind that I discovered Will, the man I had loved all my life, the man in whose arms, naked, loved and wanted, I fell into a dreamless, peaceful sleep.

CHAPTER 31

When I woke up, my eyes, bleary with sleep and champagne, were only inches from Will — from his own wide-awake, soft, dark eyes. How long he had been so closely watching me, I had no idea.

"Sleep well, Cleo?"

There was a hint of a tease in his voice and a smile flirted around his lips. More seriously, he told me that it had been snowing — still was snowing.

"Snow? You are teasing me, Will." After all this was England, not Canada. We were on the Somerset coast. It couldn't snow here. I half-heartedly struggled, lifting my head to see over the pile of musty blankets we had slept under. In the grey light of the morning I could see, through the small window of that tiny room that it was snowing hard.

"It is still snowing," I exclaimed. "Huge flakes — how amazing Will. Does it often do this in December?"

Will pulled me into his arms. "I think it's just for us," he said, kissing me gently on my head, my neck, my lips. "We're prisoners here, Cleo — no escape — you can't leave me now, not in this weather." He was kissing me again and although his voice sounded light, the words 'you can't leave me now' echoed in my head. Was he thinking of his wife who had left him by dying? I could not ask him what he meant, for it would mean talking, confronting, understanding what was happening between us, in the context of our real lives. The sensible life I had planned with Vince, and Will with his life with Gloria and hunting.

Will stopped kissing me. He propped himself up on his left arm, which had been around my shoulders. I was warm under the blankets. Will, half sitting, was more exposed to the iciness of the room. I could feel the rough texture of his farmer's hand as he gently pushed my hair from my face.

"You look very serious — anything wrong?" he asked.

"No, Will, I was just thinking about Dad, and if they'll be worried," I lied. I wanted to tell him the truth. I wanted to say, 'I'm worried about us, what it means, about you hunting and me hating that, worried about you being with Gloria, about me going back to Vince, where I belong — back to that place of safety.'

Will was reassuring me. "I'm sure Felix will guess we have stayed at Rook, and if he gets through to Rook on the 'phone they'll tell him we are safe."

"Will!" I feigned fury. "You knew! You knew all the time we were coming here, didn't you? You told them at Rook, you rotten seducer, you dragged me here when you knew I'd had too much champagne. You told them, didn't you?" I was laughing as I accused him. "Who did you tell, Will? Not Joan — not your mum? Surely not your mum or aunt?" The thought sobered me and I stopped hitting him with the cushion that I had pulled from under his elbow. Will was laughing too, defending himself from my feeble attempts to suffocate him. We rolled around, fighting and laughing.

"No, honestly, Cleo, I didn't tell them, well only George and Simon. Told them we might end up here."

"You seducer!" I accused again, falling back amongst the ruffled bedclothes, waiting with confident anticipation to be seduced, determined now to be conscious only of the present, to pay no heed to my fears about Gloria and what she and Will had done together, or about Vince and what we meant to each other, or about the things I hated about Will's life. No, this was our time. However long or short, it was ours alone.

The knowledge that I wanted to give myself wholeheartedly to the moment translated into a passion beyond my wildest imaginings. This snowstorm time seemed specially sent for us. That Will shared my feelings seemed only natural, as we loved each other tenderly and with passion.

The intensity of the falling snow had ceased, for we woke to the midday snowscape bathed in sunlight. Will made some tea and lit the fire. We were quiet as we drank the hot, sweet liquid. I dressed, pulling on a thick sweater of Will's uncle's, which hung warm around me and smelled of pipe tobacco. Starving, we searched the cupboards for food, unearthing a small tin of baked beans and one of hot dogs. I tried not to think about where the meat had grown or how it had been killed before being made into sausage meat. I glanced at the writing on the label, "Doesn't look like this comes from one of your organic home-grown pigs," I teased.

Will grinned. "Beggars can't be choosers and I'm starving," he said as he heated them with the beans and we feasted happily. An unopened packet of oatcakes, well past their sell-by date, that I found in a tin completed the meal.

Later Will looked about for footwear so we could venture outside. The sun was already sliding westward as we walked through the snow to where the Land Rover was almost hidden under its white covering.

"I've got some eggs in here somewhere," Will remembered. "I was supposed to leave them in Crediford. Mum promised them to the old lady who lives around the corner from the bank. I'm afraid I forgot, so at least we can eat eggs."

We walked to the road, seeing that nothing had passed that way, realising that until the snow melted or the snowplough came we were stuck.

"It doesn't usually last long by the sea anyway," Will said, "but we shall just have to hole up here till tomorrow, then if it's still like this we can walk to Rook Farm. It's only a couple of miles."

Despite the sunshine and the thick socks and fishermen's boots that Will had found for me, I was cold as we struggled through deep snow along the cliff to where we could look down to the sea. The sun, shining on the waters, glistened against Will's rock.

"It's magical," I said. Will and I stood there, up to our knees in snow, basking in the light of the setting sun for moments before turning for home, to our little house. I, feeling wildly free, was thinking only of now and the delight of being with Will in the tiny cottage above the sea, surrounded by a snowy landscape that kept us secret from the world.

Will re-lit the fire, which crackled to life. He piled it with dry wood from the shed at the side of the house. I found a bottle of olive oil and used some to scramble the eggs that should have been delivered to the old lady in Crediford. There were jars of dried herbs, salt and pepper to add to the meal. I found another tin with digestive biscuits, not quite stale.

"I hope your uncle won't mind," I said to Will as I watched him reaching to the back of a shelf, bringing down a bottle of single malt whisky and pouring two large ones into glasses for us.

"No, he won't mind — anyway I gave it to him for his birthday," Will grinned, "specially to keep here. He likes coming here on his own. He writes a lot, he likes the peace and quiet."

"Everyone needs quiet," I said, "everyone needs space and time alone."

We ate our scrambled eggs. Will had lit some candles. They flickered, casting shadows on the walls.

"It's very peaceful here," Will remarked, taking my empty plate and putting it on top of his on the hearth. He took my hand in his, leaning back against the sofa, which acted as a bed head, for we were sitting on our makeshift bed, comfortable on sheepskins and blankets in front of the fire.

Will's hand holding mine felt so right, so warm. I sipped some whisky, asked him to tell me about what he had said to me before the wedding, about having told his cousins things about me and Peter.

"It was mostly about you," he admitted. "I used to pretend we were brother and sister, friends — that I could tell you things. It's strange really, but in my mind you became very important. My cousins loved my stories about you, though hardly any were quite true. The few times I saw you I just exaggerated the tales — they were always asking for more Cleo stories! When you lot left Burrow it was awful. I told my cousins about it, especially Susie. She felt really sorry for me. 'Poor Will' I remember her saying, 'Now he hasn't got anyone, except us.'" Will laughed, squeezing my hand. "See, Cleo? I was your secret admirer. You were a wonderful fantasy."

I was amazed by what Will was telling me and began to recount my own feelings concerning him in those far off, childhood days. "So you see, Will," I said, "I did not only admire you, I wanted to be you."

We talked far into the night, sometimes laughing — and for my part, crying — our way through times we had known, as separate people who were yet mysteriously interwoven at a time when we were still young children. In trying to make sense of the world we had, unknown to either of us, used each other, needed each other. Now, in this snowbound place, in the light of the dying embers of the fire, we consummated again with a gentle passion our feelings for one another. Now we could express ourselves not only in words. With Will's strong warm body, heart to heart against mine, I heard words in my head, words my mother had once read to me from the Bible. 'Where your treasure is, there also is your heart.' And for the very first time, I knew that my heart and treasure were found.

The next morning we woke to the drip, drip of melting snow. The sky was grey and low clouds hung over the sea. Will was first out of our cosy bed, making tea. He smiled.

"It's over," he said. "Our little retreat is no longer cut off — the snow's gone." The spoon he was using rattled against the side of a cup. "Each day is so different," he added seriously, looking out of the window.

I tried not to imagine something ominous in his words, but in my head as we tidied the house, folding blankets, cleaning the fireplace, washing our plates and cups, I kept hearing his words 'it's over, it's over' — dismissing them as often as they came into my head.

Will whistled as he swept the floor, shaking the rugs out of the door. I wondered how he could be so cheerful. I dreaded the return to Burrow, my normal life, perhaps picking up my mask again.

"Gloria will be back, hopefully," Will remarked. "Hope she will exercise Trojan today, or he'll be over-excited on Wednesday."

"Where's the meet?" I asked, casually.

"Burrow Cross," Will told me. He stopped what he was doing, looking anxiously at me. "Don't worry, Cleo, I'll take the hounds away from Burrow when we move off — away to the other side of the valley. We'll draw the Coombes — keep away from Burrow."

Although glad that the hounds would not be swarming around Burrow, Will's words struck me like an arrow. The reality of his life, with his horses, his hounds. How could I share that part of him, that big part which was so far removed from my own? I realised that despite our closeness we had not broached the subject nor had we talked about Vince. Had our time together been simply a short reprieve from our problems?

We were both quiet on the drive back. As we neared Burrow, Will put his hand on mine.

"It's been incredible, Cleo. I'll never forget Suzanne's wedding and our wonderful time together." I looked down at Will's hand on mine, longed to ask about the future, about Gloria, about how he viewed their relationship — our relationship — but I was afraid, dared not risk a question; for I knew I was too confused myself to demand clarity from Will. When we finally arrived at Burrow, I climbed down from the Land Rover, telling Will not to come in now, for I knew he was anxious to get back to the horses and to make sure Monty was all right.

Will helped me with my things. The house looked quiet and to my relief no one came out to greet us. They must have been out of earshot.

"Cleo," Will took my hand, "let me take your things."

"No Will, you'd better get back to Kessel and," I hesitated, almost stammering, "thank you for taking me to the wedding."

"We have things to talk about," he said seriously.

"Yes, I know."

"Wednesday night perhaps? After hunting. Can you meet up then, Cleo? After darts, perhaps?"

I agreed.

"See you at the meet, Cleo?"

"Maybe," I told him.

Our communication had become somehow stilted — his voice and mine distant — light years from what we had experienced in the cottage.

The closeness we had known had vanished. I began to wonder if it had been a dream. I looked into his eyes, saw the disquiet in them, and could not speak.

"I'll phone you after hunting," he said. I nodded my head, and he was gone. I watched the Land Rover bumping over the track until it turned the corner out of sight. A light switch had clicked and the world had gone suddenly dark.

The back door was opening. Kate rushed to meet me.

"Cleo, Cleo, it snowed," she shouted. "Did you have snow too, Cleo?"

I told her that yes; we had snow. Kate greeted me as though I'd been away for months, not just a weekend.

"Vince is here," she shouted.

What!

"Where?" I was stunned.

Dad and Nadine joined Kate, all three at once telling me the news that Vince was in England, in London at a conference, unexpectedly, and wanted me to go to London, because he was only there for a couple of days and then he had to fly back to Canada. But yes, he was still coming for Christmas.

"Good news, eh?" Nadine was saying. "Your fiancé in London, it is so exciting, no?"

Felix was in the background, lighting his pipe. He waved the match to and fro, as he always had done, as far back as I could remember. Back and forth his hand was moving, and the flame dying then kindling again, until the movement of the air doused it altogether. Such a small thing, but now it seemed so significant. So utterly absorbing. We all watched for the second or two it took for the flame to extinguish and for the first time ever I wondered why my father did this, why he did not simply blow the match out.

For a moment I caught his eye, he was looking at me with the look that said, 'I'm not going to ask any questions'.

"Here's the message, Cleo," he said, handing me an envelope with the name of a London hotel written on it. Vince was to be there at 7 p.m.

"He is longing to see you," Nadine added, her eyes sparkling.

CHAPTER 32

I must give myself something to do, some definite goal. Tomorrow I would see Vince, not Will as we had tentatively arranged. I did not know, could not think what would happen, how it would be.

Tired as I was I could not rest or relax, could scarcely eat the delicious food prepared by Nadine. Kate had gone to school for the afternoon, having been to the dentist in the morning. With lunch over I wanted to escape, needed to be alone. My thoughts and feelings jangled in my head as I pulled on my coat.

"Where are you going, Cleo?"

"Just for a walk," I snapped, grabbing my camera. Nadine looked surprised. It was, after all, quite usual for Nadine and me to tell each other what we were doing. Drawn together because of Dad and Kate, and since my episode when Peter was arriving, we had become almost sisters; though there was a prudishness about Nadine, something old-fashioned and very French, which prevented me from confiding in her, especially about this thing, this crisis of my heart.

For Nadine, I could tell, revelled in my engagement to a suitable man, longed for the wedding, had already asked me about the colours of the bridesmaid's dress for Kate. Nadine would make it. I could imagine her slim brown fingers, cool, as they sewed neat seams. Yes, Nadine is a good woman — a good ally.

"Sorry, Nadine, sorry I snapped at you. I just need to be alone. I need a bit of air and space. Do you understand?" I spoke more gently, not wanting to hurt. Nadine flashed her smile at me.

"It's I should apologise," she said. "Go on, my dear, go for a walk. Blow away the cobwebs. You have things on your mind, no? And tomorrow you see Vince again, it's all too much excitement." She was looking at me with a candid expression and for a moment I wondered if she might have guessed what was happening, but dismissed the thought. Giving her a quick hug I picked up my camera put it over my shoulder and left.

The sky pressed down on the landscape, cold, grey, damp and very dreary. I made my way carefully to the Rock. After the snow, the river was high, its waters rushing furiously downstream. I stood in the mud on the bank, taking pictures, my hands shaking. First I walked upstream, then down and back again, clicking from every angle. It was hard to keep the camera steady, and to keep from getting stuck in the muddy ground.

'Stugged,' Uncle Ted called it. The Rock and the river reminded me not only of Benjy's near death, but that memorable Sunday with Will when he had quoted the Aboriginal poem that had left me feeling so close to Uncle Ted. I felt it was getting easier for me to understand the importance this Rock held in the memory of those who were part of this landscape.

The film finished, I left the camera with my long winter coat and stood by the river, listening to the sounds I could hear coming from the Rock's mouth. I stood barefoot on the bank listening for a long time, allowing myself to become part of my surroundings and hear the music, knowing that my spirit was blending with the sound and rhythm of my ancestors.

Suddenly I found myself making the decision to climb the Rock. But could I? Could I do it then at that moment with all the turmoil in my heart? I remembered how as a child I had made the same decision and had failed hopelessly. I did not want to fail again but felt compelled to try.

'Should I? Dare I?' I asked myself. 'Yes I will do it now — climb the Rock.'

Before I had a chance to change my mind I had stepped onto the closest boulder, up to my ankles in icy water. Then drawing in a deep breath I plunged forward towards what I hoped would be another boulder underneath the swiftly running waters. Yes, my feet were on a whale back stone and I knew if I moved quickly enough, I might stay upright and if I kept moving from one invisible stone to the next I would reach the base of the Rock. But I must have hesitated too long because I felt my feet slip and seconds later I was being swept downstream. Images of Benjy nearly drowning flashed through my mind. I was being thrown about and submerged at the mercy of the full force of the river until, gasping for breath, I banged against what I thought was another rock. My arms flailed wildly as I tried to move, then suddenly I realised that the water was calmer and I was jammed within the arms of a branch that kept me from going further downstream. Though not free of danger I gained a new strength from knowing I was no longer being washed away, like a piece of flotsam, by the force of the water but was, instead, half sitting in the fork of the broken Rowan branch only semi submerged now and not far from the Rock. I saw that I had been whirled around close to the base of its great flank and that I might, if I put my mind to it, swing from a branch above me and land on the tiny ledge, which showed above the water line, jutting out enough to stand on perhaps, even if only for brief seconds. Without thinking I took a deep breath and pulled my body into a position from which I could swing onto the ledge. Gritting my teeth I then swung out over the gap between me and the Rock, but my hands, tight around the branch, stiffly refused to let go. I tried again and again pushing myself from the fork with my hands above my head holding tight to the branch, which cracked ominously at my last attempt. This time I let go, landed on the ledge and pushed my body against the granite. Sobbing with fear I grabbed at what looked like a smooth body of rock.

To my surprise I found my hands gripping small holds, thus allowing me to move one foot after the other, each time finding a foothold, and every time, I knew somehow, there would be another. I kept climbing and as I moved I felt a warm glow around me and heard an unmistakable, familiar voice emanating from the sound of rushing water. It was the voice of Uncle Ted. He was guiding me to the lip of the great hole. The home, no longer of my childhood monster, but that of the spirit of my ancestors.

I realised at last that I had climbed to the top and, as though in a dream, I found myself sitting on the lip of the Rock, my legs dangling into the great hole, listening hard, scarcely aware of my chattering teeth and ice cold limbs. Yes, Uncle Ted was here. I could hear his old wheezy voice encouraging me. 'You'm a queen girl, you can do it.' He was right; I could and would go through the Rock. Then, with a strength I had not realised was mine, I slid down, slowly, into the vast hole, reaching with my feet the protruding shelf that jutted far below, covered with turbulent water. At the same time I loosened my hold on the lip and balanced myself with my back against the Rock's sides, until I could reach for the hold that Uncle Ted had once told me was there, always had been there and always would, 'for those with the mind to trust and feel it.'

I was safely in the Rock, deafened by the thunder of water and moving to the sound of crashing music. Voices surrounded me mingled with my body, became part of me. The voices roared encouragement with my every move.

Let go — hold — let go — stretch, the voices instructed, to the tune of raging water. 'Don't be afraid, maid.' 'Trust yourself, you'm a queen.' His words echoed again and again through my consciousness as I swung through the Rock. I called back to Uncle Ted, he was above me now, and I heard myself begging my ancestors, and the gods, to forgive me and release me from the torment of my guilt.

Suddenly I became aware of the danger I had been in, and still faced, and felt my body shaking. This was where people fell. 'You have to let go — not be afraid, then swing yourself through the Rock and take hold the other side.' I could not do it — could not let go. I clung to the side. A terror took hold of me greater than anything I had known. For seconds I thought I would fall, like Betty Barton I screamed to my ancestors — begged Uncle Ted to help me. The pain caused by the icy waters was overcoming me. I was slipping — felt my hand lose its grip. But, instead of falling uncontrollably, I felt a sudden warmth, as a strong hand – a hand I felt I recognised — took my own. Gasping, I plunged through the great hole, sliding against boulders as I swung into the river — found myself on one of them, leaning back against the side of the Rock, hardly believing I had survived. Relief swept through me and I waited for my limbs to stop shaking before stepping back onto the submerged stones, until I could pull myself clear of the water and drag myself to the bank, where I collapsed sobbing.

I had climbed through the Rock. I had done what I had always wanted to do. I had nearly drowned, but I had done it.

On my way back to Burrow I remembered how Will had told me that he felt taller after swimming through his rock in his childhood. Now I really knew what he meant. Something inside me had changed, I felt calm and I knew that from now on I would be different.

CHAPTER 33

Next morning Dad drove me to the station, dropping Kate at school on the way. I had packed a large suitcase with most of my belongings.

"Heavens, it's a weight!" Dad said, lifting it into the car. "I thought you were going away for two days, not two years," he teased.

A feeling of premonition had come over me, as though he could have been right.

"It's my camera stuff," I explained. "Anyway, I'm not sure what I'll need up there in the way of clothes." Dad grunted, giving me a quizzical glance. He knew I normally travelled light — but he said nothing. For a moment I considered opening my case, pulling out some of my clothes and shoes and taking them back upstairs, stuffing them back into drawers and cupboards. I'd left my room quite bare, even taken photos from my dressing table. I felt puzzled myself, for I had no intention of staying away — I just needed my things around me.

Dad slammed the car boot shut and called Kate to hurry up. I hugged Nadine goodbye and climbed into the front seat of her little car, with Kate on my knee.

"See you on Saturday, Cleo," Nadine called as we drove slowly down the bumpy lane.

Kate chatted all the way and when Dad parked outside the school she hugged me before jumping out to join her friends, who jostled around her. I could hear their squeaking voices as they ran through the gate down the drive to the village school. Dad got out too.

"Won't be two ticks," he said. He was, I knew, going to see the headmistress of the school, having promised to do a special Arts Day with the children the following day. I sat quietly in the passenger seat. We were early for the train. I could relax. My head felt heavy, the hint of a sore throat warned me that I was heading for a cold. I told myself it was no wonder, after that icy journey to the Rock. I had managed to keep the adventure secret, though Dad had looked at me askance watching me limp downstairs this morning. I told him nonchalantly that my foot was hurting a bit, having stubbed my toe. He had looked doubtful.

Despite the onset of a cold I felt strong — still glowing inwardly for having achieved the climb — and at being alive. Having clearly looked death in the face, I felt that nothing could touch me now.

How wrong I was to think so.

Dad had not yet returned and I huddled down in my thick winter coat, pulling the collar up to cover my ears. My blue scarf was around my neck and covered my mouth. I could feel my breath warm and comforting against its woollen texture. I felt sleepy, hidden in my coat as I waited for Dad. Then I was suddenly aware of women's voices — mothers who, having taken their children down the school drive, had walked back up together, talking. They stopped by a car parked in front of ours. There was no one else about now. The women's voices carried. They hadn't seen me. Though the windscreen was misting up, I recognised Josie, who played darts on Wednesdays with Dad. I was thinking idly about her skills as a darts player when I thought I heard Will's name. I didn't move, but began straining to hear what they were saying.

"Gloria told me last night," said the darts player.

"How far gone is she?" asked the other woman, whom I didn't recognise.

"She's only a month late. She could easily have an abortion."

"Does he know — has she told him?"

"No, she said she wasn't going to till she was sure. I expect she will tonight. Don't say anything, Cindy, will you? No one knows — only Gloria and me — and now you, of course," she added. "She doesn't want anyone to know."

And me, I thought as my heart shrivelled inside my breast, wishing they would go away. But they stayed, and the darts player said scathingly: "Well, it's not all that surprising is it, the way those two carry on?"

I closed my eyes, pretended to be asleep, for Dad was coming, walking past the women.

"Morning, ladies," he said brightly.

"Hello, Mr Endaton," said the stranger.

"See you at darts, Felix?" asked the player.

"Definitely, Josie — see you tonight," Dad answered. He walked to the car and got in beside me. I wasn't sure if the women saw that I was in the car, as Dad started the engine and drove on through to the village before turning off to join the road to Exeter.

I collected my thoughts, not wanting Felix to notice that something had happened while he was at the school, that I had received a blow, a shock, which had left me rigid.

"Have you got enough cash, darling?" he asked. "You will let me know what time your train gets in on Saturday night? I'll meet you — don't worry if it's late."

He could not have been more solicitous, his tone more affectionate, yet it wasn't enough. Part of me wanted nothing more from him, was glad to continue keeping our distance. Perversely I was almost terrified that our relationship would change to the way I had always hoped or wished it could have been; a relationship where I could sit down and tell him about my feelings. Part of me wanted just that: a father who would listen, understand, as though he were a father who had never abandoned me or his family — my mother — leaving us alone without support; while he found someone he loved more than us, more than me.

I glanced sideways at him as we drove to Exeter. It was no good. He had abandoned me. It was too late, I could not confide in him — ask his advice, now, after all this time. Yet, as the train slid from the station and I waved to Dad — he, waving back with his lopsided expression, a little anxious, a little humorous, with his pipe in one hand — I felt a deep sensation of sadness.

I stood by the door, as the train crawled alongside the platform at Paddington and watched the faces of the people standing there waiting. Then I saw him — Vince — tall and strong, in a well-cut navy blue overcoat, carrying a briefcase. He was staring at the train — he hadn't seen me yet — then yes, he saw me, his face lit up and he bounded along the platform, running beside my window as the train slowed to a halt. As I stepped from the train into Vince's welcoming arms I was suddenly aware that my mind was made up. There was no longer any confusion in my heart or my head. What I had overheard about Will and Gloria this morning had shaken me, but the climb through the Rock had not been in vain. The momentous effort had profoundly changed me, as had being with Will at the cottage by the sea.

CHAPTER 34

"Vince," I said, a little nervously. "I need to talk to you — very seriously." Vince had showered, was putting on his socks. I watched as he pulled them neatly up above his ankles.

There was a bottle of Canadian rye whisky on the table next to the washbasin in one corner of the room. I went over, picked up the bottle and unscrewed its top.

"Do you still like water in it?"

"Bit early, isn't it?" Vince raised an eyebrow. "Yes, just a drop or two of water." I handed him the drink, sitting on the bed next to him and reaching for his hand. He looked a little surprised, smiled at me as I raised my glass.

"To you, Vince."

"To you, Cleo."

"I need to say something." I spoke quietly. "It's rather serious — very, in fact."

Vince swallowed another, bigger, mouthful of his drink. "Fire away," he said.

"I can't marry you, Vince — I can't go through with it. It isn't that I don't love you — I do — it's just that I — definitely can't marry you." I was sweating. Vince, instead of pulling his hand away from mine, held it tighter.

"What has happened, Cleo? Is there someone else?"

I hesitated before answering. "Not exactly."

"What do you mean, not exactly? Is there someone or isn't there?"

I found it hard to tell Vince about Will, but I did. I explained that I had spent a day or two with him, but I had no intention of marrying anyone. The moment's madness I had known was over. Speaking my thoughts aloud to Vince I believed what I was saying. I did not mention Gloria.

"I want to be alone," I told Vince. "I'm going to stay in London, get a flat of my own. A magazine is interested in my photographs. I may have a few commissions. I've decided to start a new life, Vince."

He stared at me. I saw disbelief in his eyes and his face paled.

"How can you do this, Cleo? Why didn't you write? Warn me — why Cleo? Why? Why?" He jumped to his feet, strode across the room and poured himself a stiff drink swallowing it quickly.

I watched, longing to ease his shock. I was seeing a new Vince. "I'm so sorry, Vince, so very sorry." I tried to comfort him.

He turned to me: "This is shocking Cleo, I can't believe what you're saying. After all our plans — you said you wanted children, remember? Remember what you said before you left Canada? You wanted to stay. You even wanted my kids. Why the hell didn't you warn me — tell me there was something wrong, instead of letting me go on believing you loved me?" Not waiting for my response he kicked a bedside chair with force. I leapt to my feet. "Please Vince," but he turned sharply towards me.

"Don't make it worse. I don't need your sympathy. I don't want to hear any more". I had never known Vince to be angry like this; it was frightening to see him shaken out of his usual calm self. I felt helpless and wished there was something I could do to lessen his anger.

As though reading my mind he turned to face me. "I'm sorry. I've lost it. I need to be on my own, go out get some fresh air cool down. I need time to think Cleo, you go to bed. I'll be back later on. We can talk tomorrow.

I watched him pull his coat on and leave the room.

***

I heard Vince come to bed. I had been asleep. I was hot and my throat ached. I listened as Vince threw off his coat, undressed and fell into the other bed.

The next day was painful for both of us, and that evening when he came back from the conference he looked tired and came to my side, putting an arm around me.

"I don't want to lose you, Cleo."

"I don't want to lose you either, Vince."

We dined in a small restaurant nearby. My throat was worse and my head ached. I sneezed through dinner, could scarcely speak.

Back in our room I climbed into bed hardly aware that Vince had gone out again. Later he woke me with a hot drink. He had been to a late-night shop for honey and lemons. He helped me into a sitting position and made me sip the hot liquid, before I fell asleep once more.

Next morning I woke up as Vince was leaving for the conference. He called room service and ordered breakfast for me.

I had showered and changed when he returned that evening.

"I feel a bit better," I said, studying his concerned expression

The conference was finished and the next night he would leave England. As I was still shaky from my feverish cold Vince ordered a taxi and took me to a quiet restaurant for dinner. I ate little. He seemed to have pulled himself together. He told me about Freddie and how well he was getting on at school. I told him about Kate, how different her life was from the way mine had been at her age. Vince listened to every word with obvious interest. It was as though nothing had changed between us. Then he said quietly, "I'd still like to come for Christmas, Cleo. How about it? For a moment I hesitated, wanted to say yes, yes come Vince, let's be happy, be normal, but I couldn't.

"You see, Vince, I'm not going back to Burrow." I looked into his eyes. "I need time," I told him, "time to get my life in order. I don't want to lose touch with you, Vince."

I meant what I said and as I watched him paying the bill, getting my coat for me, I wished wholeheartedly that it could be different, that I could love this kind man who was willing to give me time to think. I felt selfish; unsure how I could show him how much I appreciated him without being patronising or risk giving him false hopes.

At the hotel I sank into bed, tired and weary, with my cold still hovering and my emotions stretched. Vince turned on the TV and watched a film, which sent me to sleep. Later I woke up, aware that the TV had been switched off and that Vince had fallen asleep reading. I crept out of bed, removed his glasses gently from his face, took his book and placed it on the bedside table before clicking off the light and climbing back into my own bed.

I dreamed about my mother. I was taking care of her. She was in an armchair, sleeping, and I kept removing her book, putting a blanket over her lap, trying to make her comfortable; but it didn't work. She rejected my efforts, waking up, sighing and pushing me away.

When the morning came I felt torn apart, but pretended to Vince that, yes, I would love to go to a gallery. We walked around the Tate: had lunch there before going back to the hotel before it was time for Vince to go to the airport, for his flight to Canada.

Waiting for his flight to be called Vince took me into his arms telling me that he did not want to abandon our friendship, whatever happened in our separate lives. We clung to each other before he vanished through the doors of the departure lounge.

Tears streamed down my face. Unashamed, I boarded the bus back into London, allowing them full rein. Despite my deep sadness, I was nevertheless aware that, unconnected with what was happening between Vince and me now, I was free of a torment that had been with me all my life. Mingled with my tears, a deep certainty was growing inside me, and as the bus sped towards town I remembered some words of Saint Bonaventure, I must 'enter into myself and observe that my soul loves itself'.

I blew my nose. As the bus swung into Victoria I took a deep breath before stepping down onto London's pavements. This was the start of a new life. I was determined that it would be a life of creative adventure. Not knowing what was to come, and not realising how nearly impossible it would be to keep; I made a vow that I would never again allow self-doubts to trip me up.

CHAPTER 35

I found a bed and breakfast place in Wandsworth, while I flat- and job-hunted. I was one of only two guests. The other was a highly made-up woman who kept to herself. We scarcely met as I usually went to a restaurant in the evening and ate little breakfast. The woman sniffed whenever our paths crossed as though I represented some threat. The landlady however was friendly and it was she who told me about a flat to let in Clapham.

Two days before Christmas I moved into that flat. It was in a quiet street not far away from the common. Although completely bare of furniture, it had been left clean by the previous occupiers. The day before I had been to meet the editor of the magazine who had shown an interest in my photographic work. I took my portfolio of photos.

"Not many," I apologised, "I'm a beginner."

"Not self-taught?" the woman asked in a tone of some dismay. She peered over her spectacles at me. Her black dyed hair was cut short, above neat ears. She was eyeing me, almost with suspicion.

I was undeterred. After all, I had nothing to lose. I could always get a job in a shop or restaurant. "Yes, self-taught," I told her.

She was shuffling through the pictures — Kate on her swing, Nadine in the kitchen, Dad in his studio, painting — she gave them only a glance, then more slowly began scrutinising those she had picked out. These were the ones I had taken of landscapes as well as people and animals, sometimes with the Rock in evidence. She stared at them far longer. Then the one of Will on the moor with his dog, with the Rock in the background.

"This is particularly good," she remarked. She was looking at one I had hesitated to include. It was Will, facing the camera, the wind blowing against him, and his old Barbour had flapped open. Despite the obvious movement of the air, evident from the bent rowan tree nearby on the river bank, there was a stillness about his figure that was reflected by the juxtaposition of the tree in relation to the Rock in the water beside it, with Will closer to the camera. The clouds were in movement too and somehow this was caught in the photograph. In less than the second it takes to press the button the moment had been framed by my camera.

"I like the composition," she said. "Local farmer?" I nodded. "You've captured the essence of this person in the place where he clearly belongs, which he is part of, as much as that big rock in the background is part of — something eternal."

I listened to the editor and as she spoke my mouth went dry. This would once have been the sort of occasion when I would have longed to escape, put on my mask, certainly not wanted to stay listening, for it would have been too frightening.

"This is timeless." She flashed a smile at me. "The question is, can you repeat it? We're doing a series of articles on change and timelessness in the landscape all over Europe. I'd like to offer you the commission for the photographs — give you a trial anyway," she added. "The first one is in Scotland. The snag is you need to be on location by the day after Boxing Day. Can you make it?"

"Yes, I can," I told her without hesitation. Then went straight to the agents to sign the contract for a two-year lease on a big and wonderful flat.

With the keys in my hand, I spent the rest of the day shopping. Other people were buying last-minute Christmas presents. I concentrated on household necessities — food, saucepan, kettle, and huge cushions. I filled a taxi with my wares and told the driver to go to No 16 Ash Gardens. The taxi driver helped me take my things to the door.

"Happy Christmas," he grinned.

"To you too," I said cheerfully, though my feelings did not match my words. Stepping over the threshold of my new home I was aware that I was deeply sad about so much, wondering how Vince was coming to terms with the changed circumstances. I was homesick too, sorry to be missing Christmas with Kate, Dad, Nadine. I was unable to think about Will without my heart missing beats, a feeling of grief, which the euphoria of my new life, especially the job, could not by any means eradicate.

It had been hard explaining to Dad on the phone that I could not make Christmas. I had let him know more than a week before, but clearly he had not explained to Kate, for when I rang on Christmas Eve he sounded disappointed, as though he'd hoped I'd change my mind and turn up. "Oh, Cleo! Kate will be so disappointed," he told me.

In my new changing state of being, I felt impatient with his words, seeing in a flash of realisation that Dad was not being honest — never had been honest. That was what had always been wrong with our relationship, both of us short of integrity. Why, I wondered now, could he not have admitted that he was going to be the one who would miss me? Why could he not have wished me luck in my new job? Instead he had switched the emphasis onto Kate. This evoked a sense of guilt in me. It had taken years for me to grasp the workings of my mind in relation to my parents, and only seconds now on the phone to see the reality of the way he and I related to each other.

"Let me speak to her," I said.

Kate bubbled with excitement about Christmas. "I'm going to have a computer for Christmas," she exclaimed. "Do you wish you had one too, Cleo? You could ask Father Christmas," she told me seriously. I laughed.

"No Kate, I don't really want one at the moment. I'm going up to Scotland," I told her. "I shan't be at Burrow for Christmas." I waited to hear the disappointment in Kate's voice. It wasn't there.

"Will there be snow in Scotland?" she asked.

"Very likely," I said.

"Will's made me a sledge and he's mended your house, Cleo, and it's lovely, and he said I could have it, play in it, keep it till you come home."

I listened to my young sister, imagining her in the little granite hut that Will had rebuilt. The thought gave me an ache that was hard to bear. I had winced at the mention of Will's name.

Kate's enthusiasm touched me. She chatted on about Will and how he had put the stone with my initials on it inside the hut. How he had covered the roof with sticks and mud and moss. In my mind's eye I could see him lifting the stones into place. Even on a cold day he would have rolled up his shirt sleeves, his capable hands working with just the right stones, putting them where they belonged; sweat would have gathered under his arms and his curls would have stuck damply to his forehead under his cap. His dogs would be lying down, heads on paws, near his coat, waiting for their master to finish work. For moments I relished this picture of him, wishing beyond all else that things were different and I could be there with him and Kate near the oak tree at the little granite hut.

"I'll send you a Christmas present from Scotland," I told Kate.

"Hooray! Thank you, Cleo."

When Dad came back on the phone I told him that Kate sounded fine. "Have a great time, Dad. See you soon," I promised, and put the phone down.

It was late and I heard the bells ringing for Midnight Mass. I was in a reverie about everything I'd left behind on Dartmoor. The image of Will as described by Kate, mending the little granite hut, seared into my heart and I ached too deeply to weep. There was nothing I could do but experience the hurting of it all and prepare myself for Scotland. In less than thirty-six hours I would be boarding the plane for Aberdeen. In starting my new life, the old pains would heal in their own time. No point adding fuel to my sadness by dwelling on Will or Burrow. Now, I reminded myself, I must prepare for a new era

CHAPTER 36

It was while I was in Scotland that I realised I was pregnant.

The job had lasted longer than expected. Already six weeks had passed since my arrival at Aberdeen airport and we had driven miles in all directions, through all kinds of terrain in rough weather and, sometimes, glorious sunshine. I worked with different journalists, driving everywhere in a hired car. They dashed off stories about people, ranging from remote crofters in the highlands and islands to disc jockeys in the more southern towns. I followed them around, clicking my camera. From behind the camera's lens I discovered I could reach inside the people who inhabited a particular landscape. I began to love the job, despite sometimes being emotionally drained by the sadness I could sense behind the soft-spoken words and gentle smiles of some of the subjects.

The editor liked my work and sent me on other commissions. I got on well with the journalists, and became used to being on the move in all weathers. The journalists came and went, but I stayed almost a permanent fixture in a Perth, Dundee or Aberdeen hotel, having access to studios in all these places, where I developed my work, never feeling any sort of pull back to my London flat. Everything I needed was with me there in Scotland: my camera, my clothes and then there was the distance, the space, the miles, between me and Dartmoor with all its memories, hurts and unfinished business. There was no doubt I had failed in my mission with Dad and since the knowledge that the one man I had truly fallen in love with was with another woman, I cringed at the thought of ever facing any of them again. Yes, I had thrown myself at Will and now felt my face red and hot at the memory of my behaviour with him. I even felt sorry for and guilty about Gloria. I had been a temptress drawing Will away from her without even a thought of anyone but myself, and now, as a result I had caused Vince pain too. I was better off staying in Scotland working at weekends, rather than going south. Even London seemed too close to the West Country.

It was during a weekend, that it began dawning on me that an early morning nausea was becoming too frequent to be the result of mere pressure — too much work late at night — but something else. Of course — I was PREGNANT — a strange, joyful shock shot through me at the thought of the possibility of becoming a mother and that Will was the father.

Later, sitting in a doctor's surgery in Inverness waiting for his words of confirmation, which I hardly needed, I cried. The doctor was consoling and seemed relieved to hear that my tears were not from regret. All the same I was shaking as I hailed a taxi to take me back to the Hotel. I lay on my bed all afternoon with my thoughts in a tangle of disbelief and horror followed by surges of joy at the prospect of Will's baby nestling inside me. Anger and frustration took over then. To tell anyone about this baby was impossible. No one must know. Not Dad or Nadine and especially not Will who would already be celebrating with Gloria the conception of their baby. How odd it felt thinking about the other woman carrying my child's half brother or sister. I wept with self-pity and sometimes anger and sometimes for reasons beyond description.

At work tears came easily, flowing like tap water. Photographing the old couple that held hands standing on the shores of the North Sea, the wind blowing their sparse hair in thin strands above their dignified old faces, I wept, unable almost to see through my misted-up lens.

The editor sent me to photograph a very remote croft, on a Hebridean island, its inhabitants an ancient father and ageing son, both named Angus. They told me that they still fished, milked the cow and grew a strip of barley alongside one of hay and another of potatoes. Now, in winter, the boat was upside down far up the shore and the men spent more time sitting by the smoky peat fire.

The journalist who had been detailed to write the feature had not turned up, so I had driven alone to the croft and spent the morning photographing the Angus men. They had known we were coming and had politely dressed in their best clothes. Like people from another century they stood looking surprised and solemn towards the camera, their white shirt-collars, studded, wound around sinewy necks, reddened by weather, like their faces, leathery and lined.

I gently encouraged them to ignore me, loosen their ties, and do what they normally did on a winter's day here.

On the shore, which sloped away from the croft's land, cows stood with their backs to the sea, chewing seaweed driven up the beach by the high tides.

The two Angus men loosened their ties and went about their business. They moved the cow that would calve shortly, to a sheltered spot closer to the croft, carrying forks of hay from the byre to give her. They shifted bricks of peat, from the pile in the yard to the entrance of their home. I followed them, shadow-like, and they became relaxed, absorbed in their work, and I invisible. We were like dancers moving in unison from one task to another, bending dipping, turning in tune with the cold blustering wind as it whistled and moaned around the low buildings and upturned boat, before changing key with a high whip-like sting as we moved from the slight shelter of buildings. Our bodies bowed to the salt stung tufts of yellowed grasses, through which we moved. The neat black cattle stood, backs against the wind and waves, unmoved, long suffering; content to chew the salty seaweed.

Again and again my cold fingers pressed the shutter release, clicked film after film. The subjects were familiar to me. I began to feel at home, as though I were filming Uncle Ted. Taking shots of the father and son close-up or distant, with the backdrop of the mountains and the sea, reminding me strongly too of Will's Exmoor heritage, with its close proximity to the ocean, also wild though having a softer aspect. The tough landscape with which these men had to contend, and their appearance, as though chipped from the very land they inhabited, contrasted with their gentle island voices.

My ease of weeping I put down to my growing condition. Indeed this was the emotional charge. I was grateful to be able to feel so deeply, as though what was happening to my body enabled me to understand what I was experiencing creatively. The tears were merely the immediate expression, the release.

I think I managed not to show how moved I felt, hoping they would think my nose blowing was a result of the cold wind. I think so, for they finished work for the morning and invited me across the threshold of their home.

Indoors it was dark at first, until my eyes adjusted from the clear island light, bright despite the cloudy day, contrasting with the dimness of the croft's interior. Again I was reminded of Burrow and Uncle Ted. Old Angus even wheezed like him and his eyes glinted brightly as he poured a glass of single malt whisky and handed it to me. He called me child too. 'Bairn' he said, but his tone was the same as my Dartmoor Great Uncle's. The language similar, the warmth, the depth of understanding, all familiar as he told me to sit by the fire. They gave me a slab of cheese with hard bread taken from a cupboard with glass doors. They carefully produced a packet of Highland Shortbread, 'from the supermarket' they said proudly, patiently unpacking the tough plastic. Taking a pretty, green and pink china plate with gold rim from the same cupboard Angus, the younger, arranged the biscuits in a way that told me how things must have been before his mother died.

I began to write things down in my head, the men's movements, with what reverence they poured the three small glasses of whisky — 'Gold' the old Angus called it, handing it to me like communion. I absorbed not only the smooth, peaty alcohol, but also the atmosphere, the smoky smell, the pungency of the men themselves who were steeped in these scents.

I felt at home there in the dark kitchen, with its heavy wooden table, the small window, the open fireplace and range, and next to that a gas cooker presumably fired by the huge torpedo tanks I had noticed fixed to the leeward side of the croft.

There was a telephone on the windowsill, and in the corner, covered with a velvet cloth, dark green, with a bowl on it presumably to keep the cover in place, was a small television set. "Yes," they told me politely, when I asked if they enjoyed watching television, "yes, it is very nice." I felt that they could not have criticised it, for that would have been in their eyes very impolite, an insult to me, a visitor. I guessed they saw me as part of that world, the one seen on the television.

Back at the hotel I wrote reams about the day with the two Angus men, their home, and their landscape. Shedding tears as the words poured onto the paper, as though my very writing might destroy what had always been sacred. It was with a strange feeling of reluctance that I sent off what I had written, with the pictures, before leaving for my next assignment.

Later, in London waiting to see the gynaecologist, I picked up a copy of the magazine I worked for. There were my pictures, the two Angus men, with their croft and the wild landscape of the mountains behind them. The editor had been uncharacteristically complimentary about the work, and I had been commissioned for dozens of assignments all over Europe, writing as well as photographing.

Now, reading the article in the quiet atmosphere of the waiting room, I was struck with a terrible feeling of guilt and sadness. I did not like seeing these two wonderful beings shining out of glossy pages. The thought of them being everywhere — all over the world perhaps, on planes, in hotels, waiting rooms, looked at, crushed in recycling bags, gawped at by all and sundry — evoked an anger in me that helped me decide there and then not to use my skills this way again. I would take photographs of trains, horses, mountains and perhaps people, but never again would I dig up, scrape and gouge out their souls. It was like pulling Uncle Ted out of the earth, shaking the soil from his bones and holding him up for people to see. No — such ancestry was destined to be secret, and it was up to the descendants to keep the secrets, letting out only what was appropriate to those who were able to appreciate the sanctity of existence.

I did not weep then, as I waited for my turn with the doctor, who wanted me to have scans and regular checks. I refused the scans.

"At your age there's a risk."

"Risk of what, Doctor?"

"Risk of a malformed child."

"I'll take the risk."

No, I did not weep, but a longing crept into me, which I tried to push away. A longing for Burrow, for my ancestors and more than anything a longing to relive the days I had known with Will, be with him, share this secret of mine, which was also his.

CHAPTER 37

I dreamed frequently of Will. He was always near the Rock. Uncle Ted appeared often — they seemed to be talking to each other and I would reach out with a sense of longing, wanting to hear what they were saying. When I woke up from these dreams it was shocking to find myself alone in the flat in London.

Sometimes I considered letting out my secret to Dad. Telling him about the baby — about Will. I had told him about my work, but not about anything personal, or where I lived. Only three close people had my address: my brother Peter, who was safely ensconced in his life in Australia; Vince, who never broke a promise; and Lucy, who kept my spirits up when, on the phone, I expressed doubts about having a first baby at thirty-seven. Vince, too, knew about the baby; but I kept that secret from Peter as well as everyone at Burrow. This was a decision about which I felt no guilt. During my travels abroad I sent letters full of anecdotes about whichever place I was photographing. Usually I found a present to send to Kate or Nadine, and left them poste-restante addresses so that I did not lose touch entirely with them all.

I travelled from one place to another, from Ireland to the southernmost tip of South America. It was easy, during those months, to keep up the façade with Dad and the family. When I finally stopped work six weeks before the baby was due I did not even tell them I was in London.

I wrote to Peter. He, I knew, would understand about my wanting to keep private, distanced from Dad. After all, Peter had done the same; only he had moved himself permanently to Australia, making a much bigger distance between him and Felix even than I had.

Vince phoned often, wrote regularly. He told me news of Freddie, who was growing 'apace'. He showed interest in my work. We talked at length about this. He would sound really excited if he came across something of mine in a Canadian magazine. He offered to be with me when the time came to give birth. I said "No — no, dear Vince. Thank you, but Lucy is coming to stay. I shall be fine." Lucy was to come a week or so before the due date. She and Paddy would stay in London for a month, their children spending all summer in the Ontario lakes with Lucy's parents, and the vast family of uncles, aunts and cousins.

***

I lay awake — the traffic's roar intermittent, in the early hours of Sunday. Holding my hand on my expanded tummy I realised that the little creature inside was less active than before. I was restless, eased myself from bed and pattered across the room. The August night was hot, reminding me of Canada, humid, thundery. The sash windows, flung up high, were held open with a wooden coat hanger. The curtains, white muslin, moved imperceptibly in the night air. I left the room, walked along the hall to the kitchen. Opening the fridge I took a bottle of apple juice and poured it into a tall glass. The kitchen looked neat and clean. I felt relieved to have done all that housework the day before, making everything seem ordered, the round kitchen table, so often piled with photographic work, was empty except for a jug of sweet-peas from Jane, the girl downstairs, who loved working in our shared garden. Their scent filled the warm air.

I wandered through to the airy sitting room, between the bedroom and the kitchen. Some of the things from my Toronto apartment were there: Indian rugs and large cushions. Vince probably paid a fortune to ship everything across the Atlantic. All my books were there, it was a comfort to have them in the tall bookcases. The flat felt big for one person.

I sank into the sofa, sipped the apple juice, and breathed deeply. Later feeling more relaxed; I went back to bed. On the bedroom wall hung the picture of Will with the Rock in the background.

It hung opposite my bed close enough for me to gaze at it when I was feeling strong. Sometimes I took it down, turned it away from me, and leaned it against the wardrobe. Sometimes it was too painful to look into his face, in that landscape. I had to admit the editor of the magazine was right: it captured Will and the texture of the granite in the Rock.

Sometimes, looking at the picture, I was there with Will in my imagination, so strongly that I felt that if I put my hand out I would feel the fabric of his coat, or the roughness of the Rock. At such times I would long for the picture to come alive, for Will to step out of that landscape into my room, put his arms around me. I imagined his smell his presence, felt his hand stroking my face, gently, gently loving me.

But my eyes were filling, my body shaking with an indescribable loneliness. I put my hand on my expanded tummy, felt Will's child moving inside me. I was sure it was a boy.

'I don't suppose I will ever tell him the whole story,' I thought to myself, holding my hand on my stomach, but I did tell him out loud that the picture on the wall was his father and that I had loved him, wanted him to be the father. I told him what a fine man he was.

To myself I acknowledged my nostalgia for that day when I had pointed the camera at Will — 'I want to shoot,' I had cried into the wind and Will had laughed at the words, his whole face lighting up. That was when I had captured the moment.

The picture was being highlighted by the headlights of a passing car as it beamed across the ceiling, briefly illuminating the face of the man I still held in my heart.

That night I slept fitfully waking and sleeping, dreaming of Will — longing for him as never before. At one point my feelings became so strong I felt tempted to break the silence — the secret — go to Burrow, the next day perhaps, or tell Dad everything, talk to Will about what was happening. But it would be impossible, for one thing Dad and Nadine were in Paris; Nadine's mother was ill again. Occasional cards came from Dad, with snippets of news such as 'Monty is staying at Burrow for a few weeks looking after everything for us. He has a long holiday now and Will's mother is back at Kessel so she will keep an eye on him'. He never mentioned Will. I supposed he would be busy with the summer work, a busy season on the farm at Kessel.

Neither did Dad mention Gloria. Why would he? I asked myself. Once, unable to bear the strain of not knowing, I had walked to a phone box, telephoned the pub in Crediford, asked to speak to Gloria. I had no idea what I was going to say, and it was a relief when a voice I did not recognise answered. I didn't give my name. "Sorry, she's not here today," said the voice. "I could give you her boyfriend's number, but she may not be there either. Can I give her a message?"

"No — no thank you," I said, "I'll phone another time."

"Who's speaking?" asked the voice. But it was too late. I was replacing the receiver, my hands shaky. I returned to the flat lonelier than ever.

That night, trying to sleep, I heard the kitchen clock whirring three o'clock and, at a low ebb, gave in to a shallow sleep.

CHAPTER 38

From where I sit outside the front door at Burrow I can see and smell the roses and honeysuckle climbing rampant up the walls of the house. How quickly the new top floor and thatch have settled. How fast the garden has grown its lupins, delphiniums and hollyhocks. There is no trace of burnt grass or rubbish from the fire. No trace of the tragedy, of that terrible destroyer. There are lines though, etched on my heart and face, dating from that year, that late August when Toby was born.

It is four years now and Toby, sturdy and sure of himself, is playing with Kate, his eleven-year-old aunt, my little sister. She is making a daisy chain and Toby is watching, engrossed. Every now and then his chubby brown hands pat the grass and he picks a daisy and hands it to her to join the growing garland. I am feasting on the sight of them both. My camera for once is not handy but my sketchbook is at my feet. Quietly I pick it up and with a soft pencil sketch the children. Every stroke on the paper expresses the love and tenderness I hold for them both, every line of their hair and faces. In Kate I weave the unmistakable reflections of our father Felix; the hair of golden wheat. The hands so fine and certain are other reflections, this time of Nadine. In Toby I trace the indelible strength of our Uncle Ted, the artistry of his grandfather Felix and the gentle darkness of his father Will.

Suddenly the spell breaks and the children are calling and running. "Cleo, Cleo," they shout. "We are going to help Monty". They run across the lawn and climb the low wall to the lower garden. I watch as they clamber over the gate onto the moor. I see Monty marching down the hillside with Will's flock of fifty Dartmoor ewes, their growing lambs bouncing beside them. Reluctant to leave the cool summer slopes of the moor, they stop to graze, but the dog Barney paces behind them sometimes snapping, irritated by their slow descent. He pants, tongue lolling from his mouth, head down close to the ground intent on his mission. He eyes them meanly, disdainfully. He is from the best bitch Will ever bred and I marvel watching how cleverly he does his job. Not a stray lamb or wandering ewe to be seen, just a tidy baaing bunch of sheep, moving a little faster now as they near the farmyard.

Lazily I watch, one eye open, as Monty unfastens and shuts the moor gates. From time to time he and the sheep drop out of sight as they negotiate the shallow gullies that criss-cross the land here and there, dry now in summer, sheltering an occasional wind-bent rowan tree.

Today it is Toby's birthday. Every year the memories sweep over me. Indeed I relive every moment often enough in my mind, but on his birthday the memory is especially vivid.

***

It had all started at the flat with Peter's phone call, that night when I had been so low and sleepless. The ring had startled me awake, it was scarcely light.

"Peter," I gasped in surprise, "What on earth...?"

"I'm in Paris, stopped at Dad's flat with -" I gave him no time to finish, interrupting him angrily.

"Do they know you're talking to me? I didn't want anyone to know where I am except you, Peter. I thought I was safe with you being so far away in Australia. I asked you not to tell Felix or anyone. You're the only one who knows my address." My voice was shaking; I was breathless.

"Hang on, Cleo," Peter said. "Dad knows I'm phoning you. I haven't told him where you are. But this is urgent, there's something I have to tell you. Something has happened, at Burrow Farm."

I sank into a chair, my heart beating hard. "What's the matter at Burrow?" I managed to ask, my anger gone, my mouth dry, for I could tell from Peter's voice that he was about to say something terrible.

"There's been a fire. The place is almost gutted. Thank God no one was there, as far as we know anyway, and the animals are safe. Dad only heard an hour ago, it had only just happened. He's trying to get a flight over now, but being the high season it's not so easy. He may have to drive if he can get a space on a boat, but it will take a while if he does. I'll come over after the conference tomorrow. I'm not due to fly back to Australia for another week." Peter sounded almost excited at the prospect of coming to England. "Anyway," he added, "what's all the mystery? Dad's been pretty worried about you vanishing like that, and now it's lucky I'm here.

"Dad said," he continued, "that a chap from another farm saved all he could at Burrow, but was hurt quite badly in the process. Dad thinks it could have been Will, that boy we used to see riding around the moor on a white pony, the one we used to envy — remember? You must have come across him when you were there. Dad seems to know him pretty well but as he didn't catch the surname he can't be sure it's him. Without giving me time to answer Peter kept talking.

"Anyway, whoever he is, the poor chap's in hospital."

My heart missed several beats and I felt faint.

"Yes, I met him once or twice." The words came out in a whisper. It was an effort to make a sound at all. I stopped myself from telling him that the boy on the white pony was almost certainly Will, the man from 'another farm,' but forced myself to speak.

"I'll go down there. I'll go this morning, Peter. I'll try and book rooms for you. At the White Duck in Crediford."

"Better book one for Dad too."

"I'll try."

I knew I sounded half-hearted about seeing Dad and, from his silence, could sense Peter's bewilderment. Replacing the receiver I stared into space for moments before I could make myself move. So, Peter too still hadn't forgotten our Will, the boy on the white pony.

Toby was kicking hard. I placed my hand on my belly and spoke soft comforting words to him. I dressed carefully, my hands shaking as I buttoned the loose shirt that would hang down comfortably over the bulge that was Will's baby. Distressed as I was about Burrow Farm, it was Will I was thinking about. 'In hospital', Peter had said. 'Quite badly hurt.' All because he tried to save Burrow. How typical of him.

I left a note for Jane who lived downstairs. Where would I be without Jane? I knew she would understand and I told her I would phone from Crediford. Crediford! What a place to be heading for in this early August dawn light. The place I felt I could not to return to. Burrow, the place I had always longed for, cared about, turned my back on, and now it was gone. Burned down — destroyed. An involuntary sob came from my heart to my throat, and as if to protect my baby from my feelings I put my hand automatically on my belly again.

I had always imagined that if I had a child it would be born into a happy atmosphere with a loving mother and father. Vince could have been the answer to that dream, though I knew I had been right to break away from him. In a conventional sense our lives would have been perfect, yet I would have been sacrificing mine for the sake of a conventional peace, which with all its compensations would have been, for me, living a lie. Falling in love with Will had made me see this so clearly.

Leaving the flat I noticed the suitcase, all packed neatly with the things needed for a delivery in hospital. Spontaneously I grabbed it and took it to the car 'just in case'.

Driving through the emerging day my mind was occupied with thoughts of my father — his distress — and Will. How badly hurt was he? He would not want to see me. No doubt Gloria would be with him. Comforting him. I hoped so, for as envious as I was of her closeness I could not bear to think of him lying hurt in hospital without someone who cared about him. I wondered was her baby born — or had she had an abortion? I shuddered.

I had just driven over the border from Somerset into Devon and was getting cramped and tired behind the wheel and pulled off the motorway, finding a country road that led down a lane to a small village. The pub was quiet, just opened. I sat in the shade of a big beech tree, sipping water. 'Dartmoor sparkling spring' it said on the label and my heart lurched for it made me feel I was going home. Yet as 'home' it was denied me. Why had I come? Why should I support my father? Or Will, for that matter. I felt confused, sitting there, uncomfortable from driving. After all, life in the flat in London was calm, ordered, and my present work, doing portraits of children, and the routine of each day was good for me. Even my emotions, tied up with carrying Will's child, were more or less in check. Now this sudden crazy upheaval, this dash to Devon, was throwing my whole being into turmoil. Why was I doing it? Well, I would have to find out. I swallowed the last of the water and before going to the car, went to the loo.

Horror of horrors! There was blood on my pants. Help, what should I do? Tell the barman — call the police — 'phone Jane, 162 miles away — stop at the hospital in Exeter? It was only a drop of blood, nothing perhaps to worry about. I could feel Toby kicking in his usual way. He hadn't dropped or anything. Perhaps it was quite usual to have a show of blood at this stage. I wondered whom I could ask. The bar was almost empty as I walked back from the 'ladies'. Just a couple – a man who wore a clerical collar and held a half pint glass in his hand, and standing next to him a woman in a tweed skirt and straw hat, sipping sherry. I certainly couldn't ask them. They would be kind and concerned and take me over completely.

I spoke to Toby as I got back into the car. "Stay put, please, please," I begged. "We'll be back in London tomorrow night and you can be born any time, just for twenty-four hours or so stay quietly, wait, please, please, Toby."

I turned the key and started the engine. "You see, Toby," I said, "I need to comfort your Grandfather Felix and find out about your da … father." I could not say dad. It was too casual, too familiar, too cosy. For Toby's father could never be his dad. Will need not even know about Toby.

I should have gone to Crediford first, booked rooms at the pub for all of us. Instead I bypassed the little town, unable to think of anything but what had happened at Burrow. Once there, I would hear news of Will; the firemen would still be there perhaps, surely someone who would know. People are always curious about any sort of calamity, I told myself.

Despite knowing about the fire at Burrow I was unprepared for the shock of seeing it. I left the car in the yard and walked in by the side gate. Most of the longhouse was burned away, the thatch and beams collapsed, charred or burnt to ashes. One end of the thatched roof hung at an angle on the point of collapse. Rubbish littered Uncle Ted's garden, bits of wood, paper, half burned or singed.

I made my way through the debris, the smell, acrid and dank, hung in the air. There was smoke still rising from some of the rubbish. I could see no one and made my way toward where the front door should be, and stood in what was once the hallway. The top of the stairs had vanished; the lower half hung madly, leading to nowhere. Furniture was crammed into the kitchen, which still had part of a ceiling though it sagged dangerously, dripped still with water from the fire hoses. There was an eerie silence, my predictions that there would be people about were unfounded.

The reality of what had happened was creeping over me. The destruction was terrible to see. Distraught and overcome I stood in the mess and debris of Uncle Ted's garden and poured out my grief, loudly and desperately the words tumbled from me.

"I should never have left you," I cried out loud, believing this never would have happened had I stayed, instead of running away.

"I have been too selfish — too involved with my pain to care truly about you." I was shaking with anger against myself and the Gods for the terrible thing that had happened.

"Dear house," I said, my voice dropping to a whisper, "I always loved you. Oh, God, why did this happen? Was it to bring me back? To bring me to my senses? And what has happened to the only man I have truly loved — did you burn him too? Oh, house, forgive me."

I was crying uncontrollable tears now and a hot liquid was trickling down my legs — blood. I swayed, almost falling. Tripping through the mess of debris I staggered from the ruined house, back to the yard and the car. I would drive to Crediford, but it was too late, I was dizzy, I was going to fall. I crawled into the orchard sobbing. The trees were becoming blurred. "Oh, God, I'm dying — bleeding." The grass thick with clover cushioned my hurting body as I sank to the ground. I was losing concentration.

I knew I had done another terrible thing. I had put my child's life in jeopardy by coming here. This was unforgivable. I cried out as pain seared my body. I tried to take my shirt off to hold it between my legs to stop the bleeding — but my strength was ebbing.

A shadow, a man's shadow fell across the sunlight as I lay moaning. The man leaned over me, wiped my face and I saw it was him — Will.

"Will," I gasped. He smiled encouragingly, his hands moving deftly around my body, removing my clothes. I cried out as, enveloped in a joyful pain, I gave vent to a push of relief. Will was carrying me now, over rough ground. My tears flowed onto his shoulder, the smell of his naked skin giving me strength. He was breathing hard, holding me safe to him as he climbed the orchard wall; I had an arm around his neck, could feel his hair on the back of my hand and knew in my heart where he was taking me, for I could smell the gorse and hear the swish of heather against Will's legs, felt the quickening of his paces as we reached the brow and started the descent down the hill down, down, on and on, faster and faster towards the River, towards the Rock and the Magic Pool. He carried me as though I were light as thistle-down, never faltering, then he slowed and my body shook with sobs of relief as he lowered me gently into the magic waters of the pool. His arms were wound around me still and we lay together allowing the water to flow around us. He supported his body over mine, covering me, his voice soothed and loved me. "I love you, Cleo, love you, love you, sweet girl. I will always love you, be with you."

I was crying — the grief of my life pouring from me as the water flowed over us. It was as though we were making love, in pain and pleasure combined. Thus Will entered my body as though to pull his child gently into the watery world. The rapture was held timelessly as again and again I cried out with love and total fulfilment, as I gave myself entirely to Will and his child. In a moment of ultimate joy I felt Will move with me, the water bearing away the blood, bearing my pain. Now my body was cushioned on the soft moss-covered stone that lies near the Rock. I gave myself one last time to the water and to Will and felt the child slither warmly against my inner thighs to be bathed in the clear, clean waters of the magic pool and into his father's welcoming arms.

***

The next thing I remember was opening my eyes and finding myself in a bed in a bright airy room, with roses in a blue vase on a table by an open window, through which came the scents of summer, hay and honeysuckle. Although it was still early morning, it was hot. Then I remembered — Oh, my God! My baby — Will. Turning my head I saw Felix beside me. He leaned over me. There were tears in his eyes.

"Hello, Dad," I whispered. "Where's Will? Where's our baby?" My voice was hoarse with straining. "Where is he, Felix?" I felt anxious now and struggled to move, but my father restrained me.

"It's all right, darling, he's here. Your little son is here," and Felix went to the other side of the bed and picked up the sleeping babe from a small cot and placed him in the crook of my arm. I looked closely at him, he looked so beautiful, so dark-haired, so strong-featured, so obviously Will's son.

I looked up at Felix. "I am sorry, Dad, truly sorry not to have told you about him. Your grandchild. He wasn't due for two more weeks and I felt compelled to come when I heard about the fire and Will. Thank God he's all right. I was so shocked, though, to see Burrow. Where's Will, Dad? He was so wonderful you know. I don't understand what happened about him and Gloria but I know it was all a terrible misunderstanding; for what happened at our son's birth told me everything is all right between us. He was with me all through the birth. He must have brought us here. Am I in hospital? Which one is it? Will must be exhausted, I was oh so foolish to think he didn't love me. I've always been so stubbornly independent. Dad, you always said so. I am sorry, Felix, so sorry to have caused you so much confusion." I realised that I was hardly making sense with my gabbling.

Felix's eyes were swimming, the blueness, never dimmed with age, shining through.

"Oh Dad, all these years apart from you have been such a waste. I am so grateful to you deep inside, and have hurt myself as well as you by being so stubborn. Please forgive me."

The tears in Felix's eyes began to spill over his face.

"It's me who needs forgiveness," Felix said with difficulty, "and you will need to be very brave to hear what I have to tell you."

For a moment there was no sound in the room. I heard a dog bark in the village. The cottage hospital was on the edge of it and in the distance a tractor and combine harvester were humming their way around a field. I smelled the roses and glanced down at Toby. I wanted to relax, feel at ease, now surrounded with the love that I had denied myself all my life.

- 201 -

But intuitively I knew something was not right. My newfound joy was draining from me as I studied the stricken expression on my father's face. "What is it, Dad?"

There was a tug at my heart as I wondered what he was going to say. I realised that I had hardly given him time to speak but had rattled on, talking about myself, never giving him time to break in and answer me.

Now he said: "I wish I didn't have to say this. It's about Will." My heart lurched.

"Will? What's wrong with Will?"

"Will cannot come here, Cleo. He risked his life to save Monty, who was staying at Burrow, looking after our animals. He succeeded. Saved the calves and dogs too, but it was at great cost."

I stared at my father — had he gone mad? Was I dreaming?

"He took my clothes — washed me — Toby was born in the water by the Rock in the magic pool. I remember it — he was there — it was Will — we love each other — we are going to be together, Dad, always from now on." My words faded on my lips and a terrible realisation came over me. Had I been dreaming?

"How did I get here, Felix, who brought me here? And what do you mean, he saved everything 'at great cost'? Cost of what? He was there with me, yesterday afternoon, soon after I arrived. He picked me up, carried me to the pool." I stopped speaking, drew in a deep breath. Felix's head was bowed, and then he lifted it and looked me in the eyes.

"Darling girl," he said. "I want to believe you. Now you must listen and believe me. Firstly you were brought here by two walkers, both men. They found you in the orchard and carried you to safety, brought you to the hospital in their car."

I was struck dumb by his words.

"Secondly," Dad faltered for a moment and took my hand in his, "Will was badly hurt in the fire and was taken to the hospital in Exeter, asphyxiated by the smoke fumes. I don't know any more than that except the medics feared it was too late to save him."

"He's not gone?" I stammered. "Not d-d-d ... not dead? Felix, Dad, tell me he's all right." My voice was rising and Toby struggled a little in my arms, I was clasping him too tight in my desperation.

"I don't believe it, Dad," I cried out. "Don't believe he's gone, where is he? I must go to him." I was struggling from the bed, and Dad was trying to restrain me.

"Peter's gone with him, don't distress yourself, Cleo, think of Toby."

"I am thinking of Toby," I protested. "He needs Will and Will needs me." I was out of bed. "Where are my clothes?" I wailed. Felix tried to stop me but I was like someone possessed, frantic, as I made a swift search for my clothes. They had been neatly placed in the drawer beside the bed. Putting Toby down, I quickly dressed, then wrapping him in a blanket and grabbing a bundle of nappies from a pile on a table, stuffed them into a bag, and demanded that Dad take me and Toby to Exeter.

My mind was in a whirl, knowing that Will had been with me at Toby's birth. How could he now be dying? And what about Gloria? I'd somehow forgotten about Will and Gloria. Their relationship was not the issue for me now. What mattered was Will and his important role in the birth of our son. Despite the confusion of it all there was one thing that was absolutely crystal clear to me and I wanted to focus on it — Will's life was at stake — and I knew deep inside that Toby and I needed to be with him.

As we drew near to the hospital, Felix told me that Peter had telephoned earlier. "It's not good news, Cleo, you must steel yourself," he warned.

Peter greeted us outside the little side room in the intensive care unit. He looked solemn. He held me close for a moment and took little Toby into his arms.

Will was lying in the bed, unconscious with a contraption — a life support system — attached by wires and tubes.

I watched the screen above the bed, which was making a strange beeping sound and realised that his heartbeats were being monitored and without the machine he would already be dead.

The room was dark, the curtains over the closed windows drawn, it was warm, too warm. I went to Will's side and leaned over him, whispered his name, but there was no response. I spoke into his ear again and again, told him about Toby, told him I loved him.

Toby was beginning to cry. Peter who had been holding him outside the room brought him to me. I wanted to let Will know he had a son. Joan came into the room. She looked pale and drawn. She put her arms around me and led me away from Will to an empty waiting room.

Briefly she told me that the doctor had said that Will had been clinically dead at one point. "There's a little Indian nurse here who told me that it was as though his spirit had left his body for quite a few minutes."

I know when that happened, I thought, but said nothing.

Joan continued: "He is suffering seriously from the effects of smoke inhalation. They've given him oxygen and the life support system is keeping him alive," she said shakily. "The doctors have suggested the possibility that we might want it stopped, in due course, and his healthy organs used to help another poor soul — some other poor victim."

"No. No," I protested. "Not yet, please, Joan."

I would have no say in the final decision, I knew that and knew also how pragmatic Joan could be and altruistic too. As Will's next of kin, she would be the one to decide.

"Don't worry, dear," she said, putting her hand on my arm. "I'll not make any rash decisions. I shall talk everything over with you, believe me." Although relieved I was shaken. Then Joan folded back the blanket that covered her grandson and beamed down at him.

"He's Will's, isn't he, Cleo?"

"Yes," I whispered avoiding her eyes, unable to explain further. Will's mother put her hand gently on Toby's forehead and said, "To tell you the truth I am very, very happy about the little one. I always thought it would be lovely if you and Will could have got together." Her eyes were full of tears and Toby opened his eyes and seemed to look up at her. She smiled. "He is very like Will, Cleo."

We were both tearful and Toby too. I sat on a hard hospital chair unbuttoned my shirt and put Will's child to my breast, while my heart ached with the pain of his father's loss.

Joan suggested firmly that this was no place for Toby and I agreed to let Dad and Peter take us to Kessel. "There's plenty of room, dear," she said. "Gloria and Bill are there looking after Monty and the animals."

"Gloria?" I asked, astonished.

"Yes, and her husband." She must have seen I was puzzled for she said, "You remember Bill, from the pub in Crediford? Didn't your father tell you they got married? They're having a baby too."

We walked back to Will's room. I stood by his bedside for a few moments, my grief welling up inside me. I reached for Will's hand, recognised the feel of it, but it was cool and unresponsive. Before turning away, I leaned forward and kissed the space between the tubes and his dark curls and with tears pouring down my face, feeling drained and exhausted, was helped out to the car by Peter and Dad.

Gloria smiled when she saw the baby. "I'm so glad you've got him," she said as she led me upstairs to Will's room. It was the big double one he had once shared with Maria. Gloria must have guessed my thoughts.

"It's not like it was when his wife was alive; he changed it completely, Cleo." She looked anxiously at me, gave a tentative smile.

"Thanks, Gloria, you are being very kind," I told her warmly.

"You don't mind being in here, do you? I thought it might help you — bring you some comfort."

The room looked as though Will had only just left it. He must have jumped out of this very bed before rushing to the fire. Some of his belongings were on a chair, but Gloria had made the bed for me. I put Toby down on Will's bed and turned to face her. She put her arms out and we embraced, clinging to one another, shocked, silent and dry eyed.

Gloria made me get into bed. "What about you?" I asked, "You must be tired out."

"I'm fine," she said, blowing her nose hard. "Bill is wonderful, spoils me; and my sister Jennie is here now, arrived this morning. She's taken over the horses — you see, I could be having my little bundle any time now — due in a couple of week's officially." She picked Toby up and laid him down beside me.

Toby and I slept for several hours. Gloria appeared with a cup of tea just as I was feeding him. She sat on the bed.

"Joan phoned," she told me, adding hastily, "but there's no change."

Gloria helped me bath Toby. For a short time it was as though life was all right. I went back to bed and began to feed Toby. Gloria had joined us and began, hesitantly, to tell me about Will and what had happened after I had left and didn't return for Christmas.

"He was awfully upset," she said. "He confided in me, how guilty he felt about your fiancé; he was very sad and told me how jealous he felt. He also said that the worst of it was he was missing you and felt bad about not being able to say sorry. He said that he loved you more than anyone or any thing." Gloria searched my face and I could tell that she sensed how fragile I was feeling.

I had listened intently, wondering if I should tell her about what I'd overheard that day outside the school and how I'd got it so wrong, but decided not to. What I said was, "Gloria, I always thought you and Will were sort of — well you know — more than just friends." Gloria looked astonished.

"What me and Will? No, never. We were just good mates, that's all, Cleo, just good friends. Bill used to get a bit jealous about Will flirting with me, but he knows now that Will was like a big brother to me and we have been just friends, that's all. I've fancied my Bill ever since I met him," she explained, "ever since I moved down here. Ever since Maria —

and all that awful time. I was friends with Maria, you see," she added thoughtfully.

"When she went — died I mean, he talked to me a lot. I think I was the only one he talked to about her, back then. Mind you I used to lean on him too ... about Bill. It was Will who made Bill realise how much I loved him and wanted his child. He's always been a bit of a lad." She smiled ruefully. "But I reckon he's more grounded now, and over the moon about this kid." She put her hands on her big tummy. "He's as devastated as me about Will, there's nothing he wouldn't do to help."

I felt drained now, listening to her words. Blamed myself for being so incapable of communicating my feelings to Will or Dad for that matter. All this might have been avoided had I been less rigid about letting the people I loved know that I cared. I had been afraid to risk exposing my true feelings. All my life I had kept my pride, my safe place on thick ice, now thinning to cracking point; it was now too late to show Will that I was not the cold-hearted person who could cut herself from those she loved. Will had been the one person to glimpse the other part of me, the part that was unfamiliar even to myself, but my pride had been my enemy and my mask had locked me in a strange prison.

I cried myself to sleep holding Will's baby warm against me, feeding him from time to time, when he awoke. I was made to stay in bed for the next few days. Gloria and Jennie coming in and out of Will's room to give me nourishing food and kind words, though I knew they were holding back the truth about the hopelessness of Will's situation.

Dad and Peter went back and forth to the hospital each day, coming to my room to report. They would coo over Toby, hardly looking at me, and I knew that my worst fears were being confirmed each time they came back, with vague noncommittal words about his condition, which never seemed to change.

Joan had asked Dad to dig out of the attic a cot, one that was used for Will as a baby. Putting our baby into this small wooden rocking bed on the kitchen floor was a great comfort to me. I could imagine Will there, with me, looking down at our little son asleep.

One morning I was up and dressed and took Toby downstairs to the kitchen. Dad was there alone and I begged him to tell me the truth about Will's condition.

"Don't be too hopeful, Cleo" he said. "Will is in a terrible crisis and getting worse."

I wanted to go that very moment to be with him. "I feel strong now, Dad, I'm able to cope with whatever comes." My words belied my true feelings. I knew that I would find it hard to be anything but devastated at Will's death. "I must see him Dad. Please take me now."

Dad suggested I speak to the nurse in charge so I phoned and she told me it would be better not to disturb him but if there was any change she would phone me at once. Joan was staying in the hospital and she also spoke to me in the evening, promising that she would phone. "He's heavily sedated, Cleo," she told me gently. "It might be best if you sleep as much as you can dear and bring Toby in first thing in the morning."

Reluctantly I agreed it was best and took myself wearily up to prepare Toby for the night. Gloria had prepared some soup and we all sat silently around the table. I forced myself to eat for Toby's sake, and hugged her goodnight. Neither of us was able to speak but I drew some comfort from our being together in our shared grief. Dad was arranging Peter's return flight. He had cancelled his return to Australia several times.

The moon shone into the bedroom waking me from a very light sleep. I felt restless and longed for the morning when Dad would be taking Peter to the airport and me to the hospital. Joan was to look after Toby while I spent time at Will's bedside.

I crept out of bed without waking Toby and looked out of the window. The full moon lit up the yard and I could see Will's dogs, Rip and Barney, lying by the Land Rover. I went downstairs quietly and opened the door into the kitchen. That too was awash with the white moonlight. The shadow by the window was Felix. He seemed unsurprised to see me.

"I've been thinking," he said, in a low voice. "I think we should go to the Rock, take Toby with us and go to the Rock."

Seeing my surprise he told me how he had been worrying about me and about Will for a very long time and that he blamed his inability to talk about it entirely on himself.

"I have been so sceptical about the Rock and about our heritage, Cleo, but in my heart I knew I was on the wrong track — simply didn't know how to right things. Perhaps if I'd known my father, if he hadn't been taken from me — he might have taught me to understand the importance of our heritage better. I mean the important things in life."

I stood riveted by my father's words. In the quiet moments that followed I was aware of seeing, through Will's kitchen window, the huge moon, hanging in the clear night sky. The trees had turned to statues. Nothing moved. Dad broke the spell. "He was Uncle Ted's brother when all's said and done. But as you know, Cleo, I treated Uncle's tales with a big pinch of salt and now I really regret not having taken notice of him and of his stories."

As I listened to my father I realised that something deep inside me was changing. The possibility that he may have suffered as much as my mother was dawning on me. I was beginning to see that my poor fatherless father had never been able to express his thoughts and feelings either. He was just the same as me, or indeed Mother, only he had hidden behind a different mask — different from mine — but he had suffered the same kind of need. The difference was that he had sought expression through his art and drawn comfort from arty friends, drinking or having affairs, whilst I had simply switched off, acting out my life aloof from reality, well hidden behind my mask. Mother had chosen to escape into illness, mental and physical. Poor Mother had no means of escape, only death.

I thought about how Dad's father and Uncle Ted had received such different educations; but no one knew what my grandfather's approach to Ted's superstitions might have been. The young child, Felix, had missed out by not having a father's influence, and after his death his mother had not encouraged the family connection. Once my father was at boarding school she had married an American and Dad had spent his holidays in that country. Though he never spoke about that time in his life I had known he was reluctant to even mention my grandmother, who had died when he was still at university.

It was becoming clear to me from what Dad was saying, that, in his heart he had wanted to be as close to our Dartmoor heritage as Ted. He had, all along, wanted to share my own deep connection with this heritage.

None of this had occurred to me before now, but it was sinking in as Dad explained how upset he was at the prospect of Toby being fatherless, just as he had been.

We would both make a pilgrimage to the Rock, now, in the middle of the night, just the three of us, Dad, Toby and me. He explained that it had to be us because we were the ones most involved, the ones who understood.

I had never heard my father speak like this before, nor had I seen such a clear expression on his face. It felt almost frightening to witness this huge change, yet for the first time in my life I felt the tight bands that had kept me from my father loosening. Was it possible that our pilgrimage was to be the start of something incredible? Something that involved all of us? Would the Rock provide a healing for us? For Will? Could Dad and I succeed in saving Toby's father? I prayed so, and at that moment determined that the years I had wasted in actively not understanding, even almost hating my father, were over.

Silently we got into Will's Land Rover. The dogs jumped in the back eagerly. The moonlight was bursting its brilliance over the land. The moor was bright enough to drive without headlights as we moved slowly as near to the Rock as possible. Then we walked. Toby, well wrapped, was strapped to my chest in a makeshift sling, which Dad had invented on the spur of the moment from a flannelette sheet drying above the stove at Kessel. Together Dad and I strode over the heather, and down to the Rock.

I had no thought of what would transpire, but a feeling, almost of elation, enveloped me as we came close to the great dark moonlit edifice. At last we were there together, Dad and I, with baby Toby, fast asleep against my heart. We stood on the banks of the slow-running summer stream. Even the muddy places were almost dried out.

Dad sat down with me beside him, on the soft bank opposite the Rock, our feet resting on a boulder below us. The ripening rowanberry trees, stunted from constant exposure to the buffeting upland winter winds, seemed to join with us in the silence of that moonlit landscape. In the distance a small herd of ponies were standing like statues on the slopes of the hills, which stretched for miles, partly shadowed, mysterious in the moon washed landscape joined seamlessly to the sky; and Dad, Toby and I were part of that seamless ness — we were all one.

"This is a sacred place," Dad said quietly. "Holy and powerful. Although there has been tragedy here, I believe we can turn it into the opposite."

Listening to Dad was like hearing Uncle Ted talk. He even slipped into the Dartmoor tongue, that musical soft lilt of speech which I had loved in my childhood, but which had almost died out now, except in the remotest areas of the moor.

We fell silent watching the river as it moved without hurry, yet with a glittering urgency, ruffling against the stones, reflecting flashes of sparkling light, from the vast moonlit summer sky. I gazed out at the Rock, marvelling at its glistening blackness. We sat for a long time and then, as the moon got lower in the night sky, I saw a different light, glancing like a shaft from an old lantern, its beam shot across and around the Rock and I felt Dad stiffen and knew he had seen it too. There came a sound, as though a string on a violin was being played on one solitary note, very high-pitched, so high-pitched I strained to hear it. It had an ethereal quality, the sort of note I imagined a bat might hear, but that would not normally be audible to the human ear. I was breathing in the unmistakable scent of Uncle Ted. His tweedy smell. I found myself calling to him, as I had in my dreams.

I silently prayed, asking the Rock to rattle the ancestors awake, to gather them in force to Will's bedside. My heart pleaded and begged, for these ancestors were his too. I implored his father, as well as those ancestral spirits of Dartmoor who had saved Uncle Ted in the war. I called to my grandfather, Felix's father, beseeching him to stir from his place and save my man, my child's father, from death — to change the history that was being so painfully written at that very moment, and which the doctors seemed unable to do.

I don't know how long we stayed there, but I became aware that the sky had changed, that the moon was lower, and the music had ceased. It was as though we had been away somewhere, or asleep. Dad looked at me and I asked him in hushed tones, "Did you hear the sound too and did you see the light?"

"Yes, I most certainly did," he said in an awestruck voice. He helped me to my feet and we went back to the Land Rover, where Rip and Barney were waiting, lying down with their heads on their paws but their ears pricked. They greeted us with wagging tails and leapt back into the vehicle.

We drove slowly back to Kessel just as the moon was vanishing and dawn was cracking across the sky. The feeling of hope in my heart made me forget just how tired I was. Dad looked gaunt. A feeling of love and compassion for him swept over me and I put my hand out and touched his whitened knuckles, gripping the steering wheel.

"Things can only get better, Dad" I comforted, and he smiled gratefully, his lopsided familiar old smile.

But when we swung in front of the house, lights were on in the kitchen. Peter came out to help me with Toby. I felt rooted to my seat unable to move for I could see from Peter's ashen face that he had something terrible to tell us.

"Joan has just phoned — wants you to come at once," he told us.

"Why? What is it, what's happened?" I knew from Peter's expression that the news was bad. It was unbelievable after what Dad and I had experienced that Will was worse. I had so hoped that my prayers would somehow have worked — cured him — and now Peter was warning me that his chances were nil. That the doctors had done all they could and that Joan wanted me there — thought it would be right to bring Toby to his dying father's bedside.

Gloria thrust a hot thermos of tea and some nappies into my arms. Peter had made bacon sandwiches.

"You must eat," he urged, "or that child of yours is going to sap your strength."

I hugged him before he got into the driver's seat. "Thanks, Peter, thanks so much for all your help."

"Don't worry, Cleo," he whispered, "I've cancelled my flight. My place is here with you." I climbed into the back seat and Dad handed Toby to me before getting in beside me. Thank God for families, I thought, as trying to control my trembling I suckled Will's baby son, and we sped off into the early morning to be there with Will in his last hours.

Joan's eyes were bright with tears when she met us, in the corridor near Will's room.

"The doctors say not to get our hopes up," she warned. "They say this often happens."

"What often happens?" I asked impatiently.

"Coming around, dear. Did Gloria get the message to you? She said she would run outside and catch you before you left — you must have just missed her."

"What do you mean 'coming around'?" I demanded.

"Coming around for a while and then losing consciousness," she answered quickly, adding "apparently it's not only the smoke that's causing his coma but the blow he must have received to his head from a falling beam, when he was scrambling out of the house to safety. They say it's still very touch and go."

I thrust Toby into her arms. "Call me if he cries, Joan, Dad, Peter? Please?" I hurried away from them, down the corridor, into the ward and the little anteroom and stopped, breathless at Will's door. The doctor was leaving Will's room.

"Are you Cleo?" he asked

I nodded, hardly daring to speak, as with a faint smile he told me I would be the best medicine. Gently he took my arm and steered me to Will's bedside. I saw with a sweeping rush of relief that the life support system was no longer being used, yet Will was breathing evenly. I noticed his chest rising and falling in a steady rhythm. I stood beside him then gently, very gently, bent forward and kissed his cheek.

His eyes were gradually fluttering open. I guessed he was trying to focus. Then he seemed to recognise me and slowly his lips moved and opened into a slight smile. I took his now warm hand in mine and leaned close, for he was trying to say something. I bent down close to his face, and heard his whispered words: "Love you, Cleo." Then, closing his eyes he squeezed my hand with something of his old strength before falling back to sleep. My aching heart was changing. The doctor drew me aside and explained that Will had fought hard and it now looked likely he would survive. There was hope now — real hope. I tiptoed away down the corridor to fetch Toby, for I knew that when Will woke next he would want to hold him.

CHAPTER 39

This afternoon we have all been to the Rock for a picnic tea. Will and Monty joined us for the birthday cake ceremony down at the river, by the magic pool. We were all there: Dad, Nadine, Kate, Toby, Monty, Will and me. A moment in time, Toby's fourth birthday, and my mind returned to that moment when Will and I together had welcomed our son into the world.

"You were born there, "Kate said, pointing to the pool.

"Yes, I remember," her small nephew replied.

"So do I," Will said softly, putting his arm around my shoulders.

***

Now the children are in bed. Toby loves staying here. I have said goodnight to him and Kate. Tonight Will and I are going out for a celebration, just the two of us. The anniversary of the fire and Will's survival and Toby's birthday.

I can hear Dad's voice through the open window of the children's bedroom, as he reads Toby's favourite story, the one about a frightening monster who turns out to be kind. I can picture them as I stand under the window, watering Dad's garden. Toby's big, brown eyes will be wide with anticipation as he listens to every word. Kate will be on the bed, leaning against Dad. Though grown out of this story she will be listening too — loving it — loving the process of being read to, sharing with Toby the excitement and relief when the monster shows its true colours.

The shadows are lengthening now. The watering finished, I walk down to the orchard, where Skylark is grazing. Will has ridden out to the high moor to check on the cattle. It is a busy time, and they need to be seen each day. We farm both places now though Kessel is where we live. Today I had ridden over to Burrow on Skylark with Toby in front of me demanding to 'gallop gallop.' I had allowed him to hold the reins and felt his dark curls against my cheeks as we cantered along the track to Burrow, my arm tight around his waist.

Skylark whinnies and canters towards me. I stroke her neck. On an impulse, I decide to ride out to meet Will. I collect the bridle and Skylark lowers her head, inviting me to put it on her. I lead her to the gate, climb up and slide onto her back. I love the feel of her warm body moving under me. With my legs close to her sides she canters across the orchard, glides over the wall to the moors beyond.

Will is sure to be hurrying back now, not wanting to be late for our 'date'. I stop and wait, savour the moment on the hillside, Skylark knee-deep in dark heather, facing toward the river and the Rock. We are silent. I can feel the mare's sides heaving from the steep pull up. Suddenly she holds her breath. Head high, she stares across the valley to the hill on the far side of the river, quivering with anticipation, as though it was a winter's day, and she following the hounds, watching them work. For seconds I watch with her, see something moving: a white pony – tail streaming behind — mane flashing in the half light of this hazy summer dusk. On the pony's back is a child — a boy, wearing a cap, urging the pony onward. I blink several times, barely breathe, as I watch them cross the skyline, enveloped now in the last lingering light of the summer sky. Then Skylark whinnies, shakes her head, she has seen something else. It is Benjy and Will cantering down the hill. They are out of sight for seconds before they cross the river to appear again racing towards us. A slight breeze catches my breath as they draw up beside Skylark and me.

Will is smiling. "I hoped you'd meet me, Cleo." He has not taken his eyes from mine. Sliding from his horse he stands beside Skylark and carefully pulls me from her back. He lets the horses loose, their heads bend down at once to the tough grass. Will holds me in his arms, kisses me gently, then lifts me and carries me down to the river. Down to the Rock, to the magic pool where I know we will love one another with a celebratory passion, giving thanks to our ancestors and the gods for the miracle of Toby, the miracle of the Rock.